"A luscious erotic ... des
with an alpha male ... le."
... Pick

"Cheryl Holt . . . weaves this erotic romance like a master."
—Romance Divas

"A wonderful, amusing battle of the sexes."
—*Midwest Book Review*

FURTHER THAN PASSION

"Fa... a keeper ... Holt has finely tuned the art of
de... t
w... s
re... h
p...

..._)_

"F... of
l... *un*
... es
... at
... c-
... a-

..._ew_

More . . .

TOTAL SURRENDER

Best Sensual Novel of the Year
—*Romantic Times* Magazine

"Cheryl Holt is something else again. I was totally blown away by *Total Surrender*, a tale both erotic and poignant. Sensational characters, and a very compelling read that readers couldn't put down unless you're dead! It's also the dynamite sequel to last year's *Love Lessons* . . . don't miss this author. She's a sparkling diamond."

—ReaderToReader.com

"A lush tale of romance, sexuality, and the fragility of the human spirit. Carefully crafted characters, engaging dialogue, and sinfully erotic narrative create a story that is at once compelling and disturbing . . . For a story that is sizzling hot and a hero any woman would want to save."

—*Romance Reviews Today*

"A deliciously erotic romance . . . the story line grips the audience from the start until the final nude setting, as the lead characters are a dynamic couple battling for *Total Surrender*. The suspense element adds tension, but the tale belongs to Sarah and Michael. Cheryl Holt turns up the heat with this enticing historical romance."

—*Writerspace*

"A very good erotic novel . . . if you like a racy read, you'll enjoy this one!"

—*Old Book Barn Gazette*

St. Martin's Paperbacks Titles
by Cheryl Holt

Too Hot to Handle

Further Than Passion

More Than Seduction

Deeper Than Desire

Complete Abandon

Absolute Pleasure

Total Surrender

Love Lessons

TOO TEMPTING

~ TO ~

TOUCH

Cheryl Holt

St. Martin's Paperbacks

TOO TEMPTING TO TOUCH

Copyright © 2006 by Cheryl Holt.

Cover photo © Kristin Zabawa Photography

ISBN: 0-312-93798-9
EAN: 9780312-93798-0

Printed in the United States of America

St. Martin's Paperbacks edition / March 2006

St. Martin's Paperbacks are published by St. Martin's Press, 175 Fifth Avenue, New York, NY 10010.

10 9 8 7 6 5 4 3 2 1

1

LONDON, ENGLAND, 1812 . . .

"Do you feel sorry for me?"

"Dreadfully sorry, darling."

At the sound of voices, Ellen Drake halted in shuffling her deck of cards. She'd been anxious for a quiet interlude and a chance to rest after a trying day, but apparently, no privacy was to be had. She was huddled in the shadows of the earl's library, hiding and playing solitaire at a writing desk that was situated behind a large potted plant. She peeked around it.

From her discreet location she couldn't see who'd entered, but it was a man and a woman. Considering that they'd sneaked away from the crowded party—as had she—and that they were cooing and purring, it was obvious that a romantic tryst was commencing.

When the man spun the key in the lock, Ellen's suspicions were confirmed. He was bent on seduction, and his partner eager for it to happen.

Of all the rotten luck!

Ellen glanced about, searching for a rear door by which she could escape, but there wasn't one. She was trapped, and the sole means of exit was her bumbling into the middle of the torrid scene, which she was loathe to attempt.

Though she'd been in London but a few hours, she was aware of how the members of the Quality were prone to amorous mischief, and she couldn't bear to witness which wife was consorting with which husband. She had a firm moral constitution, had had a decent and respectable upbringing, and when she knew a person had a penchant for adultery it was difficult to be civil.

Her host, Alex Marshall, Lord Stanton, was the prime illustration of how arduous it was to pretend nonchalance. A decade earlier, when she was a girl of eighteen, Stanton had been in the country, merrymaking at a local estate. She'd stumbled upon him in the woods, doing all sorts of things he oughtn't with a neighbor's daughter. Ellen had never forgotten a single detail of the spectacle, so how was she to exhibit any courtesy toward him?

For months, since the moment she'd learned that she'd be traveling to London and staying in Stanton's home, she'd been panicked. In light of her post as a lady's companion, she couldn't have refused to accompany her employers, Rebecca and Lydia Burton. Nor could Ellen voice her opinion as to why she was opposed to Rebecca's betrothal to Stanton. As the disaster unfolded, she could only observe and stew.

As she was a spinster who'd been forced to make her own way in the world, Ellen's reputation had to be beyond reproach. She could never mention Stanton's base character, for then she'd be compelled to recount how she'd spied on him.

Fortunately, during the brief period they'd been in his house, Stanton hadn't deigned to appear, so she'd avoided meeting him, and she hoped to delay an introduction for as long as she was able. Rebecca was Stanton's cousin, their marriage arranged when they were children. Rebecca had spent most of her twenty-two years waiting for Stanton to decide he was ready to tie the knot, which he finally had, so at his behest they'd scurried to the city to set the process in motion. Rebecca was thrilled and excited, but Ellen was convinced that Rebecca would be miserable with such a rampant libertine for her husband.

"The nuptial noose is tightening," the man was commenting. "I'm about to have my wings clipped."

"Poor dear," the woman soothed. "Matrimony can be so tedious."

"Can't it, though?"

An engaged man! Ellen fumed. *Who was about to be wed! The cad!*

There was a lengthy pause, a rustle of clothing, some giggling; then the woman said, "You're a beast to lure me away from the festivities."

"Why did you let me?"

"You're so . . . tense."

"Oh, I'm definitely *tense,*" the man agreed. "Very, very tense. I need to relax. And soon!"

"I thought I should offer my assistance."

"Oh, you should!" the man replied. "You absolutely should."

Each sentence was punctuated by intervals of silence, and though Ellen would have poked her eyes out rather than look, her curiosity was piqued. What—precisely—were they doing?

She leaned farther to the side, discovering that the ribald scene was every bit as tawdry as she'd envisioned.

The couple were wrapped around each other so completely that they might have been glued together.

The woman was a short, buxom brunette, while the man was tall—six feet at least—with a fit, muscled physique. He had dark hair, and though Ellen couldn't see his face, she was sure he'd be handsome as the devil.

He was cupping the woman's buttocks, and as they writhed and wrestled, Ellen rippled with equal parts disgust and exhilaration.

Don't watch! she scolded, declining to be drawn in to the squalid rendezvous, yet she couldn't stop staring.

Once prior, she'd viewed such licentious conduct—as a girl in the forest when she'd glimpsed Lord Stanton—and evidently, naught had changed since that shameful day. Maturity had neither bestowed wisdom nor granted heightened judgment. She was as intrigued as ever by sexual endeavor.

What was the matter with her?

At twenty-eight, she was resigned to her situation. Circumstances had guaranteed that she would never marry, so why was she enthralled? Was she secretly pining for a beau? Had she a lusty aspect to her personality to which she was oblivious?

How peculiar! How terrifying!

She'd often heard that a woman needed to wed, that—after a certain age—it was unhealthy to shun matrimony. She'd always scoffed at the prospect, but what if the stories were correct?

What if she had a buried need for male companionship? What if it became worse with time? Could she grow crazed from unfulfilled desire?

"We really shouldn't be dallying," the woman contended.

"But I can't predict when I'll manage to slip away again. This could be my last chance. You wouldn't ask me to pass it up, would you? It's like ordering a starving man to ignore a feast, a thirsty man to walk by an oasis."

Ellen rolled her eyes. She hadn't had much experience with men, her deceased father and her tormented brother, James, being the two main examples, but she recognized the statement for the banal remark it was. What sane female would succumb on the basis of such drivel? If Ellen were the one being seduced, she'd insist on something a tad more romantic!

"So . . . my participation would be an act of kindness?" the woman queried.

"Think of it as your Christian duty to a deprived soul," he advised. "As I said, it may be my only opportunity."

"Then we shouldn't waste it."

Instantly, the tryst was pitched to the next level. They were kissing with a mutual fervor. Her arms were draped around him, her leg, too, a heel anchoring him as she stroked her foot up and down his calf.

His crafty fingers were fondling her bosom and ultimately slithering under her clothes to caress and pet. With a smooth yank, he tugged at the bodice so that a breast was bared. He pinched and squeezed; then, stunning Ellen to her very core, he dipped down and sucked at the nipple. The gesture was so surprising, and so unexpected, that Ellen clamped her hand over her mouth, lest she gasp aloud. Though she'd previously seen Lord Stanton frolicking, and thus assumed herself an expert in libidinous affairs, that assignation had entailed a great deal of enthusiastic kissing and hugging, but nothing similar to this.

She was so naïve! She'd had no idea that a man would do such a thing to a woman, that a woman would enjoy it, and her body responded with an impatient zeal. Her breasts were inflamed, her nipples throbbing, and she suffered from the strongest urge to massage them.

Cheeks burning, temperature rising, she was so hot that she worried she might ignite, and she could scarcely keep from fanning herself.

The lovers were next to a fancy sofa, and they lay down and stretched out, so they were shielded from sight. Ellen couldn't see what was transpiring, but there was heavy breathing, sighs and murmurs, more rustling of fabric.

What was occurring?

How frustrating to have her analysis stymied by a piece of furniture! She was desperate to know all, her salacious tendencies raging, and she had to physically grip her chair so that she didn't sneak over for a closer look.

"Oh . . . oh . . ." the woman panted. "Oh . . . Stanton, you're so good at that!"

Stanton! The annoying Romeo was Lord Stanton? The swine!

As if she'd been doused with icy water, Ellen jerked to reality. Fury replaced curiosity. How could she not have guessed it was he?

Over the years, there had been appalling rumors about him, and she'd believed them all. He was a wastrel and roué, who trifled with any willing female, but beyond his profligate habits, Ellen was positive he was a liar and perhaps a thief, as well.

That fated summer, when he'd been loafing in the country, a countess's ring had been stolen. In Ellen's opinion, everyone who'd been staying at the manor was a suspect—Stanton included—but her sixteen-year-old brother, James, had been accused instead. He'd been naught more than a boy, the estate agent's son, and he'd been sentenced to twenty years hard labor and transported to the penal colonies. The disgrace and shock had killed their widowed father, so Ellen had been left all alone in the world to fend for herself.

Her cherished family had been ruined by the calamity, and she blamed Alex Marshall and his affluent friends.

Plus, he was engaged to Rebecca! Since he'd been too lazy to arrive on time, she was down the hall, entertaining his guests. No wonder he couldn't be bothered to join them for supper. He was too busy dishonoring himself with every hussy in attendance!

Ellen was so angry that if she'd been holding a pistol, she'd have marched over, aimed, and shot him through the middle of his black heart.

So far, she'd remained hidden, but she was finished with wallowing in the corner. If Stanton presumed he could behave so despicably toward Rebecca, he was in for a surprise. He wasn't going to philander! Not if Ellen had anything to say about it.

His wicked ways were about to end!

She reached for her cards, split them in half, then shuffled—slowly and loudly—each card falling with a determined snap. It was a new deck, the paper crisp and stiff, and it made a brittle noise that echoed off the high ceiling.

Across the room, the woman hissed, "What was that? Did you hear it?"

After a brief hesitation, Stanton replied, "No."

There were whispers, more shifting on the sofa, so

Ellen shuffled again, and she started to hum, stridently and out of tune, but impossible to disregard.

Lord Stanton's head popped up over the edge of the couch. "What the devil?"

"Stanton? Is that you?" Ellen asked, acting as if they'd been acquainted forever, which, in an odd way, they had been. "I hadn't realized anyone was in here but me."

"Who are you," he barked, "and what are you doing in my library?"

"I'm playing solitaire," she answered evenly, "but it's so boring. Would you care to let me beat you at another game of gin? It's been an eternity since I've taken any of your money." She was fibbing—they'd never socialized in the past—but it was amusing to pester him.

"Gin?" he sputtered. "You want to play . . . gin?"

"Unless you'd like to suggest something else."

His expression was comical. He scowled at Ellen, gazed down at his Jezebel, scowled at Ellen, then grumbled, "Bloody hell."

The woman pushed at him, tossing him on the floor in her frenzied effort to right herself. In seconds, they were both standing, their backs to Ellen, as they straightened clothing and tucked in bodily parts.

Ellen rose and sauntered over, only to ascertain that she knew the woman—the circles of the Quality were quite small—and, she hoped, to shame her into better conduct.

"Why, hello, Mrs. Farthingale," Ellen greeted with a cold calculation.

"Have we met?" Farthingale inquired.

"Have you forgotten me already?" Ellen prodded. "I'm Rebecca Burton's companion."

"You are?" Farthingale gulped with alarm as Stanton muttered, "Dammit!"

"We were introduced when you were visiting her last autumn."

"Oh yes," Farthingale claimed, clearly not recollecting at all. She paled. "How marvelous to see you."

"Isn't it, though?"

"Alex . . . that is, Lord Stanton . . . was helping me with my dress. It . . . ah . . . came loose."

"Dresses can be so *tedious,* can't they?" Ellen commented. "Like matrimony."

"We slipped away to . . . ah . . . to . . ." Farthingale halted. There was nothing she could say to extricate herself from the mess with any aplomb.

"I'll just be going," she finally mumbled. "If you'll excuse me . . ."

She slinked away, groped at the key in the lock, then bolted into the hall. As she went, Ellen and Stanton were frozen in place, watching her flee, but once the door shut, Stanton whipped around.

He advanced until they were toe-to-toe, until his boots dipped under the hem of her skirt. He towered over her, every inch of his six-foot frame aching to wring her neck.

When she'd spied on him a decade prior, she'd seen him from a distance and had figured he was handsome, but she hadn't grasped how attractive he would prove to be up close. She was disconcerted, by his height, by his demeanor, by his blatant masculinity.

He appeared dark and dangerous, his black hair swept off his forehead to reveal high cheekbones, an aristocratic nose, a sensual mouth. His shoulders were wide, his chest broad, his waist narrow, and he had lanky legs that were braced with fury.

He was studying her, his blue, blue eyes roaming

across her face and torso, and she was uncomfortable with the intoxicating scrutiny. She felt too short, too old, too skinny, too . . . too . . . ordinary, when she suddenly didn't wish to be. She yearned to confront him in a stylish sapphire gown that would match the color of her eyes and set off the blond of her hair. She craved silk gloves, a lace shawl, tasteful jewelry, and she shook off the foolish whimsy.

From where had it sprung? Why would she pine to be all that she was not? And for *him*, of all people? She loathed him and all he represented.

"What is your name?" he seethed.

"Miss Ellen Drake."

"How long have you been in here?"

"The entire time."

"Gin indeed," he ultimately griped. "I've never seen you before in my life."

"No, you haven't," she agreed, grinning, "but you've definitely seen me now. And"—she arched a brow— "*I* have seen you."

He loomed until there was no space separating them. She'd never been so near to an adult male, so she hadn't understood that the experience could be so invigorating. She reeled with excitement—but dismay, too. She found him intensely intriguing, when she didn't want him to be, and she pulled away, which he wouldn't allow.

He moved with her, very much like a hawk stalking its prey.

"Are you threatening me, Miss Drake?"

"Not at all, Lord Stanton. I'm merely stating the facts."

"To what end, you aggravating tart?"

"Tart!"

He snorted with derision. "There are a few other terms I could call you, but I don't think I ought."

"Minding your manners, are you?"

He ignored the taunt. "What is your relationship to Rebecca?"

"As I said, I'm her companion."

"She has no companion."

"Oh yes, she has," Ellen asserted, "and if you don't reform your scandalous behavior, I'll notify her of what I've witnessed."

He evaluated her again, searching for her petty secrets and apparently locating them all. He chuckled. "No, you won't. You'd never hurt her."

"I wouldn't consider myself to be *hurting* her. I'd be doing her a favor."

"A favor!"

"Yes."

"But I'm the catch of the kingdom," he mocked, "and Rebecca has me on her hook."

"You are so vain!"

He stepped in, and she stepped away. They were like a pair of dancers, gliding across the floor. They continued on until she bumped into his desk and could go no farther. She was wedged against the polished oak, her bottom perched on the edge, and he leaned in so that she was tipping over, and his firm palm between her shoulder blades was all that kept her from being prone.

"You don't like me, do you?" he asked.

"Not a bit, and I wish Rebecca didn't like you, either."

"Why, you arrogant, uppity—"

"Uppity!"

"How dare you malign me! If you are who you say you are—and I admit that I have grave doubts as to your veracity—you're living under my roof, employed by my cousin, and friend to my fiancée, which indicates that you have more audacity than anyone I've ever met. I ought to talk with Lydia and have you fired."

"If you try, I can promise that my farewell to Rebecca will involve a vivid description of Mrs. Farthingale's bosom."

Ellen didn't know where she'd garnered the courage to spar with him, or why she was bent on provocation. He brought out her worst traits, making her bold and rash. Their wrangling gave her an exhilarating sense of power. She felt as if she could do any wild thing without repercussion.

"Listen, you cheeky little—" He paused in mid-insult and reined in his temper. With an undignified scoff, he sidled away. As if his cravat had shrunk and was choking him, he tugged at it. "How much?"

She sat up. "How much . . . what?"

"Don't play dumb—which you're obviously not. What will it take for you to be silent?"

"You suppose I'm blackmailing you?"

"Well, yes." He shrugged. "I don't want to upset Rebecca. Neither do you. So name your price. Cash? Baubles? A few new gowns from Madame LaFarge?"

She let her own gaze wander down. He really was a fine masculine specimen. How sad that so much low character could be wrapped in such a pretty package.

She smirked. "Celibacy."

As if she'd struck him, he blanched. "Celibacy!"

She wasn't certain what *celibacy* entailed, but the mysterious deed included some of what he'd been doing with Farthingale. "Yes. I would have your word on it."

"Not bloody likely."

She nodded, latching on to the idea with a particular relish. "It shall be celibacy till the wedding, and your complete devotion to Rebecca. Or else!"

"Or else what?" Struggling for calm, he pinched a finger and thumb to the bridge of his nose. "Miss Drake, is it?"

"Yes."

"I realize you're a spinster."

He uttered *spinster* as if it were a vile disease, and she was incensed by the denigration. "By choice, Lord Stanton. Absolutely by choice."

"You probably hate all men."

"Not all," she assured him. "Just some."

"I only meant that you're in no position to fully grasp the nature of the male beast."

She glared at the couch where he'd enjoyed his torrid embracing. "Actually, I think I *grasp* it quite well."

"I shan't be officially engaged for another month, and the wedding won't roll around till six months after that. You can't expect me to . . . to . . ."

"Can't expect you to what?"

A muscle twitched in his cheek. Murder gleamed in his eye, and she was positive he'd have throttled her if he could have figured out how to conceal the crime.

"I'm calling your bluff," he said. "Go ahead and tell her. Lay bare the entire sordid episode. I dare you."

"I will," Ellen insisted. "I swear it. I'm not joking."

"I'm betting you are."

He assessed her, taking her measure, and she had the strangest impression that he knew everything about her, that he could read her mind. There was no way to keep him from discovering that she would never hurt Rebecca by passing on such terrible news.

"Good evening, Miss Drake," he stated. "I won't say it's been a pleasure to make your acquaintance, because it hasn't been, and if I'm very, very lucky, I shan't suffer the misfortune of speaking with you ever again."

She'd lost the upper hand—and so quickly, too!—but she was determined to get it back. He seemed to have a genuine fondness for Rebecca, so perhaps she could use it to stir his dormant conscience. "Have you no feelings for Rebecca, and how the information will wound her?"

"I have many *feelings* for Rebecca, but they are none of your concern. Just as my personal affairs are none of your business. I am a man, Miss Drake. Not a eunuch. Go blackmail someone else—if you can find anyone who's not already weary of your tiresome company."

With that deftly hurled slur, he strutted out, leaving her to dawdle in the quiet, to fume and stew about how weak she was. She'd never had any control. Not over her fate. Not over her circumstances. Not over her income or her reduced status. She was dependent, beholden, alone, and the tedium of her situation reared up as though it were a living, breathing creature that was suffocating her.

What she wouldn't give to be free and self-sufficient. She was like a slave who yearned to break out of bondage, and the fierce burst of discontentment rattled her.

When had she grown so dissatisfied? So unhappy? Long ago, she'd accepted her dreary lot. Hadn't she?

Stanton was correct: She would never confide in Rebecca as to what she'd seen. But if he thought she'd let the matter rest, that she'd ignore him as he gamboled with every strumpet in London, he was in for a huge shock.

Celibacy she'd demanded, and celibacy it would be. Stanton's life was about to change—drastically!—and she was the one who'd make it happen.

2

"Do you feel sorry for me?"

Alex grinned at his dancing partner, Lady Melissa, as he ushered her down the row of couples.

"Why? Because you're about to become engaged to Rebecca Burton?" She laughed. "She's pretty, sweet, and rich. So my answer is no. I don't feel sorry for you in the least."

"You're too cruel," he murmured as the song ended.

She was beautiful in an icy, detached way, but they'd never been lovers, for she only trysted when she was between husbands, as she was at the moment. She was a gold digger who married sickly old men, but those who'd previously bedded her claimed she could make the most limp cock stand up straight. Alex was sure her spouses had died happy.

He should be so lucky!

While he didn't have many scruples, he had a few, and he intended to be faithful to Rebecca—once the engagement was official. He hesitated and reconsidered. Well, maybe when the wedding was near.

The prim, puritanical Miss Drake aside, no sane person would expect him to forgo pleasures of the flesh for seven months. Such extended abstinence wasn't healthy.

"Of course, I'm not cruel," Melissa was saying, "and a man must utilize his *assets*. Or lose them."

"And don't forget," he added, "if we don't philander now, when we're both free, who knows when we'll have another chance? Have I mentioned the date of my betrothal ball?"

"Three times."

"Has it been that many?"

"The women of London will be devastated by the loss of your charming company." Her torrid gaze swept to his crotch, where she enjoyed a leisurely inspection. "I suppose I could take pity on you."

She flashed such a sultry, tempting smile that his toes curled. He leaned in and whispered, "Meet me in Lord Banbury's library in five minutes."

"I can hardly wait." She licked her lips, vividly prompting him to recall the stories he'd heard of her particular prowess. She'd devised more thrifty uses for her devilish tongue than the King had gold coins.

Melissa was the cure for what ailed him, and he planned to wallow in whatever succor she chose to afford. His cock stirring, he slipped through the crowd and disappeared down a deserted hall.

Though others might envision seven months to be an extended period, to himself the interval seemed a pittance, the distressing event approaching with the speed of a runaway carriage.

He'd never wanted to wed. His parents' despicable example had cooled any interest. They'd detested each other, had fought and insulted and clashed, and for the last few years of their wretched lives they kept separate residences.

On his deathbed, his father had sworn that Alex's mother had been unfaithful, that her infidelities had been the cause of the breach. He'd contended that Alex's younger brother, Nicholas, was not his child, though the law and the church insisted he was.

Alex didn't know the truth, but he and Nicholas didn't look alike, and rumors still abounded as to who Nick's actual sire might have been.

What Alex *did* know was that he'd never put himself through such drama. He would never allow himself to care for a woman, would never let anyone matter so much. He absolutely would not have emotion or passion ruling his life.

If his title hadn't weighed so heavily, he might never have married. He was fond of Rebecca, but he thought of her as a sister. Plus, she was so gullible and trusting. Compared to her, he felt aged and exhausted.

How could they find common ground? On what basis would they proceed?

The fact that they were family could only carry them so far. What would they talk about over the dinner table? What would they talk about in bed?

He paled. The notion of having sex with her was extremely disconcerting. He couldn't imagine removing her clothes, or telling her what to do with her body, hands, or mouth. The prospect was downright incestuous.

He sneaked into Banbury's dark, isolated library. He lit a candle and locked the door, but he resisted the urge to search for the intrepid Miss Drake. The snippy harridan had rattled him, had poked and prodded at his sense of honor and integrity, and he'd spent the entire day stewing over her remarks.

Was he wrong to seek carnal diversion? With the wedding so many months in the future, was he cheating on Rebecca?

He hated rumination, hated to be fretting and fashing over what his path should be. He never lamented or regretted. As a rich, powerful nobleman, he was a mini-god in a world of mortals, and if he couldn't do what he wanted, when he wanted, what was the use of any of it?

Miss Drake be damned.

Momentarily, Melissa crept in from the verandah, and he rippled with excitement. She was a renowned lover. No exploit was too nasty, no conduct too excessive, and in his current state a dissolute, raucous coupling suited him just fine.

Melissa snuggled herself to him, and he could feel every delicious inch of her. She slid her hand between them, petting and massaging with adept skill.

They were situated next to a couch, and they lay down and stretched out, with her draped across him. He plucked at the bodice of her gown, ready to liberate her breasts from the confines of corset and chemise, ready to suck at one of her delectable nipples, when a cracking noise sounded from across the room.

They both froze.

"What was that?" she asked, frowning.

"I don't have any idea," he replied, though he was all too afraid he knew. He sighed and peeked over the back of the sofa.

It can't be, he mused. *It simply can't be!*

Yet there she was.

Miss Drake was seated at a table, shuffling her cards, and she grinned malevolently.

Was she following him? Spying on him? The bloody woman! What did she want? How could he make her go away?

"Hello, Stanton," she called. "Fancy meeting you here."

He flopped down to cower in the safety of the shadows.

"Who the hell is that?" Melissa hissed.

"You don't want to know."

"Stanton," Miss Drake summoned, "I'm bored. Would you join me for a game of gin?" She clapped the deck together, the brisk cards clacking like the rolling of a pair of drumsticks.

Melissa glowered as if he'd invited the annoying interloper, her scowl apprising him that their rendezvous was over and he shouldn't depend on it resuming any time soon. Then she jumped up and raced to the safety of the patio, vanishing so quickly that she might never have been there, at all.

His temper raging, he counted to ten, then to twenty.

What should he say? What should he do?

His private life wasn't any of Miss Drake's business! He'd commanded her to desist, but she hadn't heeded his edict. Had she no concept of his supremacy over her? Of his authority and influence? With a snap of his fingers, he could ruin her.

Not that he would. But still . . .

He stood and whirled around.

"Miss Drake, how in Hades did you find me? And why would you presume it was appropriate for you to look?"

"You have the worst language," she retorted. "You forget that you are in the presence of a lady."

"A *lady*! A tyrant is more like."

He stomped over, not sure what he intended. To shout at her? To paddle her? To . . . to . . . send her to bed without supper? What—precisely—was his plan?

He hadn't a clue, but he had to take action.

He went behind her chair, boxing her in, and he bent down, a palm braced on either side so that she couldn't slink away.

She shifted to gaze at him over her shoulder, and suddenly their positions were much too intimate. An arm was pressed to his chest; a wayward curl tickled his ear. Her lips were mere inches from his own, and he was forced to note what he'd been too aggravated to perceive the night before.

She was stunning.

Her hair was blond, a sort of golden wheat, with strands of auburn. Her skin was creamy, her cheeks rosy, her nose pert, her face heart shaped and pleasing. She was slender and willowy, thin where a woman should be, but rounded where a woman should be, too.

She stared at him, her fabulous blue eyes wide and intrigued. They were a strange hue, a sapphire that seemed almost purple against the lavender fabric of her dress. Those devious eyes delved and probed, digging deep, burrowing down to his petty, depraved core.

It was a bizarre, charged encounter, where he felt as if any incredible thing might happen. He could confide any secret, confess any sin, pose any question, and she would comprehend exactly what he was saying.

When he started fantasizing about her bosom, speculating as to what it would be like to stroke her cleavage, the peculiar instant was broken. He leapt away and out of range, but he couldn't escape. She stood, too, not cowed in the least.

"Have you no decency?" she demanded. "No shame? Rebecca is down the hall in the ballroom, hoping someone asks her to dance."

"She is not."

"She is. We arrived a short time ago. What if she'd strolled in and caught you?"

A vein throbbed at his temple. His jaws ached from clenching his teeth. "Miss Drake . . . Ellen . . ."

"It's *Miss* Drake to you."

"Ellen, I . . . I . . ." *I what?*

He hadn't any notion how to finish the sentence. She'd driven him to speechlessness. He wasn't about to debate his conduct, nor would he parlay over Rebecca's abrupt appearance at a location where he'd never expected her to be.

What was left to discuss? Nothing.

"How many lovers do you have?" she queried.

"How many?"

"Yes. Is it a dozen? A hundred? A thousand?"

He laughed. "A thousand? You certainly have an elevated opinion of my prowess."

"I swear you have a woman hiding around every corner."

"Why, you sassy minx! You've been in London what? A day and a half? How could you possibly level such an accusation?"

"I may have been here briefly, but I've already stumbled on you in two compromising situations. And I haven't even been trying! I shudder to think what I'd discover if I set my mind to the task."

"I am not a scoundrel!" he felt honor bound to contend.

"You couldn't prove it by me." She frowned and

sobered. "I like Rebecca very much. I don't want her hurt."

"You assume I do?"

"I *assume* you're a pompous scalawag and you'll do whatever you wish, despite the consequences."

She was too near the mark, too proficient at reading his character. Regardless of his protestations, he was an unrepentant cad who thrived on pleasure. His reputation was so disgusting that he'd always been glad Rebecca and Lydia resided in the country, where they'd never overhear any risqué stories.

He glanced away, hating to witness her condemnation, hating to acknowledge that she'd so validly assessed his base nature. Praying for guidance, for patience, he conjectured over the best course, though he couldn't believe that he'd expend an ounce of energy worrying about what she thought.

In his world, people acted out of selfishness, with veiled motive and purpose, so he couldn't fathom why she was in such a dither.

"Why does any of this matter to you?" he inquired. "You can't tell me you have any loyalty to Lydia, and your tenure with Rebecca will end with the wedding. If you keep irritating me, I'll have you fired—sooner rather than later—so why hound me?"

"Rebecca loves you," she bluntly claimed.

The idiotic statement was like a punch to the gut. His marriage was being made for accepted reasons— money, property, family—and sentiment wouldn't be a factor. Any ludicrous feminine views Rebecca had to the contrary were stupid.

"Then Rebecca is a fool," he responded.

"She thinks you walk on water."

"She's mad."

"Dreams die hard, Lord Stanton," she said. "I won't stand idly by while hers are dashed."

There was a lengthy silence, and they tarried in the candlelit room, the noises of the ball scarcely discernible, and he was surprised at how close he felt to her. He sensed that she'd known trauma, had struggled with many ordeals, but had fought her way through, so that she was tough and resilient. What heartbreak had made her so strong?

He was overwhelmed by an outlandish desire to touch her, and he reached out and traced a finger across her bottom lip. The contact jolted him. Sparks shot down his arm, running from himself into her. The air around them was alive and unsettled, and he seriously pondered leaning down and kissing her. It seemed the normal conclusion.

She endured the intimate caress, holding perfectly still as he trailed across her chin, down her neck, but as he dipped lower, she lurched away.

He was shocked. What had been his intent? If she hadn't moved, would he have gone farther? Might he have fondled her breast? Might he have slipped a hand inside her dress?

He'd insisted that Rebecca was mad, but perhaps *he* was the one who was deranged. He was no better than a rutting dog.

Miss Drake was embarrassed, and she fumbled with her deck of cards, stacking them and stuffing them into her purse.

"You're always playing cards," he murmured, unable to devise a more pithy observation.

"I'm often alone." She shrugged. "It passes the time."

As she voiced the admission, she looked so forlorn

and tragic, and he was near to comforting her by pulling her into his arms. He was so curious about her, about her past, when he couldn't deduce why he would be. He didn't even like her, so why the piqued interest?

"*You* could be my paramour." The scandalous proposal popped out before he realized he would utter it.

She gasped. "What did you say?"

"Despite how you beg and nag, I won't stop philandering before the wedding. So why not entertain me yourself?"

The concept was ridiculous, but with an absurd urgency he was desperate for her to agree. He was outrageously attracted to her. They shared an unusual affinity, a type of strident connection about which most people could only dream.

Sex with her would be extraordinary, like naught he'd experienced prior, and preposterous as it sounded, he wanted her more than he'd ever wanted anything. Be it wrong, be it crazed, he yearned for it to transpire.

"No." She chuckled wearily. "You insult me by asking."

"Give me a good reason why you won't."

"Rebecca is my friend. It would be so wicked."

"Ah . . . a loyal and moral soul."

"I like to imagine that I am."

"How refreshing."

He stepped in, trapping her against the table. She was positioned so that the front of his body was pressed to her side, his waist to her hip, phallus to thigh. At the exciting proximity his boisterous rod leapt to attention, though she was too unschooled to comprehend how she'd affected him.

He nuzzled her nape, enchanted by the warmth of her skin, the hint of a subtle perfume, and he was tickled when she shivered. She was as enthralled as he was, himself, their physical magnetism blatant and impossible to ignore.

"Do it for me," he whispered, on some primal level recognizing that if she refused, he'd be losing out on something grand. "Do it for yourself."

Her beautiful eyes troubled, she eased him away. "I met you once, years ago. You don't recall, do you?"

"No, I'm sorry."

"What you just requested . . ." She halted, not possessing the terminology for salacious discussion. "Why did you suggest it?"

"Why not?" The comment was flip and cold, but he declined to explain, declined to furnish her with any intimation of how stunning he deemed her to be.

"Why not indeed?"

"An affair between us would be wonderful."

"I doubt it," she asserted. "I don't even like you."

"On that point"—he grinned—"we're in complete accord."

"Quit behaving so badly," she pleaded.

Her appeal was sincere, and it tugged at his conscience. He considered relenting, letting her have her way, so he could see her smile, but he didn't.

They could have engaged in a lengthy quarrel—about male needs and preferences, about aristocratic marriages and illicit liaisons—but he could talk until he was blue in the face and never make her understand.

"I can't."

"Do it for me." She tossed his own words back at him. "Do it for yourself."

"I won't."

Her temper flared. "Then we're at loggerheads."

"I expect that we are."

An awkward silence ensued. She studied him, checking for flaws and finding too many; then she threatened, "I'll be watching you."

Regal as any queen, she turned and marched out.

3

Ellen was squashed into the corner of the packed, stifling ballroom when she observed Lord Stanton creeping toward the exit. At the same moment, a blond beauty slipped onto the verandah. The pair was likely departing for a tryst—Stanton seemed to prefer secluded libraries—and Ellen rippled with exasperation.

She couldn't say why she was determined to spy on him, or why his conduct bothered her. Why should it? What was it to her if he acted like an ass?

The answer was beyond her. Normally, she was a rational, prudent person, who was versed in the peculiarities of the Quality, yet for obscure motives she couldn't define, she was obsessed with him.

The explanation had to be rooted in her past. He and his friends had destroyed her family, and the ramifications of their perfidy went on and on. Though James had been sentenced to twenty years of hard labor, he'd recently escaped from captivity, with half his sentence served, and had returned to London.

She hadn't seen him but had received several furtive

letters, which indicated he wasn't the charming, innocent boy he'd been but a ruthless, cynical man who had
too much money and no valid accounting for how he'd
come by it. Every time she thought about his current
perils, she panicked all over again.

From the morning of his arrest, her life had been a
long string of disappointment and toil, and she was
slowly realizing that unhealed wounds from that episode
occasionally gripped her and ruled her actions.

She wanted to have something go right, wanted to be
in control. Her need to manage a satisfactory conclusion
for Rebecca had taken on absurd, monumental propor-
tions. Plus, Stanton was just so annoying. He presumed
he could perpetrate any vile atrocity and get away with it.

Which was true, but that didn't mean she had to
meekly accept his antics. He'd had the audacity to propose indecency to Ellen, herself. She was still reeling
from the strange suggestion, and she'd spent many frenzied hours struggling to deduce why he'd done it.

Had she furnished some subtle indication that she'd
be amenable? Or was he simply the sort who would philander and no reason was necessary?

She peeked about, but no one was paying any attention to her, and she tiptoed away to locate the library. It
was the only door in the lengthy hallway that had been
closed, and she spun the knob, delighted to find that
Stanton hadn't had the foresight to lock it.

Was he so eager that he couldn't delay? Or was he
certain that Ellen wouldn't waltz in behind him? Had he
considered Ellen, at all?

The notion—that he might have disregarded her—
had her furious.

She sneaked in but didn't spot anyone. A candle

burned on a nearby table, but the rear of the room was dark. She peered through the shadows, when there was a feminine moan, followed by a male chuckle.

They were already prone on the sofa and shielded from her gaze. Apparently, he hadn't wasted any effort on the formalities!

"Do you feel sorry for me?" he inquired, and Ellen shook her head with disgust. How many females had listened to the feeble quip? Why couldn't he devise a more original romantic volley?

"Oh yes, you poor dear," the woman replied. "Matrimony can be such a fetter to one's amusements."

"Can't it though?"

Why did women succumb to his charms? Why would they race off to be alone with him? What was the allure? Ellen had heard whispers about the adventures of courting, and she had to admit that she was curious.

What secrets did they know that Ellen, as a virginal spinster, hadn't had the chance to learn?

The previous evening, when he'd touched her mouth, he'd given her a hint of the physical bliss he could trigger. Whenever she recalled the wild incident, her heart pounded. What had he been trying to accomplish? What if he'd kept on?

The question haunted her. If she hadn't shied away like a timid child, if she'd let his exploration continue, where might she have ended up?

"Oh, Stanton," the woman gushed, "you're so naughty."

"You're awfully wicked yourself."

The rendezvous was progressing more rapidly than the others, and Ellen wondered if it was due to Stanton being in a hurry, or if the woman was easier to seduce than the others had been. Whatever the source of the escalation, Ellen was resolved to bring about an even faster finale.

She'd commenced harassing him because of Rebecca, but somewhere between the first tryst and this one, she'd begun doing it for her own enjoyment. It was so entertaining to interrupt him. Though she recognized it as a pitiful comment on her dull life, she loved sparring with him. She existed in a world of females, in an odd purgatory between servant and houseguest—she wasn't quite either one—so she didn't cross paths with many men, especially none like him. He was extremely intriguing.

She pulled her cards from her reticule, sat down at the table, and started to shuffle.

There was a pause; then the woman queried, "What was that?"

He sighed. "Don't ask. Just go."

"But . . . but . . ." the woman sputtered.

"Trust me. We're finished for now. But we *will* dally again. I promise you."

Seeming intoxicated and disoriented, his partner tottered up and glanced around. As she caught sight of Ellen, Ellen flashed a feral smile that was so vicious the woman gasped and fled onto the verandah.

Feeling smug, Ellen rose and watched as Stanton uncurled from the couch. He appeared grim and forbidding, and she suffered a wave of disquiet, though not out of fear for her safety.

She'd exhausted his patience, and he was ready to commit mayhem, but he wouldn't harm her. For some reason, she understood him well, when there was no basis for a heightened discernment. He was irritated and enraged, but he'd never lash out.

He walked toward her, advancing with the grace of

a large African cat, and her stomach tickled, her senses whirled. She'd never have a beneficial effect on his character, so she was on a fool's errand. Yet she'd been swept away by righteous indignation and couldn't back down.

He approached until he was directly in front of her, and he stepped in so that she was pressed to the table, so that she was trapped between it and him. Exuding menace and wrath, he towered over her, and she was dizzy with absorbing the emotions coursing through her.

He was providing her with a glimpse of what enticed his paramours, of why they were so quick to sneak off with him. She was mesmerized, held spellbound by his rapt focus. She'd never been so keenly studied, as if he could bore through to her very essence, and she was stunned to discover that a vain, feminine part of her was thrilled.

When he stared at her, what did he see? She hoped he saw a vibrant, mature woman, with a pretty face and pleasing shape, but she was fairly sure that, instead, he perceived the tedious, discontented lady's companion that dire circumstances had forced her to become.

She was so pathetic! So dreary in her need for approval! She'd never been arrogant about her looks or personality, so why was she fretting over her attributes? Why should his opinion matter in the slightest?

"We meet again, Miss Drake," he said.

"Yes, we do, Lord Stanton."

His torrid gaze was locked to hers; then slowly, it descended to her mouth, lingering there, leaving her with the distinct impression that he was considering kissing her. Which was preposterous.

As a female—with no family and no prospects—she'd

never so much as had a gentleman caller, and as far as she was aware, she'd never driven any man to ponder such an intimacy.

What would it be like to be kissed by him? It would probably be splendid, would probably be something she'd like to try more than once, and the notion scared her to death.

She hadn't spent much time daydreaming about amorous affairs. She wasn't even certain how one went about kissing, and the thought that he might instigate such a deed, that she might be anxious for it to occur, had her flummoxed.

She was twenty-eight years old. How could she have failed to appreciate that she was so desperate for male notice? What was special about Stanton that he had her mulling such conduct?

He frowned, as if deciphering a difficult mathematical equation. "I can't figure you out."

"What would you like to know?"

"Where do you come by the impudence to harass me?"

"I guess I'm just brimming with daring."

"Are you?"

"I'm not afraid of you."

"You should be."

"An idle threat, Lord Stanton."

He leaned closer, his torso connecting with hers, their tummies and thighs melded, their feet tangled. She could perceive his heat, could smell the starch in his shirt, and the soap with which he'd bathed.

He had her off balance, and she was falling back. She steadied herself by grabbing the lapels of his coat.

He was trying to bully her, with his authority and position, but there was nothing he could do to her that hadn't already been done, and the realization made her feel free and reckless.

"You're very brave," he stated, "and very conceited."

"Conceited? I am not."

"You presume you're smarter than everyone else, that your view is the sole one that's valid."

"I won't apologize for being correct."

He snorted with derision and eased her down. She was stretched out on the table, and he was hovered over her. She couldn't deduce how she'd landed in such a shocking situation, or why she'd allowed him to wrangle her into it.

More surprisingly, she had no wish to wrestle away. Her mind was screaming for her to fight and flee, but her body declined to obey any commands. It was delighted to remain right where it was, as if comprehending that whatever was about to transpire was something she needed very much.

He came closer still, his lips mere inches from her own, his warm breath flowing across her cheek. Somehow, he'd wedged himself between her legs. Her thighs welcomed the outrageous placement and spread of their own accord, so that he could step in and touch his loins to her private parts.

The contact was exhilarating, her womb seeming to shift and stir, her nipples throbbing with each beat of her heart, and she grappled with an ancient yearning she didn't understand. She attempted to pull her legs together, to force him away, but he was lodged tight, and her struggles were futile.

"You're so determined to keep me from philandering," he said.

"Well, you can't behave yourself, so I'm simply encouraging you to remember what's at stake."

"That being?"

"Rebecca's happiness."

"You're so concerned about her."

"She's my friend."

"And your employer," he mentioned. "Your loyalty is a tad excessive."

"Only someone of your low standards would believe so."

"Do you know what I think?" He looked like a cat about to swallow the canary.

She gulped. "No, what?"

"You're lonely."

"Hah! My life is very rewarding."

"And I'm positive that your pestering me has nothing to do with Rebecca. You're craving a bit of adventure, a bit of excitement."

"How absurd."

"You're adamant that no one revel, that no one have any fun. Why is that?"

"I'm not against re . . . re . . . reveling *per se*."

"You're not? I'm so glad to hear it." He chuckled. "Have you ever been kissed, Miss Drake?"

"No." She was agog, so swept up that she was like a puppet that couldn't budge unless he tugged on her strings.

Was he going to kiss her? Was she going to let him?

"You loudly proclaim that chastity should rule, that people should curb their impulses at all times. But it's recently dawned on me that perhaps you've never had to learn how difficult it can be to practice restraint." He cocked a brow. "Especially when it's what you want very, very much."

"You're spewing rubbish."

"Am I? Let's see how adverse you are to dallying. Let's see how adept you are at controlling yourself when moderation is the last thing you desire."

Overcome by his intensity, she turned away, and he nuzzled at her nape. She hadn't known the spot was so sensitive, and she shivered, goose bumps cascading down her arms. He was in no hurry, nibbling in a leisurely fashion that drove her wild, and she mustered a tiny amount of sanity and pushed at his chest, but it was like shoving a boulder.

"Have you any idea of the activities men and women enjoy?"

"No . . . no . . . I . . ."

"I'll show you. I'll give you a little taste."

"You mustn't . . . you . . ."

She was babbling like an imbecile, and she'd meant to complete the sentences but couldn't. He'd bitten down and was sucking at her skin. She couldn't speak, couldn't object or rebuff him.

"Lovers experience physical pleasure," he murmured, as he trailed up her neck, across her cheek. "They can become obsessed and unable to ignore their passion. Is that how you'll be when I'm finished with you? I wonder. . . ."

He found her mouth, his lips alighting on hers, and she was stunned by how sweet and how gentle he was.

She'd expected to be grabbed, to be mauled, so she was unprepared for his tender advance. If he'd been rough, if he'd been demanding, she might have located the strength to fend him off, but as it was, she was enchanted. It had never occurred to her that an embrace could be so precious.

"Kiss me back, Ellen," he whispered.

As if she was his slave, she had to obey, and tentatively, she reached out and hugged him, by the small gesture granting him permission to continue.

"Yes," he soothed, "that's it."

He increased the pressure, his tongue flicking out, tracing across her bottom lip. Asking. Asking again.

She grasped what he wanted, and she opened wide and welcomed him inside. Their tongues tangled, working in a combined rhythm that thrilled, that terrified.

She'd leapt into an inferno. She pined for things she couldn't name, was frantic for a relief she couldn't describe, and she had no clue how to stop the spiral, no desire to have it wane.

His hands were busy, and she vaguely noted that he was removing her combs and soon her long, curly tresses would swing down. She couldn't pin them up without assistance. What would she do? How would she get home from the party without being seen?

The panicked thoughts floated away. She didn't care. Not about her hair, not about being detected. The only factor that mattered was Stanton and what he was doing to her. The rest of the world had ceased to exist. There was just him and her and the quiet, secluded room.

"I love your hair," he said as he jerked the last comb free.

His compliment pricked at a forlorn place in her heart. She was flattered, elated that he'd noticed a personal detail, and she drew him nearer. He grew more bold, massaging her breasts, caressing the mounds through the fabric of her dress, but it felt as if he were touching her bare skin. He squeezed and fondled until she was writhing with agony.

She couldn't breathe, couldn't think, and she was even more troubled. At that moment, she'd have done whatever he suggested, despite how perilous or reckless.

Before she recognized what he planned, he slipped his fingers into her bodice and slithered across to toy with her nipple. The sensation was like nothing she'd ever imagined, like nothing she could have explained. She knew she should wrench herself away and flee, but what sane woman would want him to halt? What woman would have the fortitude to say no?

In some foggy section of her mind, it dawned on her to recollect that he was a skilled roué, who regularly practiced seduction, and she was merely another ninny who'd sneaked off to be with him. Alarm bells were ringing, but softly, warning her that she'd jumped in much further than she'd ever intended to go.

She had to gather her wits, had to extricate herself from the shameful predicament, but she was too captivated, and she couldn't conjure any reasons to desist.

The exploit rattled her, made her brood and ache. Where would it end? *How* would it end?

Suddenly Stanton eased away, his naughty hand sliding out of her dress, his delectable mouth separating from hers.

"What is it?" she asked, disoriented by the abrupt cessation.

She gazed up at him, deciding that she'd never witnessed a more beautiful sight. His blue eyes were glowing with lust, but also with what she was certain was a good deal of fondness. She'd never been scrutinized like that, as if she was remarkable and unique, and she could have stayed there forever, watching him, and reveling in his attention.

He was as disturbed by the encounter as she was,

herself. His respiration was labored, his skin flushed, his lips moist and swollen from their kisses.

He appeared perplexed, as if he couldn't figure out how he'd come to have her sprawled across the table, how he'd managed to immerse them in such a sordid endeavor. The incident had escalated so rapidly, had hurled them to a dizzying height, and Ellen felt as if the earth had tipped off its axis.

She was positive that if she stood, the floor would be tilted, that she wouldn't be able to find her balance. She hadn't fathomed that such feelings could engulf her, that she'd have no willpower to resist the onslaught, and she could hardly keep from embarrassing herself by latching on to him, dragging him back down, and commencing anew.

"Isn't kissing . . . splendid?" He grinned, a dimple creasing his cheek. He looked delicious, dangerous, and more handsome than any man ought to be.

"Yes, I hadn't realized . . ."

"No, you hadn't."

He rested his palms on her shoulders, and he stroked them down, taking a slow, leisurely journey across her bosom, her breasts, tummy, and thighs.

"I . . . I feel all ragged inside," she confessed.

"Of course you do, and I bet you're wishing I would alleviate your distress. I could, you know."

"Please. . . ."

It was a prayer, a plea for mercy. As if she'd been struck by lightning, a riotous energy had been dumped into her, but there was no extra space to contain it. It was rolling around, making her crazed, making her yearn for . . . for . . . what? How was she to bear up when she was filled with such a swirling, discomfiting anguish?

With a final swipe up her torso, he straightened and began adjusting his clothes. The playful lover had vanished, his tender expression gone. He was sophisticated, urbane, and completely unaffected, while she was reeling, her hair a mess, her gown twisted, the hem rucked up. She felt as if she were a towel he'd wrung out and hung on a hook.

Every piece of her, down to the smallest pore, was humming with an undefined hunger that needed satiation, but she had no idea what remedy was required.

"Are we . . . are we finished?" she dared to inquire.

"Yes."

"But you can't leave me like this!"

"I mean to *leave* you exactly like this, you aggravating strumpet."

"Strumpet!"

"I believe we've settled the question—once and for all—as to what sort of female you are deep down."

"What are you implying?"

"You're no different from any other. You'll spread your legs as quickly as the next woman, if the right man glances in your direction."

"I will not!" she protested, though why she bothered was a mystery. He was absolutely correct: She was a trollop! How humiliating! How humbling!

"Now that your base character has been established," he continued, "maybe you'll think twice before pointing your pious little finger at anybody else."

With that, he turned and strolled out. He was calm and composed, providing no hint that he'd just ravaged her beyond redemption. He shut the door with a determined click, abandoning her to mull and stew, and she dawdled on the table and stared up at the ceiling.

She needed to sit up, to restore her condition and slink away before anyone saw her, but she couldn't move.

What had come over her? What had she done and why? With Stanton of all people!

She groaned with dismay. The man was a sorcerer, which would explain his diabolical appeal, and she clung to the rationalization as if it were a lifeline. The only other alternative was to admit that she'd been smitten and had allowed herself to be seduced, but she was too mortified to acknowledge the truth. She'd go to her grave denying that anything untoward had occurred, denying that she'd been complicit.

With enormous effort, she slid to her feet, but she was unsteady. She collapsed to the floor and huddled on the rug, her skirt pooled around her. Her deck of cards—the ultimate symbol of her solitary existence—had been scattered during the foray, and a few of them drifted down, falling around her like autumn leaves.

She picked one up, and it was the Knave of Hearts. The smirking face seemed to mock her for her scandalous conduct. As if it were afire, she pitched it away; then she pulled herself up.

She had to escape the mansion, had to find a way to notify Rebecca and Lydia that she'd departed. Then she'd race to Stanton's town house. It wasn't far, and if she was lucky, she could make the trek without discovery. She would hide and regroup while she figured out how to carry on from this second forward, for without a doubt, she couldn't ever meet up with Stanton again.

She went to the hall and peeked out. Espying no one, she scampered away toward the nearest exit and the darkness beyond.

4

"Fetch me some tea," Lydia Burton barked at the recalcitrant maid, "and be quick about it, or the next person I talk to will be Lord Stanton."

With her mention of Cousin Alex, the girl scurried away, and Lydia fumed and calculated how she'd retaliate. She'd had a lifetime of plotting revenge, of exacting it with cruel and malicious glee. She was generally a quiet, unobtrusive individual, so those who crossed her assumed she was harmless, but they discounted her at their peril.

There was a mirror across the dining parlor, and when she caught a glimpse of her unattractive face, she refused to suffer any regret. She'd been born ugly, with mousy hair, beady eyes, a sharp chin and nose, and at age thirty-five her condition hadn't improved.

Her body was peculiar, too, with her shoulders hunched and her hips too big for the rest of her, so that on the bottom she was shaped like a fat pear. On the top she was flat as a board, her breasts having never developed as they ought.

She couldn't count how often her father had lamented

over how homely she was. When the insulting oaf had died, she hadn't grieved a single second, and she was still having the last laugh, spending his money and managing his properties.

On his deathbed, she'd received particular delight in tormenting him with how she'd squander it all, how he wouldn't be around to stop her, and she liked to think that her malevolent words had pushed him over the edge and into the great beyond.

The maid arrived with her tea, and after she set it down, Lydia gripped the girl's wrist and pinched the skin hard enough to leave a mark.

"If you ignore me in the future," Lydia warned, "I'll have you whipped, then thrown into the streets and hauled off as a common vagrant. No one will ever hear from you again."

The maid's eyes widened with dismay, and she dared to sass, "The earl would never let you."

"Well, the earl would never know, would he?" She flashed such a dangerous, feral sneer that the girl ran, giving Lydia the distinct impression that she'd have no further trouble in that quarter. She smiled, relishing the discreet exhibition of power.

It was so rewarding to lord herself over others, to wreak her petty retributions, and she sighed with pleasure.

Noise erupted in the hall, and she smoothed her features as Rebecca strolled into the room. Rebecca was aggravatingly elegant—she seemed to glide rather than walk—and Lydia's elevated mood vanished in an instant.

She couldn't bear to be reminded of Rebecca's perfections! Her flawlessness, next to Lydia's dour ordinariness, was like a seething, livid monster that was eating Lydia alive.

Rebecca was everything that Lydia was not. She was pretty, with rosy cheeks, shiny brunette hair, and expressive green eyes. Her looks, coupled with her petite size, curvaceous anatomy, and kindly manner, never ceased to annoy Lydia.

Why did Rebecca have to be so sweet? So wonderful? Why did she possess so many positive female traits, while Lydia possessed none?

"Hello, Lydia," Rebecca chirped as she waltzed in, grabbed a plate, and filled it with food. She never waited for the servants to assist her, claiming she didn't care to disturb them. "Isn't it a fine morning?"

"It's supposed to rain," Lydia countered. She loathed Rebecca's chirpy attitude and constantly strove to quash it.

"Is it? That's too bad." She peeked out the window, checking the street, which was dry. "We could stay at home and invite guests over to play charades. Wouldn't that be fun?"

"I abhor charades."

"You do not," Rebecca scolded, though merrily, as she sat down. "You're just being contrary."

"The clothes you ordered are ready. If you want to wear the emerald ball gown Friday night, you have to have a final fitting. You can't be dawdling in the house."

"Duty calls then," Rebecca said, chuckling. "I shall force myself to the seamstress. Will you join me? When I was there the other day, she had several dresses that would be flattering on you. Why not treat yourself?"

"Why not indeed?" Lydia's fury sparked, but she tamped it down. "I've employed a companion for you so I needn't be bothered."

She tried never to be seen in public with Rebecca. Rebecca was so stunning, and Lydia was so plain, that there was always nattering about what an odd pair they were, and Lydia wouldn't provide fodder for the gossip mill.

Rebecca would be the belle of every soiree she attended. People would wax on about how dazzling she'd been, and the notion of all those compliments being spewed was like a wad of bread wedged in Lydia's throat.

When Rebecca was a baby, Lydia had frequently contemplated sneaking into the nursery and smothering her in her sleep. She never could figure out why she hadn't.

"What are your plans with Cousin Alex?" She'd had loads of practice at hiding her emotions, so no one would ever guess how much she detested him, too. "Are you going riding?"

"Not if it rains!" Rebecca teasingly responded.

"Don't be smart." Lydia spoke as if they were mother and daughter rather than siblings. With Lydia being thirteen years older and having raised Rebecca, she behaved like a stern parent.

"Oh, Lydia," Rebecca retorted, "you're being such a stick-in-the-mud. Are you feeling all right? Have you a headache?"

"No. I'm merely weary of the engagement preparations. You're aware of how much I hate London."

"I realize that, and you're a dear to have accompanied me to town."

"It's not as if I had any choice. I couldn't let you travel alone, and you certainly couldn't reside with Cousin Alex by yourself."

"No, I couldn't, and I'm grateful to you."

"Are you, Rebecca? Are you really?"

"Yes, Lydia."

Rebecca offered the charming smile for which she was renowned, and Lydia yearned to slap it off her face.

It was the height of affront for Lydia to watch and help as Rebecca completed her betrothal to Alex. Originally, Lydia was to have been Alex's bride, but for reasons that had never been clear, their fathers had switched the girls' positions, so that Rebecca was the fiancée and Lydia was nothing, at all.

Lydia hadn't cared about Alex—she was incapable of such strong sentiment—but it galled that Rebecca would have something that should have been Lydia's. Rebecca could have had any man she wanted, and should have been required to accept Alex's younger, ne'er-do-well brother, Nicholas, but she'd latched on to Alex without a thought as to Lydia's wishes.

It was a shame Lydia couldn't forgive, and sometimes she worried that she might explode from carting around so much rage.

More footsteps sounded, and Ellen staggered in. She was severely attired in a drab gray dress. Her golden hair was concealed by an unsightly mobcap and, as if she'd been ill, she was pale and shaky.

She slinked in and obtained a single piece of toast, which was strange considering that she normally ate like a horse, taking full advantage of the meaning of *room and board.* She seated herself, while Rebecca chattered away, in her typical irritating fashion, about the fun they would have shopping.

Lydia ignored them both. She despised Ellen even more than Rebecca. Ellen was the most striking woman Lydia had ever met, surpassing Rebecca with a maturity and grace that Rebecca hadn't yet achieved. Though adequately reared and educated, Ellen was poverty-stricken and had no prospects, yet she carried herself like royalty. She was always putting on airs, and she acted as if she were a special guest or member of the family rather than a lowly employee.

Rebecca viewed Ellen as a friend and treated her as such, failing to indicate the distinction for Ellen as to her true role. Lydia had to continually chastise Ellen for forgetting her place.

"Would you mind terribly if one of the maids went with you?" Ellen was suddenly whining. "I'm not well."

Rebecca was about to reply with sympathetic drivel, so Lydia butted in before she could. "Yes, I *mind* if you loaf at home."

"Now Lydia," Rebecca interjected, "if Ellen is under the weather, I can run my errands tomorrow. It's no problem."

"You'll pick up the gowns this morning, Rebecca." Lydia's harsh tone cut off any argument. "As for you"— she glared at Ellen—"you're being compensated to attend Rebecca. Not wallow in your sickbed. Have some tea, restore yourself, then be about your duties."

Lydia rose and left, declining to linger and be badgered by either of them. There was nothing more nauseating than observing the two of them together when they were chummy and cordial.

As she stomped down the hall, she recognized that her temper was more aggravated than usual. She couldn't decide whether it was from her anger over the pending nuptials or from the fact that she'd bumped into Nicholas earlier and he'd been too cross to say hello.

Somehow . . . someway . . . she vowed to herself, she would get even with all of them. Before she was through, she would make them pay for every slight, and they would all be so sorry.

• • •

Nicholas Marshall paused outside the dressing room of the infamous French actress Suzette DuBois. She was applying her stage makeup and about to don her costume. The evening's performance would be lackluster, the actors boring and inept, the comedy stupid, but she would be magnificent.

He wasn't supposed to visit unless he'd located the funds to set her up as his mistress. She was tired of waiting and was distressing him with her insistence that she would soon search for another protector, which he couldn't allow.

He had to have her for his own! He had to! He couldn't tolerate any other conclusion.

Through the crack in the door, he could see her strutting about, her flaming red hair flowing to her hips, her thighs covered by a pair of frilly drawers, her slender feet balanced on a pair of spiky heels.

Her corset was laced tight, her splendid bosom pushed up and out. As he spied on her, she untied the strings, drawing out the moment until the suspense was excruciating; then she tugged at the undergarment and shimmied it off.

Breasts bared, she arched and stretched, the creamy mounds shifting and swaying as she rolled her shoulders. She retrieved a towel and rubbed it across her arms, her nape, her chest, tracing it round and round.

His lust spiraled to a treacherous height, and he couldn't stand to admit that she might never be his. He had coveted many things in his twenty-eight years of living, and he was adept at garnering what he craved— through fair methods or foul—but only she had eluded his grasp. The cost to have her, to support her, was simply too great.

For the thousandth time, he cursed his lot. By committing the horrid sin of being born second, his status was diminished accordingly. Then there were the rumors about his beloved mother's adultery.

Nicholas didn't resemble Alex in the least. Alex looked like their father, with dark hair, blue eyes, and a tall, trim physique. Nicholas was blond, with brown eyes, a stocky build, and a bit of padding around his middle.

Their father had taken the differences to heart, and Nicholas's inheritance had been reduced to a meager scrap, a paltry farm called New Haven. The hideous property was his sole possession, but the income from it was scarcely enough to keep him in clothes, let alone having his own house or carriage. He had to constantly beg Alex for money.

What was he to do? How was he to purchase Suzette's favors? He was so obsessed with her that he was beginning to fear for his sanity. She was like a dangerous disease for which there was no cure.

She turned toward him, and she scooped a dab of cream from a jar and massaged it onto her nipples. They were tiny little buds—like a young boy's—and they constricted even further as the cold ointment was slathered across them.

As she pinched and squeezed, he was goaded past his limit. He wouldn't dawdle in the hall like a supplicant, wouldn't plead for permission to enter, and he burst through the door.

At his abrupt appearance she was startled, and she frowned. "Nick, *mon ami,* why are you here? I asked you not to come back."

"I won't stay away. I can't."

"Why torture yourself? After the performance, I'm off to meet with Monsieur Delford. We're discussing terms."

Delford was an obese, aging reprobate, and the idea of his sawing away between her pristine thighs was nearly Nicholas's undoing.

"I won't let him have you!" he threatened. "I'll kill you first. You're mine, do you hear me? Mine!"

She scoffed. "I'm *yours*? If that's what you believe, you're mad."

He bristled with rage, and he grabbed her and pinned her to the wall. He leaned in, his body flattened to hers, and she struggled to escape, but she was no match for his larger size.

"I'll find the cash," he contended, having not a clue from where.

"So you keep saying."

"I will!"

"Your assurances grow tedious."

"My word is my bond!" he lied. "I'm about to be engaged."

"A likely story—that you've told me before."

"Even as we speak, I'm working on a betrothal."

"I'm not cheap, *mon cher*. To afford me, you'd have to marry an heiress, but who would have you?"

The snide question was too much for his pride, and he wouldn't be denigrated by her. For over a decade, he'd debased himself before every rich girl in the kingdom, but nary a one had been interested. He lacked his brother's title and charm, so he had to scrounge for the scraps others left behind. But he was finished groveling. He would figure something out; he always did.

She was squirming and writhing, and he clasped her arms to her sides. He bent down and sucked on her nipple.

"I know what you need," he growled. "I know what you want."

He unbuttoned his trousers, and he guided her fingers inside, wrapping them around his rigid cock. She didn't like to touch his private parts, and he had to show her how, had to force her to obey.

He flexed into her closed fist, and he considered spilling himself, but he didn't. They played an infuriating game. She tantalized him with prospects for pleasure, but she only let him have a small sample, just enough so that he returned for more.

She'd been very clear: She wasn't free, and he had to pay for his privileges. If he desired her, he'd have to arrange his financial affairs.

"Get down on your knees," he ordered. "Lick your tongue across me—as you did the other night."

She shuddered with distaste. "I don't like to."

"I don't care."

He tried pushing her to the floor, but she wouldn't go. She claimed that when he produced the money she'd do whatever he demanded—that she'd take it in the mouth, that she'd take it in the ass—and the opportunity to have her at his mercy, to attempt such perverted deeds, was agonizing to contemplate.

"I hate doing it with men," she declared. "If you brought me a woman, she and I could dally—while you watch."

She repeatedly mentioned how much she liked women, and the notion tormented him. He was determined to demonstrate how it could be between them, to change her depraved preferences.

"No women for you," he scolded. "You'll ride my prick, and you'll enjoy it. Now get down."

Though mutinous, she finally dropped to her knees, and her compliance had him feeling omnipotent and invincible. She pulled his phallus from his pants and licked across the end—once, twice—then she lurched away and stood. While he was in a wretched condition, she was calm and composed, and acting as if nothing had happened.

"There'll be no more," she asserted, "until you move me into my new house. Unless, of course, Monsieur Delford moves me into one first. What is your plan, Nick?"

"I told you: I'll kill you before I let Delford have you."

"How will you stop him?"

She shoved him away and marched to her mirror, where she went back to fussing with her makeup, and he was incensed by her disrespect.

He clutched her around the waist, ready to bend her over the chair and have her against her will. After all her derision, after all the waiting and worrying, it would be so satisfying to proceed.

"Let me go!" She elbowed him in the ribs.

"You'll have no one but me," he vowed. "No one!"

"You are a dreamer."

He tightened his grip, and she squealed with alarm, which delighted him. Her fear was thrilling, and he'd instigated a bruising kiss when a stagehand poked his nose in and inquired, "Are you all right, Miss DuBois?"

Suzette yanked away. "I'm fine, Tom. Would you escort Mr. Marshall out? I must finish dressing."

The boy held the door, and Nicholas hesitated, then stomped out. Suzette called after him, "Two weeks, Nick. I want your answer in two weeks."

He huffed out the rear of the theater, and he hovered in the dank, smelly alley.

Two weeks . . . two weeks . . . The words rang like a death knell. He had a fortnight to procure a fortune, and the only single, prosperous female he hadn't pestered was his obnoxious cousin, Lydia. She was so disagreeable that, even with her enormous wealth, she couldn't entice a suitor.

He tarried in the shadows, ruing the past, pondering the future, when he thought of Lydia again, and he couldn't get her out of his head.

Yes, she was repugnant, and homely as a mud boot, but she was also stupid and slow—and pathetically lonely—which he deemed an advantageous combination.

With no trouble at all, he could coax her to any conduct he commanded. After all, how could she refuse him? A swift wedding would have to follow.

Could he do it? Had he the stomach for such a revolting scheme?

Out on the street, coaches arrived at the theater as fashionable London disembarked to watch Suzette. In his mind's eye, he could picture her twirling and strutting on the stage, could envision the men in the audience as they ogled and cheered.

"Lydia . . ." he mused. "Why didn't I think of her before?"

James Drake sneaked out of the crowd, walked up behind his sister, and murmured, "Hello, Ellen."

She froze, struggling to decide whether she'd actually heard his voice.

"James!" she breathed, and she whipped around.

She was so much older than his recollections, but
then a decade had passed since he'd last seen her. In his
imagination, she'd remained the naïve eighteen-year-
old girl she'd been when disaster had struck, but then it
would be difficult to suffer such a trauma and stay the
same. He, himself, was so altered that anyone who'd
known him prior wouldn't recognize him.

At age twenty-six, he was no longer the lanky, handsome youth he'd been. Stress and adversity had whitened
his blond hair to silver, had dulled his blue eyes to gray.
He was brawny, strong as an ox, his skin tanned from laboring in the harsh sun, his face cynical and wrinkled
with crow's-feet, his smile gone.

His back was crisscrossed with flogging scars, his
shoulders slightly stooped, and he limped, a souvenir of
a leg broken during an especially vicious beating.

There was a rough edge to him, one of danger and
menace that warned others to keep their distance. He
exuded power and threat, and though he was attired as
a gentleman—his cravat neatly tied and jacket perfectly tailored—he was an imposter. Every genteel ten-
dency had been lashed out of him.

He was pleased to note that Ellen was still terribly
pretty, but her mischievous innocence had vanished. She
was so prim and proper, so mature and sad. She seemed
weary, as if she'd endured too much, and even though
none of the scandal had been his fault, he felt responsible for the changes.

Would he ever make it up to her? Should he even try?

It was obvious she yearned to hug him, and he could
scarcely refrain, either, but they were in the middle of
Bond Street, with pedestrians careening by, so any emotional display would have caused a scene. For that very

reason, he'd chosen the busy spot. He'd been nervous about his reception, and lest she turn away in disgust, he'd wanted the throng to shield him if he needed to slink away.

At learning that she was elated with the rendezvous, his jaded heart rejoiced.

Surreptitiously she slipped her hand into his. "What are you doing here?"

"You wrote that you'd be in London," he explained. "I had to see you. Are you receiving the money I've sent?" It wasn't nearly enough, but he shared what he could, when he could, and the amounts were growing.

"Yes, thank you. I bought this dress with some of it." She held out the flare of the skirt so he could observe how fetching it was.

"I'm glad you spent it on yourself." Unable to resist, he reached out and toyed with a lock of hair that had fallen from her chignon. "You look just the same."

"Liar," she teased, but her smile faded as she noticed the ring on his finger. It was a gold band, with a collection of sapphire stones in the shape of a bluebird—an exact replica of the cursed piece of jewelry that had ruined them.

"Where did you get that ring?" she demanded.

"Don't worry. It's not real."

"Then . . . why?"

"So that I won't ever forget what they did to me."

"Oh, James . . ." She sighed, clearly wanting to chastise but comprehending that he wouldn't listen. Instead, she queried, "How are you obtaining so much cash? I wish you'd confide in me."

"I work, silly. From where would you assume it comes?" He supplied nothing further, for he didn't care to expound on vice and gambling, on extortion and intimidation. She would never understand or condone his acquired habits.

His tribulations had furnished him with an interesting glimpse into his character that he wouldn't have had if his previous life had lumped on as planned. He could be ruthless, could be brutal, and he'd mustered his less savory traits to maximum effect.

He didn't mind wallowing with the lower classes of London's squalid neighborhoods. After all that had transpired, he wasn't destined to hobnob with the gentry as he had when he was a boy, but he hated that *she* had to work for a living.

By now, she should have been a matron with a successful husband and gaggle of children, mistress of a fine house, and a pillar of the community. None of those circumstances had come to fruition, and he was sure their father would never rest in peace until she was settled.

Two goals drove him: revenge—and a desire to have his sister comfortably situated. The twin objectives influenced his every move, and he would not relent until they were both achieved.

He didn't suppose they had much time to talk, so he needed to hurry. He'd spied on Ellen as her employer had flitted into a shop, and she would reappear soon. Ellen wouldn't want to be caught conversing with him.

"Tell me," he started. "Where is Father's grave located? I have to pay my respects."

She frowned, then said very gently, "There was no money, James, for a proper funeral. He was buried in the pauper's field, behind the church."

Which meant no stone had been carved, no marker had been left, to indicate that the kindly man had ever existed. It was another cross for James to bear, and it was awfully heavy. If he'd smote the dear fellow, himself, his burden couldn't have been any more profound.

The news hardened his resolve, focused his energy and determination. His family would be avenged! If it took till his dying breath, he would see to it.

Suddenly Ellen pulled away and straightened, and James glanced up to ascertain that her employer was returning.

The woman was younger than he'd presumed and extremely beautiful, with fabulous brunette hair and big green eyes. She was short but delightfully rounded in all the right spots, and she was very merry, exuding an aplomb and grace that only the very rich can convey.

She symbolized everything he loathed, and James detested her on sight. Swiftly and covertly he evaluated her jewelry, her purse, assessing value and worth, as he conjectured as to which item would be easiest to pilfer and pawn. He hoped she wasn't too attached to any of them, for one would be missing when he walked away.

"Ellen," she greeted, as she approached, "you're so sweet to have waited for me."

"It's no trouble," Ellen replied. "You know that."

"I couldn't decide on the fabric I wanted, but ultimately, I picked the blue."

"Excellent. It will be superb on you."

There was an awkward pause as the woman scrutinized James, then Ellen, then James again. Obviously, she expected an introduction.

Ellen was embarrassed, and she tried to figure out what to say, but her tongue got rolling before her brain kicked in. "Rebecca, allow me to present my . . . my . . ."

She couldn't finish the sentence, so he stepped forward, clasped the lady's hand, and bowed over it. "I am

Mr. James Duncan," he lied, providing a false surname. "Ellen and I are old friends. We grew up together in Surrey, and we haven't seen each other for . . . oh . . . ten years or more."

"Ten years! My goodness!"

"Isn't it amazing? We just bumped into each other on the street."

"After all this time?" she gushed. "How marvelous for both of you. I'm Miss Rebecca Burton," she added, making the overture herself since it was apparent that Ellen couldn't.

"A *Miss* Burton?" he inquired. "How is it that no lucky man has snatched you up?"

"One has." She grinned and flashed a ring with a diamond the size of Ireland. "I'm in London to become officially engaged."

"Really?"

This was information that Ellen hadn't shared in the few letters she'd penned. In fact, she'd been particularly reticent about her post, but Miss Burton seemed acceptable enough.

"Perhaps you know my fiancé?" Miss Burton tentatively ventured.

The question finally prodded Ellen to speak. "James, she's betrothed to Alex Marshall."

It was a shock to hear Stanton's name uttered aloud, and he was proud at how calm he acted. A thousand thoughts raced through his head, the primary one being that he couldn't believe Ellen would take a job from such people. No wonder she hadn't mentioned it!

As to Miss Burton's devoted fiancé, James had never discovered which of the spoiled, vain aristocrats had actually stolen the ring that had secured his desperate future, but Alex Marshall had been in attendance, and he was on the list of those from whom James would extract retribution.

"Congratulations," he offered to Miss Burton. "He's incredibly fortunate."

"You're very kind," she responded.

She smiled, dimples creasing her cheeks. It charged the air and lit up the space around him, and a wicked notion occurred to him, one that was cruel and wrong, and thus exactly the sort upon which he thrived.

Stanton might think he was about to marry Rebecca Burton, but now that James had crossed her path, the chances of it ever happening were very remote.

"I'd been apprised of the engagement," James fibbed, "but not about the loveliness of the bride-to-be."

She laughed. "You are a terrible flirt, Mr. Duncan."

"When confronted with such splendor," he gallantly declared, "I can't help myself."

"It sounds as if you know Lord Stanton," she probed.

"We've been acquainted for years."

The answer was literally true, if not entirely correct, and was meant to give the impression that James ran in her social circle, that he frequented the types of places where Stanton might show his smug face. The fabrication would make it so much simpler to arrange a second meeting.

"We should be going," Ellen interjected, looking grim. With a decade having elapsed, James was nearly a stranger, and she couldn't be certain what he intended.

"How long will you be in London?" he asked his sister.

"Through the summer," she stated, "but after that, I can't predict what my plans will be."

Miss Burton jumped in. "You'll stay with us till the wedding, won't you? You can't leave before then. I'd miss you too much."

"Through the summer," Ellen repeated, "then we'll see how events play out."

"I'll be in touch," he told Ellen, but the same applied to Miss Burton.

"I'd like that," Ellen said.

"Good day, Miss Burton, Miss Drake."

He bowed and departed, sliding around Miss Burton and pretending to be jostled against her as he went. The crowd swallowed him up, but as he strolled away she exclaimed, "Oh, my purse! Where could it have gone?"

He kept walking.

~ 5 ~

Miss Drake had stopped following him. Why?

Wherever Alex went, he kept peeking over his shoulder, expecting to espy her—and her damnable deck of cards—but she was nowhere to be found, and her vanishing nagged at him.

He sneaked down the dark hall toward her room, unable to halt the forward progress of his feet. What bizarre whim was urging him on? When she opened her door, what would be her response?

She'd faint, so he wouldn't knock. He'd simply enter and discover what had happened. It wasn't as if she could protest to anyone, and if she was brave enough to tattle, who would listen? He was lord of the manor, and the staff comprehended that he could act however he pleased.

Gad, but he was being an ass! This was madness, this was lunacy, this was danger and stupidity and every other cautionary word he could conjure, yet he couldn't desist. He felt as if a magnet were leading him to her.

Memories kept creeping in, as he recalled how she'd

looked, how she'd tasted, when he'd kissed her sense-less a few nights earlier. He'd done it to teach her a les-son, to knock her off her lofty moral pedestal, but *he* was the one who had been unsettled.

Since that ignominious meeting, he hadn't seen her, though not for lack of trying. He'd dawdled at home, spending many tedious hours waiting—in vain!—for Miss Drake to appear, but she'd been markedly absent.

Most likely, she was embarrassed at how her preach-ing had backfired, which was precisely the emotional state he'd been hoping to inspire. Yet he was fretting over how she'd weathered the ordeal and, if he was candid, craving the chance to do much the same with her again.

Somehow, the aggravating female had slipped under his defenses, had flustered him until he was no longer sure of what he'd meant to achieve. By trifling with her he'd unleashed an odd reservoir of want and need that he hadn't grasped he'd been harboring.

Miss Drake had put her whole heart and soul into their embrace, had joined in as if they were the last cou-ple on earth. Her enthusiasm had jangled loose a desire to return to the heady days when sex had mattered. How had the joy been lost? Why couldn't it be resurrected?

In some deeply buried, disregarded part of him, he was positive that if he kissed Miss Drake a few more times, he might find something for which he'd been searching without even realizing he was.

He arrived at her door, and without delay—where he might have taken a moment to reconsider—he spun the knob, tiptoed in, and . . .

She was mostly naked.

Her back was to him, her fabulous golden hair down

and brushed out, her feet bare, and she was dressed only in a petticoat. She was washing, dipping a cloth in a bowl and stroking it across her body.

In all his fantasizing about how he'd barge in, it had never occurred to him to wonder what *she* might be doing. He was stunned, elated at having stumbled upon the erotic sight, and too uncouth to slink out as he ought. Like the worst voyeur, he watched.

Without planning to, he must have made a noise, because she gasped and whipped around. Her cheeks were flushed, her blue eyes glittering like diamonds in the dim candlelight. Clutching the cloth to her bosom, she tried to shield what he shouldn't be allowed to view, but with scant success. She was sensuous and adorable, and the most marvelous impression of anticipation swept over him. Any spectacular thing might transpire and it would be all right.

"You shouldn't be here," she said.

"Probably not," he agreed.

"Go away."

"No."

He approached until they were toe-to-toe, and she gazed up at him, refusing to recoil, refusing to cower.

"What do you want?" she asked.

"I had to see you."

"Well, now you have."

"You've ceased hounding me"—he grinned, anxious to ease the awkwardness of the encounter—"so I thought I'd better check on you."

"I don't care where you go or what you do," she claimed. "It's none of my business."

"But your harassment was beginning to grow on me. Why quit when you're having such incredible results?"

"I shouldn't have pestered you. As you so elegantly pointed out, I'm in no condition to chastise over the weaknesses of others. I have plenty of my own flaws about which to worry."

"You're a veritable slattern," he joked.

"Don't make fun of me."

"I'm not."

"You can't stay. Be gone! At once!"

He ignored her edict and yanked the cloth away. She squealed with affront and struggled to fold her arms across her chest, but he wouldn't let her hide herself. He gripped her wrists and pulled them away so that he could study her.

Her breasts were perfectly formed, neither too big nor too little, and the appropriate size to fill a man's hands. She was breathing fast, terrified by what he intended, and the elevated respiration had hardened her nipples so that they jutted out.

"You're very beautiful," he murmured, and he reached out and caressed one of the soft mounds.

"Please don't," she implored.

"I won't hurt you," he vowed.

"I can't imagine you'll do anything else."

As he leaned down to kiss her, she turned away, so he grazed her cheek instead. Continuing on, he nuzzled down her neck, to her cleavage, across her breast, and he toyed with the inflamed tip, licking it over and over.

He couldn't believe what he'd started, couldn't understand his strange urge to be with her. The cost of seducing a chaste female was much too high, so he never dabbled with innocents. There were many wicked, amenable trollops who would execute any deed for a price, so he couldn't figure out what was motivating him.

She was a maiden, a spinster—Rebecca's companion, for God's sake—and he wasn't some violent roué who would force himself on a woman. Yet none of it signified.

He'd leapt across any acceptable boundary of propriety, but his behavior didn't seem wrong. His feelings for her were convoluted and perplexing, and he couldn't sort them out. Though he barely knew her and they hadn't spoken more than a few words, he felt as if she belonged to him, and thus his conduct was permissible, an extension of what had gone before and what would come after.

He trailed up her bosom, to her chin, to her mouth. His lips teased hers, but she was trying not to react. He could perceive her confusion, her uncertainty as to whether she should participate. She desperately wanted to—he could sense her eagerness, her yearning—but she was conflicted over her lusty nature and resisting it with all her might.

"Kiss me back, Ellen."

"No, I can't."

"Yes, you can."

Ultimately, she relented, and cad that he was, he took full advantage. She tasted so sweet, so dear. He nibbled across her skin. It was moist and warm from her ablutions, and she smelled like soap and flowers. The invigorating aroma called to his primitive side, which was begging to have her for his own.

He clasped her buttocks, drawing her loins to his, his cock needing him to press, needing him to flex. Though mentally she didn't comprehend what the gesture indicated, her body recognized what was required, and her hips responded, meeting his in a slow rhythm.

There was no predicting what might have transpired, but footsteps sounded in the hall, and they froze. He held her close, her face wedged to his chest, her pulse hammering with fear like a captured bird's.

They listened, as the strides neared, then passed by and into the stairwell.

"It was merely a servant," he whispered.

"And you think that makes it all right?"

They tarried a few seconds more, but the intimate spell was shattered, and the fiendishness of his actions swept over them like a poisonous cloud. He was chagrined, while she was shocked and appalled, and she lurched away to grab her robe from the end of the bed. With trembling hands, she jerked it on and tied the belt; then she went to the window and stared out at the stars. It was obvious she was hoping he'd leave without humiliating either of them further, but when he was around her he couldn't behave rationally.

He walked up behind her and rested his palms on her shoulders.

"I won't say I'm sorry," he told her.

"I will then. Just go."

"I can't. Not yet."

He played with her hair, sifting through the silky strands. It was the kind of hair a mermaid might have, or a magical siren who lured sailors to crash on the rocks, and after what had occurred with her he grasped how cheerfully those poor fellows had traveled to their dooms.

He felt as if he were on a ship at sea, that the rudder had broken and he was careening toward a perilous shore.

"What's happening to us?" she queried.

"We're attracted to one another, in an extreme manner that's impossible to fight."

"But I don't even like you, so how could that be?"

She chuckled miserably, and he did, too, and he snuggled himself to her backside.

"I want to visit you again," he declared. "I want to come to you every night."

"Absolutely not."

"I have to know you this way."

"You're daft to ask it of me. I'd never agree."

"I'm not asking."

She shifted and peered up at him. "You're ordering me to consent?"

"I guess I am."

"You'd ravish me? Against my will?"

"Of course I would," he boasted, not having the faintest idea from where such a falsehood had sprung. "It's the type of man I am—which can't be any surprise to you."

She evaluated him, her keen assessment digging deep. He tried to look stern and sinister but failed, and she shook her head. "You shouldn't lie to me. I can tell when you are."

He bent down and kissed her, once more. For an instant, she allowed the advance and reveled with him, but sanity swiftly returned, and she yanked away.

"Where are you from, Ellen?"

"Nowhere."

He laughed. "Everyone's from somewhere."

"Not me."

"Where is your family located?"

"I have no family. That's why I work for Lydia. I must support myself."

It was a sad confession that tugged at his conscience, that made him want to voice offers he wasn't prepared to tender. "Then who is to prevent you from dallying with me?"

"*I* am the one. It's wrong."

"According to whom?"

"You mean besides God?"

He grinned, sinful but not repentant. "Yes, besides Him."

"It would hurt Rebecca—if she learned of it."

"Rebecca would never know," he arrogantly contended.

"You can't promise that with any conviction. Secrets have an annoying habit of leaking out."

"But you're almost finished at your position with her." As they chatted, he was caressing her, smoothing his hands over her stomach, her thighs, her breasts, to vividly remind her of how wonderful they were together. "You'll move on to another job. I understand you feel a loyalty to her—"

"As you clearly don't!"

Declining to be goaded into a discussion of his faults, he disregarded the taunt. "—so how can it matter?"

"It matters to me." She whirled around, a fist clutched over her heart. "I don't have much left that's my own, but I have my integrity and my scruples. She's been a friend to me—when no one else has been in a very long while. If I betrayed her, I couldn't live with myself."

He was curious as to what had wreaked such disaster in her short life, but he was too conceited to inquire, too set on seduction to care. "What's between us, it's unique and exceptional. A person could search for all of eternity but never stumble on such bliss. You're crazy to deny yourself."

"Then call me mad, for I will never yield to ardor. I'm not that sort of woman."

"You're *exactly* that sort of woman."

"Talking to you is like talking to the furniture." She pointed to the door. "Why don't you go?"

He thought about refusing, about staying and tempting her to mischief again, which he was sure he could do without much effort. She was so vibrant, so impatient for what he could bestow. It would be simple to entice her, but she was confused by her physical desires, by her willingness to take part in carnal games.

He wanted her aroused and pining away. She wasn't aware of how unrequited passion could smolder, how it could gnaw away at one's best intentions, but she was about to find out. At their next rendezvous—which would be soon—she'd be much more disposed.

"I'll be here tomorrow night," he advised. "At midnight. Be ready to welcome me."

"No!"

"I'm not giving you a choice."

"I'll lock my door. I won't let you in."

"I have a key," he warned. "I'll use it."

He strolled out, and as he stepped into the quiet corridor she muttered a very unladylike epithet and hurled an object after him. It banged the wall and fell with a muted thump.

He smiled, tickled to note that she was in a disturbed state, and he had to admit that he was in no better condition. He was hard and aching, and he burned with a strange yearning as he speculated on how he'd manage until he could be with her, once again.

He couldn't wait, and just from contemplating their

pending meeting a burst of gladness raced over him. For
ages, his world had been so dreary, so uneventful; then
she'd barged in and changed everything. She made him
happy, made him anxious to proceed. It was a novel sensation, a type of joy mixed with lust, and he couldn't remember ever feeling quite so peculiar.

Excited and eager, he took the stairs two at a time.

6

"You're dressed like a bloody duke. What are your plans for the evening?"

"I'm off to con a lady."

"Out of what?"

James chuckled and peeked out the carriage window as it rumbled to a stop in front of a grand mansion. The windows were open and aglow with the flickering of thousands of candles, and the sounds of an expensive orchestra wafted out on the night air.

"Out of her drawers," he answered, "and her money, and whatever else I can convince her to give me."

"Lucky boy," his partner, Willie Westmoreland, replied. He glanced out, too, taking special note of the bejeweled women who were parading into the house. "Have you need of any help?"

"The idea is to be inconspicuous," James remarked, "so no thank you."

There was nothing ordinary about Willie. Not his height, not his looks, not his bearing. Though he'd been born a bastard, he claimed that his father actually was a duke—so perhaps Willie knew how they dressed—but if he had exalted bloodlines, they hadn't been of much benefit when he was transported with James. He'd been a common criminal and treated just as brutally.

They'd suffered indignities no man could describe, had endured humiliations no man could forget or forgive, and it had forged a bond between them that could never be broken.

James hopped out, grinning as he went. "I'll see you tomorrow."

"Have you an invitation to this affair?"

"What are you? My social secretary?"

"They won't let you in without one. The rich are fussy that way."

"Don't worry. There isn't a building in London that can keep me out."

"No, there isn't. You had a good teacher."

"Yes, I did," James responded, Willie being that teacher.

James ambled into the crowd, then continued down the walk. In a few seconds, he was over the hedge and strolling in the rear garden. A few seconds more, and he was in the ballroom, sipping on champagne and nibbling on a pastry.

He had the clothes to masquerade as a member of the Quality, had received a suitable education and upbringing, and the old habits quickly returned. His father had scrimped and sacrificed to send him to schools they couldn't afford, so James understood these people, how they acted, how they talked. He'd hobnobbed with their sons, had played with them at their summer homes in Surrey.

The guests wouldn't speculate over him, and if he

stumbled upon any prior associates, he wouldn't fret about detection. They'd never recognize him. He was too changed.

When he initially observed Rebecca Burton, she was dancing, though he couldn't locate Ellen, and he was glad. The less Ellen knew of his scheme, the better.

He watched from a corner, tracking Burton's every move. By being engaged, she had too much liberty, which was convenient. He'd be able to approach her without being questioned, and she'd be free to exit without others noticing.

He thought about signing her dance card—when he was an adolescent, dancing had been his favorite amusement—but after much deliberation, he decided he couldn't. As a newcomer, he'd be too visible. Plus, his ruined ankle couldn't take the strain.

The set concluded, and she headed for the buffet table. He followed her, and he rippled with an unaccustomed excitement. He was ecstatic at having the chance to speak with her, to chat and gaze into her pretty green eyes, which had him wondering if his recent trials hadn't left him a bit deranged.

Whenever he was in the mood, he had plenty of female companionship. After all, he wallowed with thieves and whores, so it was simple to find a trollop, but it had been an eternity since he'd parlayed with a woman of Miss Burton's caliber.

The last dance he'd attended had been held a few days before his arrest, and it was still vivid in his memory. There'd been so many girls present, girls like Miss Burton from wealthy, respectable families, who had teased and flirted. To his astonishment, a wave of nostalgia swept over him, as he conjectured—for the first time in ages—over what his life would have been like if he'd eluded disaster.

He shoved the silly reflection away. It was pointless to ruminate over the past, futile to wax on about what might have been, and he scolded himself to buck up, to steel himself against any heightened sentiment. Miss Burton symbolized all that he abhorred. If she was fetching, if she was sweet and pleasant, so what?

She had just grabbed a plate when he stepped in behind her, standing much too close, her skirt billowing around his legs. To ascertain who had arrived, she peered over her shoulder, and she smiled.

"Hello, Mr. Duncan," she greeted, referring to him by the fake name he'd provided.

"Hello, Rebecca." He used her given name, and it flustered her, but she didn't comment, and he took it as a propitious beginning.

"We meet again."

"Yes, we do, and you must call me James."

She gaped about, as if wanting someone to tell her it would be all right, and her consternation was an indication of how sheltered she'd been. She was so innocent, and the realization thrilled him. Her naïveté had her ripe for the plucking, would make her so much easier to seduce.

He let his masculine appreciation wash over her, let her sense his admiration and regard, and she was startled by his blatant interest. Clearly, no man had ever assessed her as he was doing.

Did Alex Marshall care about her, at all? Had he ever looked at her and seen anything besides a means to increase his vast fortune? Had he ever evinced the slightest awareness of her as a woman?

Apparently not.

James leaned in, delighted to note that she was extremely rattled.

They enjoyed an unusual affinity. He felt it, and she felt it, too, and she was perplexed by the commotion their nearness generated. The air around them sparked with energy, and he could barely keep from reaching out, from resting a hand on her waist. It would have been so natural to touch her.

He'd had his share of naughty flings, many more than a bachelor ought. Desperate situations threw desperate people together, so he'd fornicated with many hopeless women who'd lost all, who were anxious for the solace that human contact could render.

He'd learned how to satisfy a female, and he had no qualms about utilizing his dubious skills to ruin Rebecca Burton. While she'd be humiliated in the end, the journey would be marvelous—for both of them.

"I want to be alone with you," he whispered.

"What?" Shocked by his suggestion, she peeked around to ensure that no one had eavesdropped. "You're mad."

"No. I'll be outside. In the garden, behind the gazebo."

His focus dipped to her mouth, and he stared at her ruby lips until she recognized his carnal intent for what it was.

"I can't," she claimed.

"Why not? Who's to prevent you?" Before she could refuse, he added, "In five minutes. I'll be waiting."

He left without glancing back, so he didn't know if she watched him go, but he was fairly certain she'd come. He was an astute judge of character, and where she was concerned he had enhanced perception. She'd been intrigued by his bold advance, and she'd be eager to converse, if only to remind him that she was bound to Stanton.

Exactly seven minutes later, she walked onto the verandah.

"Curiosity killed the cat," he muttered. She was a fool to join him, and he was a fool to have asked, but he couldn't desist. Whatever happened, he wouldn't be sorry for how it evolved, though she would be.

She was too trusting and gullible, so she'd never suppose that there might be a devious plot in progress. In her privileged life, nothing bad had ever transpired, so it was beyond her comprehension to consider that he had ulterior motives.

She strolled into the yard and skirted the gazebo. Once she was concealed from the house, she murmured, "Mr. Duncan?"

He crept up and slipped his fingers into hers. She gasped with surprise, and he guided her off the path so that she was hidden with him. He studied her, evaluating her curvaceous figure, the nip and curve of her waist and hips. The bodice of her dress was cut low, to reveal a fabulous swell of bosom, and he was disturbed by how fervently he desired her.

It was his plan to trifle with her, to escort her down a road where she dare not travel, but it was to be a game for him, and his abrupt level of yearning had him worried. What might he do in order to possess her? To what lengths would he go to make her his own?

Any despicable behavior seemed possible, which was saying a lot. Over the previous decade, he'd proven himself capable of many nefarious deeds. When the circumstances required it, he could maim or murder, could rob or ravage, without restraint or remorse.

Could he blithely harm her? Or was there a flicker remaining of the boy he'd been, of the gentleman he'd been raised to be?

He didn't think so. His honorable tendencies had been buried, but with how she was gazing up at him his dormant conscience was stirred, and he tamped down any feelings of guilt.

He wouldn't be affected! Couldn't fret over what would become of her after he was finished! Alex Marshall deserved to lose something he valued, and what could be more appropriate than it being Rebecca Burton?

"Mr. Duncan—" she started, but he interrupted.

"James," he said. "My name is James."

"I'm engaged. I can't be out here with you."

"No one knows. It's all right." He led her farther into the shadows. She hesitated, not actually following, but not declining, either, and he soothed, "Don't be afraid. I won't hurt you."

"What is it you want from me?"

"I had to see you."

"But why?"

"Because you're the most stunning woman I've ever met." It wasn't some petty falsehood voiced to further his scheme. She was magnificent.

"Me? Stunning?"

"Yes."

She was bewildered at the compliment, and James was convinced that Marshall had never expressed any flatteries. His spirits soared. There wasn't a female alive who didn't relish being informed that she was special, and Rebecca was no different from any other. She'd soak up his praise like a sponge.

"You shouldn't say such things to me," she admonished.

"Why not? It's the truth."

"But I've been betrothed for so long that I feel like an old, married lady. I'm grateful for your attentions, but you can't address them to me."

While she was protesting his conduct, she hadn't stomped off in a huff. "You're not married—yet."

"No, but my fiancé would never approve of my chatting with you."

"Stanton can go to the devil," he vehemently declared. "Has he ever told you how beautiful you are? Or how superb you look with the moonlight shining on your hair?"

"No." She was perplexed anew, as if it had never occurred to her that Stanton ought to have been more effusive.

"You're a terrible match for him. He'll make you so miserable."

"Really, Mr. Duncan"—she chuckled nervously and tried to pull away—"you're too presumptuous."

"But I had to speak out. After we were introduced, I couldn't be silent."

"About what?"

"Have you any idea why he hasn't wed you before now?" James had no clue, but he was prepared to articulate any prevarication. He was determined to plant seeds of doubt, to spin the strands of his web.

"No, and if you're about to give me some horrid reason, I will never believe you."

"He has so many other women that he doesn't need to tie the knot. He's too busy philandering."

"You're lying."

"He keeps a mistress whom he adores, and he has no intention of splitting with her after the ceremony. Could you carry on like that? Could you turn a blind eye as he sneaked out, night after night, to be with her?"

For the briefest second, it seemed he'd misplayed his hand, that she'd slap him and flee, but her shoulders slumped and she whirled away.

"So it's true then," she mumbled.

"What is?"

"I overheard a remark once, about Alex and . . . and . . . how he entertains himself when I am in the country. I've always wondered if it meant what I suspected it did."

"If you marry him, he won't stop womanizing. He'll break your heart each and every day."

"I'm sure he will," she glumly agreed.

"I can't stand that this is to be your conclusion."

She was so wounded by the news that he felt as if he'd kicked a puppy, and he couldn't bear that he'd upset her. He drew her into his arms and snuggled her to him, and as he caught himself brooding over how marvelous it was to hold her, he chased the absurd notion away. When he was around her, he had to be cautious.

Their physical magnetism created feelings that weren't real, made him perceive facts that weren't accurate. She was merely a distraught female, one of many he'd comforted over the years. He had a soft spot for women, but he couldn't let his empathy interfere with his plans.

Yet he couldn't deny that the moment was tremendously pleasurable, and he wallowed for as long as she was inclined to linger. Finally, she shifted away. Her eyes glistened with tears, and he swiped at them.

"You don't have to marry him," he advised.

"Of course I do," she insisted. "It's all arranged. It's been arranged my entire life."

"But you don't have to go through with it."

"What would I do with myself if I didn't?"

"You could come away with me."

He was amazed by how fast they'd arrived at the dangerous juncture. It was an outrageous offer. Would it take root and grow?

She'd been groomed to wed Stanton, but deep down, was that what she wanted?

Had she ever contemplated throwing off the chains that bound her? Had she ever yearned for an adventure? Was she feeling trapped and manipulated? Or was she content to proceed down the path that had been chosen for her?

"Come away?" she mused. "With you?"

"Yes."

"To where?"

"To wherever you'd like to go."

"We'd just tot off? The two of us on a wild lark?"

"Yes."

"If you weren't a friend of Ellen's, I'd say you're a fortune hunter." She laughed at the prospect, as if it was fun to suppose he had such a base character. "I'm beginning to worry that I should be on guard around you."

"Are you rich?" he asked casually, his expression curious.

"Yes. Didn't you know?"

"No, and I don't need your money. I have plenty of my own." The assertion was a fib. He had savings that would eventually buy a house for Ellen and support her so that she never had to work again, but he hadn't reached that point.

"What—precisely—do you do for a living?"

"I'm in imports and exports."

It was a vague answer that gave no hint of the dockside thievery and smuggling that made up his criminal enterprise. He would commit any sin for cash, and he had no reservations about stealing from the wealthy sods who brought in the chattels that lined their fat purses.

"So we'd sail off on one of your ships?"

He didn't have any ships, but he was perfectly willing to let her assume he did. "Yes. We could travel to Jamaica or America or India. We could do whatever we pleased, and we'd never have to come back."

Strangely, he was excited by the lie, and he pondered what it would be like to run away with her. He thought he'd abandoned any hope of leading a normal life, but for a fleeting instant he regretted the loss of that opportunity for an ordinary existence. With a woman like Rebecca Burton at his side, a man could do anything.

"Mr. Duncan . . . James . . ." She sighed. "I've met you twice, and I've conversed with you for a total of about fifteen minutes. You're mad to presume I'd consider such an escapade, and I'm astounded that you'd suggest the possibility."

She tried to appear insulted but failed, and from her demeanor he was positive he'd touched a nerve. Perhaps she wasn't as eager for her pending nuptials as she had to maintain.

"I want you to be happy," he contended.

"I am happy."

"Are you? With a fiancé who doesn't care about you? Who doesn't love you?"

"He loves me."

"Has he ever told you so?"

"He doesn't have to."

Which meant he never had. "If you were about to be mine, I'd tell you every second."

"You would, would you? You're an incredible romantic."

"Why shouldn't I be? Especially if there's a chance I could end up with you."

She sighed again. "I should go in. By loitering here, I'm only encouraging you in your folly."

"It's not *folly*," he quietly stated.

"Yes, it is. You're wrong to have approached me, and I'm wrong to have listened."

"There's a splendid attraction between us. I feel it, and I know you feel it, too."

"But we're adults, so we needn't act on it."

"What if we did? What if we cast caution to the wind and forged ahead?"

"I'm sure disaster would result." As if cataloguing his features, she studied him, then said, "Good-bye."

She stepped away, but he had to stop her, had to provide her with a reason to sneak off in the future, and he was betting on what it could be.

"Good-bye," he replied, and he leaned down and kissed her, his lips lightly brushing hers, her warm breath coursing across his cheek.

It was extremely chaste, but it was fantastic. The world was reduced to its barest elements: him and her and the hushed night.

She was surprised by the brash maneuver, but she didn't pull away, or raise a fuss. She was very still, enjoying the sweetness of the embrace, and he speculated as to whether she'd ever been kissed and decided she probably hadn't been. Stanton didn't sound like the amorous type—at least not with her—and James was thrilled to be the first.

He held her close, their bodies melded. Her breasts were flattened to his chest, his aroused cock wedged to her belly, and though she was too unschooled to grasp what his erection indicated, her anatomy recognized that it was proceeding in the appropriate direction.

Her arms rose, and she hugged him, and the small gesture provoked him so that suddenly he desired more from her than she could ever give. He was yearning for love and companionship, for a home of his own, a devoted wife, and a gaggle of adorable children. He wanted all those things and more, and he was frightened by the ferocity of his craving.

He was the one to yank away, and he glared at her, a fiery storm of unspeakable hungers and passions churning around them.

"Don't ask me to walk with you again," she finally said. "I won't. Not ever."

She turned and ran toward the mansion.

"Rebecca!" he called, but she kept going.

He watched to guarantee she made it safely inside, and his mind was awhirl with how quickly he could finagle another rendezvous. Despite her plea that he leave her alone, he was determined to be with her. And soon.

He tiptoed to the rear wall, climbed over, and vanished.

～ 7 ～

"What am I to do?"

"Why keep pestering me? I haven't a better answer now than I had the last time you asked."

Nicholas sipped his brandy and glared at his brother. "It's not enough money for a bird to live on. I want more from the family coffers. I deserve more!"

"I won't dole it out to you," Alex insisted.

"You're a flippin' earl," Nicholas snapped. "You could share some of it if you wished."

"Perhaps I don't *wish* then."

"Bloody right."

They had the same argument at least once a month. Nicholas had been their mother's favorite, and she'd sworn he'd be as wealthy as Alex, but their father had only bequeathed him tiny New Haven. The rebuff was a burr under Nicholas's saddle, rubbing at his temper and his pride.

Why should Alex have everything, while he, Nicholas, had hardly anything at all?

"If you weren't such a spendthrift," Alex nagged,

"you'd have plenty to support yourself." He swilled his brandy, stood, and motioned to the door. "I'm weary of this quarrel. Let's join the ladies."

They'd actually dined at home with Lydia and Rebecca. The sisters were regular visitors, more like sisters than guests, so when they came to town there was none of the fanfare that attached to company. The brothers wouldn't try to entertain Lydia, for she was never happy, no matter what amusements were supplied.

"I've met someone," Nicholas admitted.

"To marry?" Alex was intrigued by the possibility.

"No, not to marry. What darling little rich girl would have me? I don't hold a title, remember?"

"You could have your choice. Stop complaining."

"I'm taking a mistress," he clarified.

"Is it anyone I know?"

"Her name is Suzette DuBois."

"The actress?"

"Yes. I must buy her a house and provide her with an allowance."

Alex frowned, then scoffed. "No."

"You have to help me!" Nicholas grabbed Alex by the lapels and gave him a firm shake. "You can't refuse. Not when this is so important to me."

At being manhandled Alex was furious, so Nicholas released him and moved away. Alex was bigger and tougher, and he wouldn't hesitate to administer a thrashing as he often had when they were boys.

"The woman is a shark," Alex said. "She'll eat you alive."

"I have to have her," Nicholas proclaimed. "I have to make her mine."

His obsession with Suzette was starting to rule his

life. He couldn't concentrate on any other topic, and his need to possess her was like a putrid tumor growing inside. He had to have her or die! Why couldn't Alex understand?

"You're mad to consider it," Alex contended. "Don't bother me about her again. I won't change my mind, so you'll be wasting your breath—and trying my patience."

He marched out so there wasn't opportunity for a caustic retort. The bastard! Always thinking he knew best! Always thinking he was smarter than everyone else!

Nicholas hated Alex, reviled his superior attitude, and begrudged him his dark good looks and urbane style. The disparity in their situations galled Nicholas beyond any sane limit.

What he wouldn't give to bring Alex down a peg or two! There had to be a way, and he was determined to find it.

Lydia dawdled in the deserted salon, a candle burning, as she listened to the noises of the party progressing without her. Rebecca had many friends, was constantly surrounded by an exuberant crowd, while Lydia was shunned and ignored. No one came to check on *her*; no one wanted to chat or mingle with *her*. It was all Rebecca, Rebecca, Rebecca.

Footsteps sounded in the hall, and momentarily Nicholas poked his nose into the room.

"Cousin Lydia," he said, "you're hiding again."

"Yes, I am. I can't abide that pompous mob."

His speech was slurred, indicating that he was inebriated, which seemed to be his habitual state. The fool had no notion of restraint, and Lydia couldn't stomach a weak man, especially one who couldn't manage his liquor.

He entered and shut the door, and she studied him suspiciously. When he sat next to her on the sofa, her brows rose to her hairline.

The randy goat! She was aware of what he intended. Years prior, another oaf just like him had feigned affection and trifled with her in secluded parlors. She'd been young and gullible as to masculine impulses, so she'd reveled in the nonsense he'd whispered as he'd persuaded her he was a genuine beau.

Of course, his attentions hadn't meant anything, and it had taken a humiliating trip to the barber to rid herself of the sin she'd committed. She'd never forgiven herself for being so stupid, but then she'd gained invaluable experience from the affair—experience that she'd used to push her father to an early grave.

Frequently she'd crept into her father's bed at night, murmuring like a harlot and doing foul deeds with him that no wife would have countenanced. He hadn't been able to resist his incestuous lusts, and she'd driven him insane with guilt and remorse, with terror over her sly threats to expose his unnatural behaviors.

She'd been wondering when Nicholas would realize she was the answer to his prayers. He always needed cash, and she was dying to be apprised of the details of his current fiscal crisis. She'd investigate later, but for now, she'd let him continue, smug with the knowledge that before the summer was through, she'd be married.

Despite how she publicly denied the prospect, it was her secret dream to have a handsome spouse she could flaunt before the members of High Society. She yearned to snatch a prime marital candidate away from the vapid mothers and simpering debutantes who routinely ignored her, judging her too ugly to be a rival. She'd show them all! She could already picture the design of the wedding invitations, could envision the decorations on her cake.

After the ceremony, she would stay in town with her new husband, would demand that he march with her down the promenade in the park as the members of fashionable London watched.

Ooh, how she would relish the coming weeks and months!

Nicholas slid closer and made a gauche move, stretching his arm across the back of the sofa.

"Cousin Nicholas?" she asked.

She pretended to be naïve as to what was transpiring, for she grasped how men liked to presume they were in charge. She was perfectly happy to let him have his illusions, but for the privilege of laying his hands on her he would ultimately have to compensate her, and she could guarantee that he wouldn't enjoy the penalty she planned to extract.

"It recently occurred to me," he replied, "that we should become better acquainted, but in a different way than we have been. We have so much to offer one another."

"Such as?"

"It's awful that you've never wed, that you've never had your own home or family."

As he spewed his male falsehoods, he was gazing at the far wall, which was just as well. If he'd been staring directly at her, she couldn't have kept a straight face.

He was such an idiot! By never marrying he thought she'd been deprived, but she'd run her father's estate, had supervised the staff and hosted his guests. With the old swine having passed away, all of it was hers—the money, the mansion, the stables, the farms—to do with as she pleased.

She didn't need Nicholas Marshall to have stability and security. But he needed her.

"I never wanted to wed," she lied, "but with Rebecca marrying Alex, it's dawned on me that I missed out by not accepting any of the proposals I've received."

"*You* have had marriage proposals?" His incredulity was revealed before he could mask it.

"Certainly," she responded, though it was a huge fib. She'd never had a single one. "What with my enormous fortune, many fellows have been interested, but I refused."

"Why?"

"I have everything a woman could desire: income, property, independence. Why would I need a man in my life?"

"Perhaps a man could furnish other things—more personal things."

"Like what?"

"I . . . I . . . suppose I could show you."

He was being deliberately enigmatic, but she knew to what he referred, and it was amusing, having him assume she was clueless. If he deemed her to be reluctant, he'd be more aroused, would force the issue, which would make it impossible for him to renege.

He went to the sideboard, poured himself a whiskey, and gulped it down. He poured another and swilled it, too; then he walked to the door and locked it.

As he returned to the sofa, he blew out the candle.

"Nicholas! What are you doing?"

"You need a husband, Lydia," he maintained. "It might as well be me."

"I don't need a husband. I don't want a husband."

"You only think you don't. I'll change your mind."

Pompous bastard! she seethed. Men liked to imagine they were the greatest lovers, that a woman couldn't wait to have them slobbering and rutting.

Without wooing or warning, he jerked her into a tight embrace and, as he pushed her down, as he came over her, she stifled a shudder. He was a big man, as her father had been, but his size didn't scare her. She was an expert at exerting control, at inspiring panic. In the end, Nicholas would drown in his own misery.

He crushed her into the cushions, and for his benefit she faked a struggle.

"Lie still," he commanded.

"I won't," she said. "I can't."

"Be silent, or our guests will burst in and discover how you've enticed me."

At the notion that anyone might infer she'd *enticed* him she nearly guffawed aloud, but she quashed her reaction, not wanting to cause a delay. She continued to tussle, though, and the wrestling excited him.

He fumbled with her skirt, raising it up, and she stiffened as he shoved his clumsy fingers inside, as he stroked them back and forth. She abhorred being fondled, but it was the price she had to pay for a marriage. However, once the deed was accomplished, she'd cut off his hand before she let him touch her there again.

"Desist!" she entreated.

"No, I have to do this."

"But I can't bear it."

"You have no choice, Lydia. I've been swept away by passion."

"I don't understand what you want," she wailed. "What are you attempting?"

He loosened his trousers and pressed himself between her legs. His phallus was at her center, but it wasn't anywhere close to where it needed to be, and she yearned to shake him. Hadn't the accursed man ever fornicated? Was he too drunk to locate the route?

Eventually, he landed in the right spot, but though he thrust over and over, he couldn't seem to enter her. His cock wasn't very hard, and she was rankled. If he stopped in mid-ravishment, where would that leave her?

"Jesus, woman," he complained. "You're dry as an old hag. Relax, would you?"

"I can't. I'm being smothered!"

He wrangled with the front of her dress, yanking down the bodice so that her flat bosom was exposed. He petted and painfully plucked at a nipple, but she wasn't concerned. The more he hurt her, the more ferociously she would retaliate—when he least expected it.

"You've got tits like a boy," he grouched.

"Quit mauling me! I don't like it."

"You'll *learn* to like it."

"Never! I never will."

Though he'd denigrated her breasts, his caressing them had worked a little magic on his phallus. It was erect, and he wedged it in. She lurched up and cried out, as a virgin ought, and he clasped his palm over her mouth.

"Hush! Everyone will hear you!"

"Oh, I can't have anyone see us like this!"

He thrust in earnest, but the liquor had dampened his sexual drive and was preventing him from arriving at the conclusion. She was in copulation hell, trapped beneath him, his fetid breath choking her.

He kept on and on and on, and she began to worry that she might expire from boredom. Finally—finally!—

he spilled himself, his disgusting seed spurting across her womb, and he grunted with satisfaction and pulled away.

"What did you do to me?" she asked.

"I've given you a taste of manly desire. I've taught you what transpires between a man and his wife. Your horizons have been expanded."

"You mean I'm . . . I'm ruined?"

"Yes, you are."

"I'll have to marry you!" she protested.

"You absolutely will, but don't fuss." He stood, arranging his clothes and hair. "It was bound to happen sooner or later. Keep it all in the family, you know."

"You're a beast, Nicholas, a cruel beast!"

"Cease your whining and straighten yourself."

He proceeded to the sideboard and downed more whiskey, conferring the distinct impression that he'd found the entire incident repulsive, and she was enraged by his arrogance.

Who was he to be revolted? He was naught but a poverty-stricken scapegrace. He was lucky she deigned to be in the same room with him.

"Promise me you won't inform Alex or Rebecca," she pleaded, sounding appropriately desperate. "They can't be apprised of what you've done."

"I have to tell Alex."

"I'm begging you not to. The shame would be too great."

"You'll get over it." He moved to the door.

"Will you . . . will you speak with him this evening?"

As if he might be growing unsure, he hesitated. "Not tonight. He's busy with company."

"Tomorrow?"

"I'll catch up with him. Prepare yourself."

Preening, he strutted out, and after he'd disappeared, she sat up.

"Stupid fool," she muttered, and she tarried in the quiet, calculating the ways she'd have her revenge—both if he followed through and if he didn't.

"Would you walk with me in the garden?"

"In the garden?"

"Yes, the garden," Rebecca fumed. "I'm positive you've heard of it. It's the green area behind the house, decorated with all the shrubbery and flowers."

Alex glanced at the dark sky and scowled. "It's starting to rain."

"I don't care. It's stuffy in here, and I want to go out!"

"All right, all right. Calm down."

He offered her his arm, which she took, and they strolled onto the verandah. It actually was sprinkling—he hadn't been lying about that, at least—and when he paused, she dragged him down the stairs and onto the path.

No one else was in the yard, so she was truly alone with him—as she never was—yet she experienced none of the thrilling rush that was so evident when she'd sneaked off with Mr. Duncan.

With him, she'd felt wild and free, as if she could commit any rash exploit without repercussion. For a few heady minutes, she'd been someone besides stuffy, prim Rebecca Burton, whose sole claim to fame was that she'd been waiting all her life to become Mrs. Alex Marshall and Countess of Stanton.

While previously the position had been exactly what she wanted, anymore it merely seemed tedious.

Recently, she'd been so restless and edgy, as if she was being slowly buried by the mundane. She was tired of plodding along, year after year, as Alex dithered over his readiness to tie the knot.

Her furtive assignation with Mr. Duncan had opened a Pandora's box of yearning and unhappiness that she usually kept closed, for she hadn't been courageous enough to peek inside. Now that she had, her worst fears were realized.

She was afraid that Alex didn't love her, that he didn't wish to marry her. There'd been rumors to that effect, but she'd discounted them. Mr. Duncan had simply confirmed her suspicions. She couldn't bear to think that her future with Alex would be as dull as the past. She was craving passion and excitement. Sometimes, her placid, serene world was so frustrating that she ached to run out on the front stoop and scream until she was hoarse.

Why . . . she was twenty-two years old and had never been kissed until Mr. Duncan had dared. She'd been pledged to Alex for two decades, and he'd never so much as held her hand.

They were such a polite, dreary couple that madcap behavior was beyond them. But with Mr. Duncan's flirtation hot in her mind, she couldn't help wondering why Alex was so uninterested.

She peered up at him. He was so tall, so handsome and masculine, yet there was none of the sizzle that Mr. Duncan inspired. Why?

The situation was driving her batty. Why wasn't Alex agog with desire? He was like a kindly brother or uncle, which was wrong. Shouldn't they be feeling some ardor? With the engagement about to officially occur, shouldn't he be luring her into isolated corners and whispering sweet nothings in her ear?

Out of the blue, he inquired, "Where's your companion, Miss Drake? I never see her with you."

"She's been under the weather."

"She'd be welcome to socialize with us."

"Of course she would be," Rebecca curtly remarked, irked that he had her all to himself and he was talking about another woman. "I've invited her down every evening, but she'd rather retire early."

He chuckled. "Is our company that unpleasant?"

"I suppose it is."

They continued on, lost in thought, and she couldn't abide the silence. Mr. Duncan was a sorcerer who'd cast a spell, and his accusations were taunting her to recklessness. Too many words were bubbling out, and before she could balk or reconsider, she blurted, "When I'm not here in London, do you consort with other women?"

"Other . . . other women?" He sputtered with surprise. "Rebecca, what's come over you? You're acting so bizarrely."

"Do you?" she demanded, determined to pry a response out of him.

"Why would you pose such an odd question?"

"Because I'm curious."

"I can't imagine why."

"You haven't answered me," she pointed out, "which is an answer in and of itself."

He sighed with exasperation. "You only visit three or four times a year, so yes, I occasionally escort others to the theater or whatever."

"That's not what I'm asking, and you know it."

"No, I don't *know it*. What—precisely—are you hoping to learn?"

She stopped and faced him so she could view his expression. "Whilst I'm away, do you make mad, passionate love to other women?"

"Rebecca!"

He blushed, and she couldn't figure out why he was embarrassed. Was he shocked by the subject matter? Or was he guilty of philandering?

"After we're married, will you practice fidelity?"

"Fi . . . fi . . . delity?"

As if he'd bitten into a rotten egg, he grimaced, and he grabbed her arm and turned her toward the verandah. "I'm not having this discussion with you. Let's go in."

Suddenly a sliver of moonlight broke through the stormy clouds, bathing her in its glow, and she remembered Mr. Duncan's romantic comments. She dug in her feet, halting him.

"Is the moon shining on my hair?" she queried.

"Yes."

"How does it appear to you?"

"What?" He was completely confused. "Your hair?"

"Yes. What color is it?"

"Brown."

"What shade of brown?"

"Very brown."

She stared at him, really *looking* for a change, and it seemed to her that he was a stranger, that this man with whom she'd been acquainted forever was someone she didn't know, at all.

A wave of fury swept over her. She was so angry that

she wanted to clasp him by the lapels of his fancy jacket and shake him until his teeth rattled.

Quite sure she sounded deranged, she seethed, "My hair is brunette."

"Well then," he said, "that certainly clarifies everything."

Wrath and hurt warred inside her, and she yanked away. "Shut up, Alex. For once in your pathetic life, just shut the hell up!"

It was the first time she'd ever cursed, and at having done so she felt marvelous.

She spun and stomped to the house.

8

Ellen trudged through the dim halls. She—apparently—was the only one in the drafty mansion who couldn't sleep. In recent days, she'd suffered too many upheavals, so she was careening between anxiety and joy. She couldn't relax long enough to lie down and get comfortable.

She was disoriented from seeing James—so suddenly and so unexpectedly—then having him flit off a few minutes later. The likelihood that he might reappear, that she might turn around and find him standing behind her, had her so agitated that her life was in total disarray.

She couldn't think, couldn't socialize, couldn't concentrate. She was too muddled, so she'd taken to hiding in her bedchamber, which, she'd quickly deduced, was a marvelous method for avoiding Lord Stanton.

After his outrageous seduction, she was in a constant state of panic, terrified that she'd bump into him in a deserted parlor and he'd seduce her all over again. Though she'd never admit it in a thousand years, she was thrilled by what he'd done to her and hoping that something similar would occur as soon as she could manage a second encounter.

She wanted Stanton in every risqué, bawdy way she could have him. He'd opened a door to a secret world she hadn't known to exist, and she was fascinated by what she'd discovered on the other side. She hadn't the fortitude to say no to the pleasure he offered, which meant that any interaction would have them racing down the road to perdition. Perhaps they already were.

Was she mad?

She'd planned to stay on with Lydia and Rebecca till the wedding, but when she was having such lust-filled thoughts about Rebecca's fiancé how could she?

She had to leave—immediately—but hadn't the funds to go. She had no money saved, and her sole family member was James—a convicted criminal on the run from the law. His whereabouts were a mystery, and she had but an obscure address for sending him stealthy notes. Dare she cast her lot with him?

What if he was rearrested? Once previous, she'd watched the law march him away in shackles, and she couldn't bear a subsequent experience. Wasn't it better to protect herself? To steer clear of anguish?

Oh, she was in a fine fettle! Fretting and stewing and not a soul to whom she could vent her woe!

She was tired of pacing the quiet house, tired of being alone with her frantic rumination. She arrived at her room and crept inside, when a male voice had her jumping with fright.

"Lock the door," Lord Stanton ordered, and her foolish heart soared with elation, even as her mind whirled with dread over what the visit portended, over what sins she might commit at his instigation.

She recognized that she shouldn't obey the command, that it would be the worst decision ever, but without hesitation she did as he'd bid her. Bracing herself, she took a deep breath as she calmly asked, "Why are you sitting here in the dark?"

"Would you rather I had a lamp burning?"

"I'd rather you hadn't come, at all. You can't be popping in and out. What if someone saw you?"

"I imagine there'd be a huge ruckus."

"First and foremost, I'd lose my job."

"I'd locate another for you." As if employment was a trivial concern, he shrugged.

"Would you? You're too, too magnanimous."

She went to the dresser and lit a candle, struggling to conceal how her hands were shaking. As the wick ignited and the flame grew, she focused on him. He was lounging in the chair, his legs crossed at the ankles. His coat and cravat were off, the top buttons of his shirt undone, so that his chest was exposed. He looked disreputable and dangerous—like a pirate or a brigand—and capable of perpetrating any nefarious deed.

His blue eyes glowed with a furious intensity, and they commenced a leisurely trip down her anatomy. Memories flooded in as to what had happened the prior occasion he'd stopped by, and on remembering her naked condition her nipples sprang to attention, throbbing and rubbing her corset. She blushed as his gaze dropped to her breasts. It was evident that he, too, was recalling every depraved moment of that misadventure.

He was drinking. He'd brought a glass and a bottle of liquor. What effect would it have on him? Would he be more aggressive? More angry? More passionate?

If he became any more amorous, there was no predicting what might transpire.

"I've been waiting for you for an eternity," he stunned her by claiming. "Where have you been?"

"I was starving, so I've been pilfering your pantry."

At her honest response, he chuckled. "Then we're even. I've been snooping through your belongings."

"How very crass."

"Isn't it, though?"

"Have you stumbled on much that was interesting?"

"Many things."

"Such as?"

"Who is James?"

She reeled, striving to recollect the contents of the letter she'd penned but hadn't mailed. What had she written? "If you've been reading my correspondence, you're even more rude than I assumed."

"Is he your lover?"

"My lover?" He almost sounded jealous, and she laughed at the ludicrous prospect. "Oh yes, I have dozens of swains. They sneak in and out when Lydia isn't looking."

"You're too pretty not to have a beau, and you're too old to have never married. Why haven't you?"

"I swear, Lord Stanton, every time you open your mouth, you say something more discourteous."

"It's a fair question. I see nothing impolite in my wanting an answer."

"Not every female has the resources to wed."

"So it's been a matter of finances?"

"Of course it's been finances. What would you suppose?"

"You don't hate men?"

"Hate men? Are you drunk?"

"Would you take a lover if you had the chance? If you could be guaranteed that no one would ever know and that you'd never be caught?"

"No, I would not."

"Why?"

"Just because you philander with every woman who walks by doesn't mean that I would behave in the same indiscreet manner."

He sipped his liquor and stared at her across the rim of his glass. "Who is James?"

"No one of any consequence."

"You're a terrible liar, Ellen."

"You may not call me by my given name. It's *Miss Drake* to you."

"So, Ellen, who is he?"

She was exasperated by his annoying superiority, but she considered the pitfalls of various replies. Finally, she divulged, "He's my brother."

"You have a brother? Does he plague you—as mine frequently plagues me?"

"I'm sure mine is much worse than yours."

"I'm going to inform Lydia that you need a raise."

"What?" she stammered, thrown off guard by the abrupt change of topic.

"You have three dresses. One is suitable, but the other two are worn to rags."

"I like my dresses very much," she was compelled to protest. She'd earned them—every single stitch—by putting up with Lydia's sniping.

"You have two decrepit pairs of shoes. One has a hole in it. You also have two pairs of stockings that are scarcely useable from having been mended too often to count."

"Have you tallied my undergarments, too?"

"Yes," he confessed without a hint of remorse. "They're entirely drab, provincially functional."

Why would she want her unmentionables to be anything *but* functional?

She studied him, and she thought about chastising him for intruding on her privacy, but any reprimand was pointless. He was a petty tyrant, who reckoned he could act however he pleased, and he could.

"If you so much as whisper my name to Lydia," she threatened, "it will be the last words you ever utter, for I will strangle you with my bare hands."

"Wouldn't you relish having a few extra pennies to spend?"

"If you talk to her, she'll be aware that you have a heightened interest in me. How would you explain it?"

"I loathe that gown," he said, rapidly switching the subject, once again. "Gray is horrid on you. It washes out your skin."

"And you'd presume yourself to be an authority on feminine attire?"

"Yes."

Naturally he would! He entertained himself by disrobing women! He was a veritable fashion expert!

"I like gray," she insisted. She wasn't about to clarify that Lydia picked and purchased her attire and it was the only color she would allow.

"If I bought your clothes, I'd choose a lavender, to match your eyes. Or maybe a red, to highlight the gold in your hair."

"Do you actually think that I'm the sort of female who would parade around in a red dress?"

"I'd have you wear it for me—when we were alone."

She gulped, besieged with images of the type of intimate relationship he envisioned between them. Her cheeks were flaming hot, and she could hardly resist the urge to fan herself.

"You suffer from the most insane flights of fancy. Is lunacy a recurring problem for you?"

"You have no possessions," he noted, ignoring her insult. "Not a book, not any jewelry, not a picture tucked in a locket. Why is that?"

She'd cut out her tongue before she admitted that nearly every item had been seized and sold to reimburse James's accuser. Many of the pieces had been part of her mother's dowry, had been in Ellen's family for generations, and that loss—coming on the heels of James's arrest and her father's death—had been too wrenching.

In the years since, with the exception of the last of her mother's personal effects, she'd shunned ownership, her intent being to never become attached to anything or anyone.

"We're not all obsessed with chattels," she retorted, "as are the rich."

"You told me that we'd met previously."

"It wasn't a *meeting*. Someone merely indicated who you were, and I saw you from a distance."

"As a boy, I was acquainted with a family named Drake. In Surrey. The father was estate agent for a friend of mine. Are you related?"

"I don't have any kin in Surrey"—which had been the truth for a decade—"so I'm positive I don't know them."

He scrutinized her again, evaluating her expression, sifting through all the lies she'd spewed, and his smirk apprised her that he hadn't believed any of them.

"Why do you keep so many secrets?"

"If I had any secrets—which I don't—why would I be stupid enough to share them with you?"

"Why indeed?"

He rose from the chair, and he crossed the small room in three strides so that they were toe-to-toe. As he approached, she experienced such a heady wave of exhilaration that she was dizzy.

She understood that she shouldn't dally with him, but how could such fervent wanting be wrong? With her whole heart and soul she yearned to leap into the inferno he ignited. Through no fault of her own, her life had taken a dreadful turn. She had so few pleasures, so few reasons to celebrate.

Would the world stop spinning if she selfishly and impetuously reached out and grabbed for some happiness?

She'd always been dutiful, had been diligent and honest. She'd never pined for more than what she had, had never bemoaned her tribulations, and where had it gotten her? Nowhere! She was a poverty-stricken spinster, with no past or future worth contemplating.

Didn't she deserve to have something good happen?

What if . . . The fascinating prospect slipped in and took hold. What if she dared? What if she walked down the road he was encouraging her to travel?

Without a doubt, there would be misery and desolation when he was through with her. She never did anything halfway, so she'd probably fall in love, but there'd be no reciprocal emotion from him.

Even if he grew fond of her, he would never deviate from his plan to wed Rebecca, and Ellen wouldn't want him to. In the end, Ellen would never see him again. She'd leave Lydia's employ, and she would be on her own, cast about by the winds of fate, as she tried to establish herself elsewhere.

She'd be forlorn and despairing, but she would have memories of the time she'd spent with him, and suddenly those memories seemed worth any price.

He traced a finger across her lips. "Be my paramour, Ellen."

"I don't know what that means."

"I'll show you."

"I'm afraid."

"It will be wonderful between us," he claimed. "I'll make it wonderful."

"Promise me that you'll never hurt me." There was no possibility of a satisfactory resolution, so it was a silly request, but she had to pretend that there could be one. "I couldn't bear it if you did."

"I never will," he vowed. "I never could."

He dipped down and kissed her, and she groaned with delight. Her body was afire with longing, fraught with pressures and torments that needed release, and she wrapped her arms around him and pulled him closer.

He deepened the embrace, his tongue in her mouth, his hands in her hair. He yanked at the combs, tossing them on the floor so that the lengthy mass tumbled down. He riffled through it, as he pushed her against the wall, as he gripped her bottom and lifted her.

Her legs were spread, her skirt rucked up, so that she was pinned to him, balanced on his thighs. His loins were flattened to her privates, the rough nap of his trousers rubbing her, and he flexed his hips in a steady rhythm.

She was like a blossoming flower, opening just for him. Her breasts throbbed, her crotch wept with desire, and her own hips responded to his, imitating his movements thrust for thrust.

"Have you any idea," he inquired, "of what men and women do when they're together like this?"

"No. Teach me everything."

He spun her and carried her to the bed, laying her down and coming over her. She could have declined, could have protested, but she didn't. It seemed as if there was a line clearly drawn in the middle of the room. It was the line between right and wrong, between sin and morality. She'd crossed it with him and was so far on the other side that she'd never be able to return to how she'd been prior.

But she didn't care. Not about her old character, or her old ambitions, or her old manner of keeping on. There was only now and how it would be after.

Once he'd finished with her, who—and what—would she be?

He was heavy, his weight forcing her down into the mattress, but she didn't mind. He was welcome and familiar, and there was none of the strangeness or discomfort that she might have predicted. It felt so appropriate to be with him, as if she'd been heading toward this place her entire life without realizing she had been.

He stared down at her, and there was a fierceness in his gaze, but a tenderness, too, and she was thrilled by it. She could have dawdled into infinity doing nothing but watching him as his potent attention billowed over her.

"I'm so glad you said yes," he murmured.

"I'm a fool to have agreed. You overwhelm my better sense. I can't refuse you."

"Why would you wish to refuse me?" he asked.

"Because you'll bring me naught but trouble."

"I'll try my best to exceed your low expectations." He smiled wryly. "We'll go slow."

"Don't you dare!"

"I want to touch you all over. I want to kiss you all over."

"Will it make me stop aching? On the inside?"

"Have you been miserable?"

"Yes, you bounder. Whatever is ailing me, it's your fault, and I insist you effect a cure. Immediately!"

"All in good time, my little vixen. All in good time."

He swept her away on a tumultuous tide of ecstasy, and she was content to follow wherever he led. His crafty fingers were busy, and before she knew it, her dress and corset were loose, and he was tugging down the straps of her chemise.

She braced with anticipation, her nipples tightening into painful buds. She was so impatient that she nearly embarrassed herself by begging him to hurry. Finally, her breasts were bared. He snuggled down and took one of the tips into his mouth, and she hissed with an agonized joy.

Driving her wild, he suckled her, and she wrestled and squirmed, striving to escape the onslaught but move closer to it, too. He was inching up her skirt, his hand trailing up her calf, her thigh. Instinctively, she recognized his destination, that relief was in sight, so she wasn't about to call a halt.

"You're so wet," he said.

"Why am I? What's happening to me?" He was brushing across her cleft, toying with her so that she writhed and moaned. "Please . . . have mercy!"

Without warning, he slid two fingers inside her, and they fit perfectly, as if she'd been designed for him to caress her in precisely that fashion. He stroked them back and forth, back and forth.

"That's it," he coaxed. "Relax."

"I feel as if I'm about to explode."

"You are."

She had no idea what he was implying, but if something didn't occur—and soon!—she worried for her physical safety. There was a stress building, the tension extreme, as her body worked toward a goal that remained out of reach.

"When will it end?" she pleaded. "I can't stand any more."

"Almost there."

His thumb dabbed out and flicked at a spot she'd never noticed, and it seemed as if all the sensation in the universe were centered there. He jabbed at it—once, twice, thrice—and she leapt over an invisible precipice, her torso in free fall, her spirit soaring across the heavens.

Someone cried out, and she was quite sure it was herself, though she was too dazed to be certain. The rapture spiraled her up and up, to an excruciating level, until it peaked and began to wane.

As she floated down, as consciousness reasserted itself, she was cradled in his arms. He was preening and smug, as if he'd explained the world's mysteries, and in a way, he had.

"What was that?" She struggled to regain her usual aplomb, which was impossible. She was mostly naked, the bodice and hem of her dress bunched at her waist, her bosom and loins exposed to the cool evening air.

He leaned in, his warm breath tickling her ear. "The French call it the *petit mort.*"

She grappled with the foreign phrase, and when she deciphered it, she shuddered at how apt it sounded. "The little death?"

"Yes."

"Can you make it happen more than once?"

"My beauty, I can make it *happen* as often as you like."

She collapsed onto the pillow to stare up at the ceiling, and she rippled with unease. Her anatomy was so keen to recommence that she felt as if she'd ingested a dangerous drug, as if she was addicted from a single application.

What had she set in motion? How fast could it whirl out of her control?

She glared at him. "This is the *secret* of the marital bed, isn't it?"

"One of them."

"There are more?"

"Many."

She was aghast. Before they were through, she'd have no scruples left, would have no self-respect. In order to repeat the experience, she'd merrily attempt any shameful conduct he suggested.

No wonder females were so carefully sheltered and chaperoned. They had to be kept from learning the truth! If she'd had any notion that such riotous behaviors could be enjoyed with a man, there was no telling what paths she might have chosen!

Without intending to, she yawned. "I'm so tired."

"Pleasure can be rather draining."

"I might take a nap. Just for a minute."

"By all means," he wisely concurred. "You should rest up for the second round."

Rapidly she drifted away, the strenuous activity leaving her exhausted. "Don't go anywhere," she mumbled.

"I won't. When you awaken, I'll be right here."

He was arranging her clothes, lowering her skirt and straightening her chemise. There was a knitted throw at the foot of the bed, and he drew it up and nestled them in a cozy cocoon, with her spooned against him.

She'd never felt so protected, so cherished. She smiled and slept, too weary to ponder how she'd ever face him the next day.

∾ 9 ∾

Suzette DuBois loosened her corset as she listened for Nicholas Marshall in the hall outside her dressing room. He stopped by before and after each performance, so she was expecting him and eager to put on a good show.

The oaf was thick as a brick—all men were, which was a fact she'd deduced early on in her nineteen years of living—but he was wealthier than most, a heartbeat away from being an earl, and he wanted her so desperately. Meeting him was the best thing that had happened to her since she'd moved to London at age ten.

As opposed to other females who traveled to the city, seeking fame and fortune, Fate had been kind to her. With her red hair and green eyes, her curvaceous figure and fascinating face, she looked exotic and foreign, and she captivated every man with whom she spoke. Her ability to fake a French accent didn't hurt, either.

She was extremely popular with the masses who laid down their hard-earned coins to watch her sing and dance, but she didn't intend to work forever. Actually,

she didn't intend to work for even the next few days, if
she could get her finances arranged.

For an eternity she'd been trolling for a rich patron,
and she was so near to achieving her goal. Nick was
about to make her every dream come true.

He pretended penury, but he was a member of a disgustingly affluent family, and he'd ultimately cough up
the money she was demanding. By allying herself with
him she saw years of profit. She'd have a grand residence, a huge allowance, fabulous clothes to wear, and
delicious foods to eat. She'd be a powerhouse in the
demimonde. People would flock to her parties, would
vie to be her friend, all in the hopes that a relationship
would bring them closer to Nick and the rewards that
could be gleaned through an acquaintance with him.

She grinned with avarice. She would have it all. And
soon.

Her older sister, Peg, stomped in and nagged, "Nell,
where are my stockings you borrowed?"

"Hush!" she scolded. "Nick will be here any second.
You must call me Suzette."

"Suzette!" Peg grumbled. "You've been *Nell* to me
for twenty bloomin' years. I'm not about to change at
this late date."

"Do you want the money I promised you or not?"

"Yes, I want it."

"Then call me Suzette—or bugger off!"

Their father—a handsome con artist—had been
French. He'd hung around long enough for his children
to learn a bit of his language and habits; then he'd vanished.

After he'd abandoned them, their mum had died in

childbirth. Nell's siblings had been scattered to the four winds, with her and Peg heading out to find employment. While Peg cursed their father at every turn, Nell quietly thanked him for the flair and charm she'd inherited. Her flamboyance had gotten her far in the world and would take her even farther.

Footsteps sounded, and they both paused, Peg's brow raised in question as to who was approaching, and Nell nodded. It was definitely Nick.

"Stand behind my chair," she hissed, and she sat and scooted around to give him a better view as she jerked off her corset and tossed it on the floor.

From the waist down, she was clad in a pair of the frilly drawers and the spiky heels that drove him wild. Her upper torso was bare.

They waited until they were sure he was peeking through the crack in the door. Then Nell reached over her shoulders and guided Peg's hands to her breasts. Peg massaged them as Nell writhed with false ecstasy.

She and her sister were no strangers to sexual dalliance, weren't adverse to philandering together—if the price was right. They'd do anything for cash, and they often catered to the odd carnal whims of various gentlemen of the Quality.

They both grasped how excited a man could become by observing two women, how quickly desire could override common sense. Nick was such an easy mark. Once Nell was through, he'd be willing to commit any deed to purchase her favors.

"Oh, *chéri*, oh, Peg," she breathed, "I love what you do to me."

"I can't resist you, Suzette," Peg claimed, and she could scarcely keep from giggling at the ludicrous charade. "Even though it's wrong, even though it's shameful, I can't stay away."

"Touch me, Peg. You know how I like it."

Peg rounded the chair and knelt between Nell's thighs. They enjoyed a passionate kiss, complete with tongues engaged. After a lengthy embrace, Peg slipped a hand inside Nell's drawers, and she stroked Nell's privates. Nell flexed her hips, exaggerating her thrusting, sighing and moaning with great relish.

"You feel wonderful," Peg murmured, slithering a wicked finger inside Nell's sheath.

"For you, Peg. Only for you."

Delighted by Peg's amorous talents, she urged Peg to her nipple. Peg was an exceptional lover, and as they carried on, Nell wished they had a few minutes alone where they could finish what they'd started.

"You'll always be mine, won't you, Suzette?" Peg frantically queried. "I can't let any man have you! Not after you've shown me how it can be between us!"

"I'm yours, Peg. Yours forever."

They'd pushed Nick to his limit, and he burst in. She and Peg whipped around in surprise, and Peg put on a magnificent display. Acting terrified, she stumbled to her feet, as Nell rushed to tug on her costume, hiding every lush detail that he wasn't permitted to see until he paid through the nose.

"Beg pardon, milord," Peg stammered, pretending she thought him to be a titled nobleman, which she knew would puff him up. "I didn't realize anyone was there."

"You bloody well didn't, you sick pervert," he admonished. "Be off, before I summon the law and have you arrested for your depravities."

"Please, sir, no," she entreated. "I'm a good girl, I am. Suzette has just . . . just . . ."

She covered her face, gave a theatrical wail of despair, then fled. Nell and Nicholas watched her go, his anger and arousal billowing off him in waves. He was titillated by the exhibition, and more keen than ever to set Suzette up as his mistress.

Oh, it was like taking candy from a baby!

"Why are you here?" she protested. "I asked you not to return."

"And I told you that you can't keep me away." He grabbed her and shook her. "I won't have you debasing yourself with that hussy, do you hear me?"

"I love Peg," she declared. "I can't live without her!"

"If you feel the need for a swivving, you'll have my fat prick between your legs, and not some whore's puny fingers."

"You have no right to order me about."

"I will have the right," he vowed. "Very soon."

She yanked away so that he wouldn't see her smile of satisfaction. "Does this mean you've found the money?"

"I . . . I . . . yes."

"What did you do? Rob a bank?"

"I'm planning to marry."

"Really?" she taunted. "There's been no gossip about your eminent self being betrothed."

"It's not . . . official yet."

"Hah! Then it's naught but a lie—as you've spewed before."

"I'm serious this time."

"Of course you are." She rolled her eyes, then feigned sympathy. "Give it up, *mon ami*! You can't afford me. You'll *never* be able to afford me. Stop torturing yourself."

"It will be arranged by tomorrow," he contended.

"Tomorrow?"

"Yes."

The stage manager was calling to the actors, the curtain about to rise.

"I have to go," she advised. "This argument is over."

She shoved past him, when he stunned her by reaching into his purse and pulling out a gaudy bracelet. He seized her arm and clasped it around her wrist, and she did a hasty evaluation.

It seemed genuine, with a dangly gold band and huge red stones that she suspected were rubies. It was likely worth a fortune, and she conjectured as to how he'd come by it. Had he stolen it? Was he that obsessed? How marvelous if he was!

Well, she hoped he—or whoever had parted with it—wasn't too attached to the pretty bauble. If it was authentic, she'd sell the gems for cash; then she'd have an exact replica created to wear when he was around.

"What's this?" She snickered, studying the bracelet as if it were the ugliest thing she'd ever seen.

"Consider it a down payment—for future services I'll demand you perform. Perhaps I'll require you and your degenerate friend to join me in my bed. Together!" As if she should be frightened or disgusted, he leered, appearing much like a pervert, himself.

"It will take more than these paltry jewels to make me consent."

"You'll have more. By tomorrow. You're about to have more than you could ever spend."

"So you say."

"So I know," he retorted.

His conviction had her thinking that maybe he was

about to wed, and she couldn't imagine what sensible female would have him. He was attractive enough, and connected to a prominent family, but his annoying qualities were so blatant. Who could tolerate him?

Had he forced himself on somebody? Had he ruined some girl against her will? If so, Nell was suitably impressed. She'd never envisioned him having the courage to perpetrate such a dastardly deed.

The stage manager hollered again, and she strolled out, her new bracelet shimmering under the lamps.

"Have you ever been in love?"

"Me?" Ellen chuckled and shuffled her cards, unable to look Rebecca in the eye and needing the distraction for her hands.

In light of the sordid meetings she'd been having with Alex, it was impossible to tarry in Rebecca's company, and at all costs, she avoided socializing. If Rebecca ever learned how Ellen had betrayed her, she'd be crushed, yet Ellen couldn't desist with her torrid affair.

Humiliating as it was to acknowledge, she was a fallen woman, so weak of character and moral constitution that she'd succumbed to the advances of the first man to evince the slightest interest.

Granted, he was more striking and dynamic than any fellow ought to be, so she wouldn't chastise herself too harshly. What woman would have been immune to such charisma and charm? Under the circumstances, who could have behaved any better? Ellen would have had to be forged of stone to resist him—at least that's how she was justifying her despicable conduct.

"Why are you laughing?" Rebecca asked.

"Because you're being silly."

"Why?"

"Who would love me?"

"Any lucky chap, and you know it," Rebecca kindly insisted. "But I'm not talking about men being in love with you. I'm curious if *you* have ever been in love."

"Have I had an unrequited, ardent *amour*?"

"Yes."

Ellen thought for a moment. "There was a boy, once, when I was sixteen."

"Were you wild for him?"

"I presumed I was at the time."

"But you weren't?"

"Well, he had the biggest blue eyes, but I believe he was more infatuated with his horses than with me. And with a neighbor—who was very rich."

"So you probably couldn't describe the signs."

"The signs of what?"

"There must be symptoms that would help a woman to tell."

"I suppose there are," Ellen agreed. "Don't the poets write about racing pulses and constant yearnings?"

Rebecca pressed two fingers to her throat, checking her heartbeat. "Mine's barely pounding."

"Perhaps your *innamorato* must be present for you to suffer any physical reaction."

For the longest while, Rebecca gazed out the window; then she said, "Do you think Alex loves me?"

"Lord Stanton?"

"Yes."

Ellen shifted uncomfortably. This was a murky bog,

into which she had no desire to wander. There was no proper way to respond. In her philandering with Stanton she was so compromised that she couldn't offer a valid opinion.

Suddenly the terribleness of her choices was battering her like bricks tumbling from a wall. She needed to flee, to slink off where no one knew her, where no one would ever discover the stupid predicament into which she'd thrown herself.

Yet the notion of going was so distressing that she couldn't contemplate it. She'd grown so attached to Stanton, was fixated on him in a wretched fashion that she couldn't conceive of severing. If she left, she'd never see him again. He was the only remarkable thing that had ever happened in her pitiful life, and she was too foolishly smitten to walk away.

She'd always pictured herself to be a smart and pragmatic person. How had she vaulted into such a mess?

Very gently, she inquired, "Does it matter if he loves you or not?"

"I expect not, but wouldn't it be wonderful if he did?"

"Would it make any difference, though? You'd still be bound to wed him."

"I might be happier," Rebecca shockingly admitted.

"You're not . . . happy?" Ellen dared to query.

The question startled Rebecca out of her peculiar mood. "Of course I'm *happy.*" She waved off her odd comments. "Don't mind me. I'm tired, so I'm a bit grumpy."

"You've been awfully busy," Ellen concurred. "All this socializing is exhausting. You should stay at home tonight and rest."

"I just might," Rebecca replied. She dawdled a tad more; then, appearing confused and anguished, she ambled away.

"What have you to say for yourself?"

"Well, I . . . well, I . . ."

Lydia watched Nicholas as he hemmed and hawed, refusing to answer Alex, and she rippled with fury. Days had passed since he'd forced himself upon her, and she'd waited on pins and needles for him to speak with Alex so that the wedding plans could proceed.

No confession had come, so she'd assumed control of the situation, had sought out Alex, herself.

It was painfully obvious that the lout imagined he could ravage her and get away without making compensation. The realization—that he hadn't intended to follow through with a marriage—had her in such a state that it was all she could do to keep from leaping up, marching across the room, and assaulting him.

As he was about to learn, he discounted her at his peril!

Her entire life, men had insulted and underestimated and offended, her father being the worst of the lot. The deviant codger had found out—the hard way—how dangerous it was to cross her. Nicholas would, too.

"It was horrid, Cousin Alex," she interjected, as the conversation ground to a halt. "If Nicholas was interested in marrying me, I don't know why we didn't simply talk it over. Instead, he felt it necessary to . . . to . . ."

"You needn't specify the details, Lydia," Alex grimly responded. "I accept your word as to what transpired."

He glared at his brother. "I'm merely ready to hear from Nicholas."

Nicholas was deathly pale. He rose and went to the sideboard, poured himself a stiff brandy, and downed it. As he turned to face them, a bleak, fake smile curved his lips. "There will have to be a wedding, I guess."

"Don't tell me," Alex barked. "Tell Lydia."

Nicholas gulped and trembled. He didn't look at her but stared at a spot over her shoulder. "Lydia, old girl, what do you say?"

Lydia gaped at him. He called that pathetic sentence a proposal? The marriage was to have been her stellar triumph, her shining achievement, but as with every man in her past, he'd wrecked it.

She stood, gripping her cane so tightly that her knuckles were white. "I'm not *old* and I'm not a *girl*," she growled, "as you would be wise to remember in your dealings with me. But yes, I will marry you."

Nicholas's knees gave out, and he sank into a nearby chair.

"How soon can you be prepared?" Alex asked her.

"A month from today."

"A month?" Nicholas croaked.

"Yes," she sternly asserted.

"It's all set then," Alex said.

"I'll have my solicitor draw up the contracts," she lied. She'd draft every deceptive paragraph herself.

"And I'll have mine inquire about the Special License. We'll have to have the ceremony here at the house."

"Rather than the church?"

She was aghast. Her ruination meant she'd never parade down the aisle, would never be a blushing bride. It was another sin to lay at Nicholas's feet.

"It would be more fitting."

"I'm sure it would be." She was more irate than ever. "I'll handle the arrangements."

"Let me know if you need anything," Alex agreeably mentioned.

"I will."

Cane thumping on the floor, she stomped out, and she ignored Nicholas, who seemed to have descended into a panicked stupor. She walked down the hall and rounded the corner, and once she was out of sight she grinned with malice.

Nicholas thought he was about to get his hands on her fortune, but he had no idea of how thoroughly she'd secured her finances. It had taken decades of clever manipulation to wrangle her father's assets away from him, and she wasn't about to part with a single farthing.

She knew more about money—how to obtain it, how to conceal it—than the most miserly banker. It would be impossible for Nicholas to receive a penny without her allowing him to have it. What hoops would he jump through to keep her happy?

It was going to be so amusing to find out!

~ 10 ~

"I'm here."

James's voice emanated from the dark shadows, and Rebecca jumped at the sound. She couldn't see a thing, and she whispered, "Where?"

"Here."

She whirled around, and he linked their fingers. Through the lace of her glove she could feel his warm skin, and she rippled with exhilaration, much more glad than she should have been, but she wouldn't tamp down her elation.

It was wrong to meet with him, yet she couldn't stop herself. When his note had been delivered, inviting her to sneak out after midnight, it had seemed to be a tether to the thrilling world she yearned to inhabit instead of the sedate, dull one where she actually resided. She was going mad in Alex's mansion, so frustrated that she often wanted to run away and never look back.

James represented all that was beyond her grasp—excitement, risk, danger—and she intended to revel in their odd acquaintance. She was tired of being a good girl, of behaving exactly as she ought. For once, she planned to do something out of character, something totally outrageous.

Her engagement was about to become a reality, and after it transpired she would lose part of herself, would be subsumed by Alex. She had this silly sinking impression that any chance for happiness would have passed her by, and she was plagued by a fierce need to grab for whatever bliss she could find, as if it might be her sole opportunity for joy.

There would be eons after the wedding to plod along in her routine, to accept that marriage hadn't changed her life a whit. But for the moment, she was free and away, not boring, tedious Rebecca Burton but someone audacious and confident, someone who was eager to throw caution to the wind.

Having eyes like a cat, James guided her down the alley. Soon they stepped into the street, where there was more light, where she could see his carriage. She scanned it, searching for a crest that would give her a hint as to his family or identity, but the vehicle provided no clues.

A tall, blond footman, attired in a fancy red livery, held the door and helped her with the stairs. James clambered in behind, and before he was fully seated the driver cracked the whip and they were off at a fast clip that had him off balance and tumbling into her.

Previously, she might have been shaken by the jarring impact, but she declined to let decorum shape her conduct. She was determined to forge ahead, to have James regard her as the passionate, madcap woman she wished she were.

"I can't believe you came." He laughed and hugged her.

"I can't believe it, either." Her venturing off with him

was the only shocking, unexpected thing she'd ever done.

"I was positive you'd say no."

"How could I refuse such a naughty invitation?"

As though she weighed no more than a feather, he scooped her up and perched her on his lap, and she was assailed by new sensations. Her bottom was nestled to his crotch, her thighs flattened to his own, and she was amazed at how breathtaking it was to be so close to him. Every nerve tingled with anticipation, and it seemed that any extraordinary event could happen.

He untied the string on her cloak, loosening it so it fell off, and she shivered, though not from the cold. He noticed immediately and reached for a blanket, and he draped it over them so that they were sealed in a snug cocoon.

"Where are we going?" she asked.

"We're having a late supper in my private quarters." When she hesitated, he added, "I didn't think we should be out in public."

"No, we shouldn't."

"I suppose we could ride around all night, but the air is chilly, and I'd hate to have you uncomfortable."

"Your lodgings will be fine."

She smiled, stunned by her words. Her visit to his home would be scandalous in the extreme, and she couldn't understand the forces that were spurring her on, but she couldn't rein them in.

She would have an adventure if it killed her!

He eased her forward, so that her chest was pressed to his. Her nipples grew very hard, and with each jolt of the coach they rubbed against him.

She hadn't known that her breasts were so sensitive, that touching them to a man could have such a stimulating effect, and her level of agitation scared her. She was suffering from a desperate need to shed corset and chemise, perhaps to have him pet the soft mounds to alleviate the ache. The urgency was terrifying, and lest she do something she oughtn't, she had to remain composed.

How did James inspire such rashness? Why was she letting him? He had her ready to leap into a conflagration from which there could be no return. She intended the outing to be a fun jaunt, a harmless flirtation, but it was so difficult to keep the encounter frivolous.

He stirred longings she didn't comprehend and didn't particularly like, and if she wasn't careful, he'd have her forgetting her place—and his. She was bound to Alex, and nothing could alter that fact, not even a dashing, daring stranger who was smitten by her for no reason, at all.

The carriage rattled to a halt, and he peeked out.

"We're here," he said.

"So soon?"

He perceived her anxiety, and he nuzzled her cheek, her ear. "Don't be afraid."

"I'm not."

The door was whipped open, and she was whisked out and into a stairwell and instructed to climb. She could smell the river, and she'd glimpsed the mast of a ship, so they were near the docks, but wherever their location, she'd never be able to find it in the light of day.

Shortly, she was ushered into a parlor, complete with sofa, bookshelves, lace curtains, and paintings on the wall. The normal furnishings dispelled her worries as to his status. He appeared to be a gentleman of some means.

Beyond the initial room, she espied his bedchamber and a bed with a carved headboard. The view made her stomach swarm with butterflies, and she twirled away, pretending it didn't exist.

Someone had prepared the space for their arrival. A fire burned in the grate, and candles established the mood. A table was positioned in front of the hearth, set with china, a white tablecloth and napkins, shiny silverware, and a bouquet of flowers. Two chairs were cozily situated, food and wine laid out.

It was the most romantic sight she'd ever witnessed, and she was assailed anew with the evidence of how drab her life was, with how little attention Alex paid her. They'd never had an intimate meal, and the lack had her unaccountably angry, but she chased away the spurt of temper.

Alex had no business popping up in the middle of her special rendezvous.

She listened as James shut and locked the door, but she wasn't concerned over being sequestered with him. Whatever transpired, it would be brought about by her own choices, and it would be marvelous.

He came up behind her, took her cloak, and hung it on a hook, and she could feel his gaze roving over her, and she wondered what he saw. He was very worldly, and likely had women guests to his residence all the time. She imagined they were gorgeous, exotic females who knew which clothes to don for such a tryst.

As for herself, she'd had great trouble dressing. She hadn't wanted to arouse suspicion, so she'd had her maid help her to bed, but after the woman left, Rebecca had risen and selected a functional gown she could pull on without assistance.

Her hair had been the major problem. She couldn't pin it up by herself, so the brunette tresses dangled in a braid down her back.

"I want your hair to be loose," he said. "May I re-move the ribbon?"

The request surprised her. From the year she'd turned twelve and had begun to wear corsets, no man had ever observed her hair flowing free. The notion of granting him permission was disturbing, but she was re-solved to explore every novel avenue he suggested.

"I don't mind," she replied.

He tugged away the ribbon and unraveled the lengthy mass; then he leaned in and bit at her nape, sending goose bumps down her arms.

"You're so beautiful."

"Oh, James . . ."

He'd rendered her speechless, and she reached over her shoulder to cradle his cheek. He kissed her palm, the simple gesture making her weak in the knees. He spun her, and he unbuttoned her gloves and drew them off, which was another unusual experience.

Her hands were never bare, and though it was foolish, she felt half-naked. Once again, he instantly noted her distress and sought to reassure her.

"I love your skin," he claimed. "It's so smooth and soft. Don't ever hide yourself from me."

He escorted her to the table and held her chair; then he sat next to her. They were so close that they were touching all the way down.

"I thought we'd serve ourselves," he explained. "So we'd have more privacy."

"That's fine."

"Are you positive?" he inquired. "I can ring for a ser-vant. It's no bother."

"No, no. This is perfect."

The dishes were covered, so she didn't know what

meal he'd arranged. The food smelled delicious, but she couldn't start eating.

She was caught up in the gray of his eyes. He was so handsome, so masculine. He exuded a rough aura that was different from every other man of her acquaintance. If he hadn't been attired so fashionably—in a blue coat and tan trousers—she couldn't have guessed how he earned his living. She might have pegged him as a highwayman.

His circumstance seemed a pretense, where he was eager to shuck off his jacket and become someone else. He was always coiled for action, as if he expected to be attacked from the rear so he needed to watch over his shoulder.

She'd noticed his limp, as well as a scar on his face, and she traced across it. "How did you acquire this?"

He shrugged her away. "It was a minor quarrel, long in the past."

"Did it hurt?"

"At the time, very much."

They stared, neither able to speak or look away, and he bent nearer and kissed her, his lips delightful and demanding. She was deluged, by his heat, by his scent, by the hard planes of his body. She couldn't think or pull away; she could only hold on.

His tongue was in her mouth, his hands in her hair. As constantly happened when she was with him, she was propelled much deeper into the passionate frenzy than she'd ever planned to go.

He slipped his fingers inside her gown and massaged her breast, pinching at the nipple, and she was electrified. At that moment, he might have persuaded her to engage in any recklessness.

With a wrenching gasp, she yanked away.

"Please stop," she begged.

"No." He was ablaze with desire and another emotion she couldn't name. "Why did you come to me?"

"What do you mean?"

"You're here in my bachelor's abode, when it goes against everything you've been taught. Will you leave him? Will you run away with me?"

"No. I never could. Alex is my life, my destiny."

"He doesn't love you!"

"He doesn't have to love me."

"And why shouldn't he?"

"It's not required!" She felt compelled to defend their staid relationship, but the statement sounded so idiotic. "Alex is just . . . Alex."

"Then what are you doing?"

"I . . . I . . ."

She couldn't put into words the strange impulses that were driving her. She'd had to be with him, had had to revel in the thrilling rush she enjoyed when in his presence.

She was surrounded by people, her world peppered with parties and friends, yet she was so lonely! When she peered down the road to her marriage and beyond, she didn't see that fact changing. If anything, she suspected she might be even more forlorn.

Tears surged into her eyes, and suddenly she was about to weep. At witnessing her upset, he appeared stricken, and he hugged her.

"I'm sorry," he said. "Don't cry."

"I can't help myself!" she wailed. "Since I've met you, I've been so confused."

"Everything will be all right," he soothed.

She struggled against a dam of despair that was waiting to burst. She was laden with a desolation she hadn't realized she'd been carrying, and she'd like to dump it on his sturdy shoulders, but she wouldn't.

He was fascinating and exciting—sort of like a prancing, untamed stallion—but she'd never be brave enough to actually ride such a wild beast. She was who she was, despite how she might secretly pine to be different.

"I wish I was who you assume me to be," she told him. "I wish I was free to do whatever I wanted."

"You are!"

"No. It's simply not in me to behave so badly."

"Stanton wouldn't miss you for a second," he scathingly contended.

Though she was certain he was correct, she declared, "You're wrong. He would be terribly shamed and hurt."

She pushed her chair away from his, needing to separate herself, to create space. When he touched her, she couldn't concentrate, couldn't render appropriate decisions.

"I shouldn't have come," she murmured, and she stood. "Would you be so kind as to take me home?"

"You can't leave yet. I won't let you. Not when you're so distraught." He stood, too, and he gestured at the table. "At least eat a bite. Have a glass of wine. It will calm you."

"You've gone to so much trouble, and I'm being so ungracious." Tears threatened again, and she gulped them down. "Please, may I go?"

He studied her, cataloguing her features, but she couldn't abide his scrutiny, and she glanced away.

"I could make you so happy," he insisted.

"No, you couldn't. You have no idea of what I need or who I am."

"I know exactly what you need. You need *me*."

He drew her toward him, his lips finding hers for the

sweetest kiss. It coaxed and urged and pleaded, and she clung to him, gripping him so tightly that if she'd released him, she'd have fallen to the floor.

It was a magical, charged instant, as though a portal had opened and she could walk through it—or not. She dawdled on a threshold between who she was and who she could be, but in the end, she hadn't the courage to step across to the other side.

"I can't stay," she whispered.

He was ready to argue, ready to cajole, but on noting her determination he sighed with resignation. "So be it."

He fetched her cloak, and she tarried like a statue as he draped it around her and tied the hood. She was overcome by the most weighty impression of conclusion, as if there were a stone on her lungs that was so heavy she couldn't breathe.

"Don't be angry with me," she implored.

"Angry? With you? I never could be." As if he might caress her a final time, he reached out, then thought better of it and dropped his hand. "Let's be off."

He led her out, and the carriage was still parked at the corner. The driver and footman were huddled together, sharing a flask, and they leapt to attention. As the footman assisted her, he and James exchanged a significant look she didn't understand. James shrugged imperceptibly but had no comment.

The door was closed, and they were away. They traveled in an awkward silence, but she didn't know how to break it. There were so many things she wanted to say, so many parting remarks she wanted to utter, but none of them seemed fitting.

After an excruciating interval, they arrived in the alley behind Alex's mansion, her one pitiful adventure cut

short by cowardice. She suffered a wave of embarrassment at how she'd sneaked off, at how she was slinking
back to Alex, with James lurking in the shadows.

She had to exit, but after she did, she'd never see him
again.

Don't go! Don't leave him! The voice rattled so loudly
in her head that it ached, and she fought the strongest
compulsion to fling herself into his arms, to tell him she'd
changed her mind, but she said nothing; she did nothing.

"I'll watch till you're safely inside," he advised.

"Thank you."

"If you ever need me—for any reason—promise
you'll send for me."

He furnished her with directions to a pub on the
Thames, which she found odd, but as this was farewell,
it wasn't necessary to question him about it.

"I won't ever contact you."

"You just never know what might happen," he
replied, and he gave her fingers a squeeze. "Good-bye."

With all the words clogging her throat, she couldn't
respond, and she lingered, absurdly hoping for a last
kiss, but the footman was observing all, the residence so
nearby.

She tugged at her hood and climbed out; then she
raced to the rear gate and flitted across the lawn to the
house. Without incident, she crept up the servants' stairs
to her room. She shut the door, went to the bed, and sat
down in the quiet, and it was as though she'd never left,
at all.

❧ 11 ❧

Alex walked the last few steps to Ellen's room, unable to believe he was being so reckless. It was wrong to persevere with his infatuation, but he couldn't stop. His nocturnal visits meant everything to him. They'd taken over his life, every minute agonizing, as he watched the clock tick toward evening and the moment he could be with her again.

He never saw her during the day. She had been living in his house for weeks, yet she was like a phantom, hiding and changing her schedule so that they never crossed paths. Should they suddenly come face-to-face he couldn't imagine how they'd act.

Her stealthy behavior was driving him mad, and though it was insane to wish it, he yearned for a relationship that included memories generated outside her bedchamber.

She would leave soon, would finish her employment and move on, and her imminent departure was eating at him, though he couldn't figure out why. She was nothing to him, and had no hold over him, other than the fact that they were compatible in their amorous pursuits. Previously, he'd never been tempted to more than a fleeting fling. He was aware of how rapidly desire could spiral, how quickly it could wane, so his libidinous habits were appalling, the practice of fidelity never contemplated.

He should have been getting bored with her, but he wasn't. How had she bewitched him? Why had he let her?

He arrived at her door and slipped inside without knocking. She was expecting him, relaxing in a chair by the window and sipping on a glass of wine. A candle burned, illuminating her blond hair so that it glowed like a halo around her head. Her blue eyes shimmered like polished sapphires.

"You're late," she said. "I was about to give up on you and go to bed."

"I'm glad you waited" was all he furnished in reply.

He wasn't about to remark on where he'd been or why he'd been delayed. They never discussed the reason she was in London, her job, or her position with Lydia, just as they never talked about Rebecca. But Rebecca was like an edifice in the middle of the room, an unmentioned, glaring reminder of how despicable it was for them to continue, of how powerless they were to fight the attraction that ruled them.

She uncurled from the chair and approached, dressed in a worn summer nightgown, a tattered robe over top, and he was so weary of seeing her attired like a pauper. He speculated as to what she'd look like in a blue satin negligee, with tiny straps and a shortened hem. Maybe he'd order one for her and present it as a gift, would insist she keep it despite how vociferously she complained.

She snuggled herself to him, unbuttoning his shirt and

tugging at the lapels to bare his chest, and she rubbed her cheek in the soft matting of hair.

"I've been thinking," she commented.

"Really? About what?"

"About you and how good you smell."

He chuckled. "Anything else?"

"Oh yes. Quite a lot," but as usual, she didn't share any of her reflections, and he realized that he'd been fishing for compliments and was frustrated when none were forthcoming.

She never explained why she'd gotten involved with him, and he hated to consider that he wasn't special to her, that she might have done the same with any man who'd pressed the issue. He'd been the lucky fellow to initiate her into carnal conduct, but strangely, he craved more than a brief dalliance.

He was plagued by their association being strictly sexual. She was perfectly happy to philander—with no strings and no promises—while he, for once, was chafing at the lack of a bond, the dearth of ties.

She nibbled up, to his neck, his chin, and he groaned as their lips connected, as her tongue found his.

A month earlier, she'd scarcely been kissed, and now, she joined in like the most experienced courtesan. She wasn't afraid or timid over the most raucous intimacy. It was as though after they'd agreed to proceed, she'd decided there would be no restraint. She'd thrown herself into the affair, eager to try whatever he suggested, and he had to slow them down, to counsel that they couldn't do all the things she asked. She was constantly begging to be ravished, and he was constantly refusing, which was a sign of how their characters had been turned inside out.

So far, he'd been relatively well behaved, had kept

his trousers on, the placard fastened, but he didn't know how many more times he could be so chivalrous.

He lifted her and spun her so that her back was to the wall, her thighs wrapped around him, and he flexed into her, receiving a modicum of relief from the motion.

"You're pushing into me again," she said. "Why?"

"I told you: I desire you. In a manly fashion."

"But you never show me what you mean!"

"If I *show* you, we can't repair the damage."

She growled with exasperation. "I detest when you speak in riddles."

"You could never marry."

"You act as if I have swains lined up at the door."

"Who knows what the future will bring? You might waltz out of here tomorrow and meet the man of your dreams."

He'd made the statement as a joke, but the idea disturbed him. Though she could never be his, he didn't want anyone else to have her, either, and his yearning for both outcomes was a further indication of how muddled he was in his dealings with her.

No resolution suited him.

He carried her to the bed, and as they stretched out he reveled in how marvelous it felt to be so close to her. His fingers were inside her nightgown, and he filled his hand with her breast. Instantly he was frantic to have her.

Yanking at her bodice, he pulled it down to reveal her bosom. He dipped down and took her nipple into his mouth, working over it until she was writhing with ecstasy.

He trailed up her leg, her thigh, to toy with her privates. With hardly any effort on his part, she came in his arms, her body convulsing with a potent orgasm. He'd never been with a woman who could be so swiftly aroused and satisfied. She had a fabulously lusty nature, and he was thrilled that she trusted him to set it free.

To muffle her cry of delight, he kissed her, and as she spiraled down he was grinning.

"I can't get over how sexy you are."

"How do you do that to me?"

"I don't *do* anything. You're easy."

She punched him on the shoulder. "I am not!"

"All right, have it your way, but just so you know, it's typically acknowledged among gentlemen that it's difficult to pleasure a female, unless she's . . . well . . ."

"Easy?"

"Yes."

She scowled. "Are you admitting that you and your male friends chat about such personal matters?"

"Of course. We're men. We're like beasts in the field. We like to strut and preen."

"So you view me no differently than a bull might a heifer?"

"A very pretty heifer—if that makes you feel any better."

"You're correct: You are a beast." Her fervid gaze roved over his torso, and she inquired, "Is it the same?"

"What?"

"When I touch your breast, is it the same sensation as when you touch mine?"

"I suppose."

"And if I put my mouth there? Would it be the same, too?"

"Probably." Her questions had his heart racing.

During their assignations, he hadn't demanded much of her. *He* was the one who tormented and teased, and she'd participated with a great relish, but she hadn't evinced much curiosity as to what he enjoyed, as to what *she* might do to him.

She scooted away and clambered on top of him. She was on her knees and hovered over his lap, and she stared down, her eyes blazing.

"An interesting notion recently occurred to me," she said.

"What is it?"

"You've taught me all these naughty deeds, but you never ask me to do anything to you in return." She raised a brow. "How come?"

"Well . . ."

"All this activity must be very stimulating to you."

"It is."

"But there has to be more on your end. I should be able to excite you as you excite me."

"You can."

She leaned down, grabbed the lapels of his shirt, and shook him. "Then why haven't you enlightened me?"

"Because if we start in, I'm not positive I can control myself."

"Have I suggested that you control yourself?"

"No, but one of us must keep a clear head."

"Why?"

"As I've already explained—on numerous occasions—if I'm too carried away, you can never marry."

"And I told *you* that we needn't worry about that situation ever transpiring."

"For another, you could become pregnant."

Obviously, she hadn't realized the dangers, and she released him and plopped onto her haunches. "From what we've been doing?"

"No, but from the rest, from what we haven't attempted, and whatever else you might think about my morals, I don't intend to get you with child."

"How does it happen?"

"What?"

"Pregnancy."

He studied her, trying to figure out where to begin, but there didn't seem to be any good place. He blushed. "I guess I'm too embarrassed to describe it to you."

"That's absurd. You can do it, but you can't talk about it?"

"Believe me: Some things are easier to demonstrate."

"So show me." Impatient to be ravished, she spread her arms wide.

"Not bloody likely."

"Alex!"

He sighed. She was right: They were adults, and they ought to be capable of having a rational discussion about intimate affairs.

"We're built differently," he said.

"Where?"

"In our private parts." He massaged her cleft. "You have an opening here, whilst I have a sort of . . . sort of rod."

She glanced at his crotch, seeking proof. "What's it for?"

"When I'm aroused, it grows very hard, and—if we were in the throes of passion—I would thrust it inside you." He wedged two fingers into her sheath and caressed her in a seductive rhythm, giving her a clue as to what he was relating. "I would push it back and forth, and the motion produces a friction that causes a white cream to erupt from the tip. This is my seed, and it plants a child."

"This . . . this flexing, how does it feel?"

"Fantastic. Like nothing else in the world."

"And you're sure a babe is created this way?"

"Yes. Very sure."

She was quiet, digesting the information; then she clutched the waistband of his trousers. "I want to look at you."

"No."

"Why?"

"A man can be too provoked, so I'm afraid to remove my pants."

"You'd never harm me."

"I would—if I was goaded beyond coherent judgment."

"I'm scarcely the type to spur you past your limits."

"You'd be surprised what I might do because of you."

"I have to see this for myself."

She flicked a button free, then another and another. He knew he should prevent her, but he was only a mortal man, and he had so few redeeming qualities, moderation not being one of them. He was beyond refusal, his untended phallus in revolt.

The last button fell away, the placard loose, and she tugged the fabric down around his flanks. In a thrice, his unruly cock was exposed. It was eager to be fondled and, having a mind of its own, it reached out toward her.

"Oh my," she murmured. She gaped, then traced across it with her finger.

Her touch was electrifying, and he shuddered as if she'd prodded him with a hot poker.

"Sweet Jesu . . ." he moaned through clenched teeth.

"What should I do with it?"

"Take me in your hand."

She hesitated, then wrapped her fist around him. He started flexing, the soft skin at the crown tightening, and he stared at the ceiling, struggling to calm himself, but he couldn't bear her exploration.

He'd wanted her for so long, with a reckless abandon that he hadn't had an opportunity to slake, and he was tired of being gallant, tired of steering her from folly.

He couldn't keep himself in check, and he shoved her away.

"What is it?" She was confused by the abrupt halt. "What have I done?"

"Nothing. Everything is fine." He pulled her to him. "Hold me."

"Why?"

"I need to spill myself."

"But . . . but we mustn't! We could make a babe!"

"We won't."

She panicked and tried to wrestle away, but he pinned her to him, gripping her shapely bottom, his erection pressed to her belly.

"Alex! Stop it!"

"I won't be inside you," he managed to spit out. "You're safe."

It was all the reassurance he had time to give. He was at the edge, and with a few brief thrusts, he came against her stomach. He flew to the heavens, his heart pounding so rigorously that he was surprised it didn't burst; then he floated down.

At his raucous performance he was too embarrassed to face her, and he burrowed into the pillow. He'd behaved like a savage, and he couldn't imagine what her opinion must be. For her first encounter with male desire it couldn't have been all that magnificent.

What was he supposed to say? How was he to act?

"My goodness"—she broke the awkward silence—"that was . . . was . . ."

As he'd suspected, she had no words to describe the event, and he wondered why he was renowned for being such a great lover, for having such a way with women, when all evidence indicated that he was an ass.

"It can be a bit wild," he mumbled.

"It certainly can."

She was riffling through his hair, massaging his shoulders, and he couldn't abide her composure. He slithered away and straightened his pants; then he went to the washbasin and returned with a wet cloth and towel. He swabbed away the remnants of what he'd done.

Without comment, she submitted to his ministrations, but when he'd finished, he could no longer avoid the inevitable. He lay down and stretched out. They were on their sides and studying each other.

"I'm sorry," he said.

She frowned. "For what?"

"For not warning you about how it would go."

"I didn't mind."

"Well, I did. The masculine end of things is a tad more . . . physical."

"I definitely concur!" She laughed.

"It can take some getting used to."

"I'm not made of glass. Don't worry about me so much."

"I can't help it."

She stroked the front of his trousers, and even though he'd just come like a maniac, the rowdy appendage leapt to life, anxious to begin anew.

"I've heard the phrase *randy devil*," she mentioned. "Is this what it means?"

"Yes."

"So you can do it again?"

"Over and over, as can you."

She considered, then grinned. "I wish we never had to leave this room."

"A marvelous idea. Let's stay here forever."

Suddenly she appeared very shy, very young. "I like it that you fancy me so much, that I can make you so aroused."

"I like it, too."

He cuddled himself to her, so that their bodies were touching, so that he could feel her all the way down. With the waning of their ardor, the air had cooled, and he grabbed a blanket and drew it over them.

Though he couldn't deduce why, every exchange was so much more vital with her, so much more precious. They were at the start of something extraordinary, and he had to pursue it to its natural conclusion. He was dying to know where it would lead.

Yet how could he proceed? What was the solution? His ties to Rebecca were choking him, the prospect of marriage more unpalatable with each passing day, but he couldn't cry off.

Rebecca was his destiny, his path. He was an earl, a peer of the realm, and he had responsibilities that no normal person could comprehend. He couldn't shirk such an important commitment; yet he was obsessed with Ellen.

If he'd been sane, which he was doubting more every second, he'd jump out of her bed and scurry away as fast as his legs would carry him, but he couldn't. He was so happy, so pleased, to be with her.

What was he to do? The choices were so dismal.

"My engagement ball is a week from tonight," he said, throwing the forbidden subject out into the open.

"Yes, it is," she replied, but she had no other remark. She was very still, her eyes unblinking, which irked him enormously.

He wasn't sure what he'd been expecting, but some display of emotion ought to be in evidence. Did she feel anything for him? He thought she did, but then he'd been wrong about women on many occasions.

"Would you be my mistress?" he queried.

"You asked me once before, and my answer is the same now as it was then."

"I can't fathom why you're refusing. I want to take care of you."

"No, you don't. Not really."

"Why would you say that?"

"We enjoy a heightened affection, but it won't last. You understand that better than I."

He fussed with a lock of her hair. "But our attraction is so splendid. We shouldn't walk away from it."

"Don't be daft. Of course we should." She slipped off the mattress and went to fetch the wine she'd been drinking when he'd arrived. She sipped on it and gazed out the window, her back to him.

"Actually," she stated, "I've been wondering if I shouldn't speak with Lydia."

"About what?"

"To inform her that I'm quitting."

"Quitting?" He was stricken by the notion, and his

pulse thudded with equal parts astonishment and alarm. "You're joking."

"No, I'm not."

She spun toward him, and he hated that she was so far away. He held out his hand, hoping she'd cross to him, that they could nestle down under the blanket, but she didn't move.

"Where would you go? What would you do?"

"I'll find another job. What would you suppose? I'm not helpless." She assessed him, then shook her head in consternation. "You can't have presumed I'd stay on."

Well, yes, he had. In his dallying with her, he'd been living in a fairy tale where naught was real, where the outside world didn't exist. Since they were ensconced in a fantasy, he hadn't pondered the future.

"You can't leave. I won't allow it."

"It's not up to you."

Her shoulders were set, her proud chin jutting out, and he rose and marched over to her. He took her glass of wine, swilling the contents, himself; then he pulled her to the bed and snuggled them down.

"You're being foolish," he chided.

"No, you are."

"You're talking as if disaster is lurking around the corner, as if we're on the precipice of calamity. There's plenty of time. We needn't make immediate, drastic decisions."

She sighed. "Have you reflected on this, at all?"

"Yes," he fibbed. He dreaded how he was fixated on her, so he'd given the situation very little consideration.

"Then you have to see that I'm in an impossible jam."

"I don't *see* anything of the sort," he mulishly claimed.

"You were determined to commence this affair, and I was complicit in its development and execution, but how have you envisioned it will end?"

Very badly, he mused, though he'd never say so aloud. "I imagine we'll . . . we'll . . ."

"You assume I'll linger in this bedchamber into infinity, waiting for the glorious moment of your arrival. How long will that be precisely? Should I remain until the betrothal is official? Until you're married? Will you sneak down on your wedding night for a quick romp?"

"Ellen," he scolded, "it's not like that between us."

"It's exactly like that. At this late juncture, don't pretend otherwise."

He was extremely vexed over how to resolve the impasse. He wished he could be split into two people, that one half of him could enter into his arranged marriage with Rebecca, while the other was free to wallow with Ellen until he could shed the driving urge he had to be with her.

Why couldn't he have what he wanted? He was rich and powerful. If he couldn't wrangle the details so that he could have Ellen, what was the use of any of it?

"Don't go," he entreated. "Please. Not yet."

"I have to. This is killing me. I can't watch what will transpire in the next few days. Don't ask it of me."

"If you depart, we'll never see each other again."

"No, we won't."

For once, he was totally honest. "I couldn't stand it."

For a lengthy interval she was silent; then she admitted, "Neither could I."

"We'll figure it out," he vowed. "Just bear with me."

She grumbled but assented. "I will."

He rolled onto her, and he kissed her, reveling,

cherishing, and they were instantly transported to the physical realm where they were so compatible, where nothing mattered but the fact that they were together and alone.

He was like a magician, juggling balls at a fair. If he could keep the sections of his life whirling about, if he didn't drop any of the pieces, everything would turn out fine.

"Trust me," he murmured.

"I don't. I absolutely don't."

She chuckled, but it was such a weary, sad sound that he couldn't abide hearing it. He deepened the kiss, intent on ignoring whatever was coming his way.

~ 12 ~

"You're what?"

"I'm tendering my resignation."

"I don't accept it."

Ellen shifted in her chair, uncomfortable with how Lydia was glaring from her perch behind Alex's desk, but she forced herself to remain calm. She understood Lydia's contrary nature, and her desire to be in control of every situation.

If Ellen begged, if she demanded, if she did anything at all, Lydia would view it as weakness, would jump on her like a wolf on carrion.

"There's no need for me to stay on," Ellen maintained.

"No need? Rebecca's not dead. She's merely becoming engaged. She shall require your services till the wedding, and perhaps for some time after. *I* may require your assistance, too, while I pursue my own nuptials."

With the mention of her pending marriage to Nicholas Marshall, Lydia preened, obviously expecting more congratulatory drivel, but Ellen couldn't figure out what to say that would sound earnest.

When the peculiar news had initially been disseminated, Ellen had swallowed her shock and offered the appropriate remarks, but she couldn't spew many more insincerities. She had no idea why a man would marry Lydia, even to acquire her fortune. While it made rational sense for Mr. Marshall to chase after the financial windfall, Ellen couldn't wrap her mind around it emotionally, and she shuddered to envision what sort of children they'd produce!

"I haven't been much help to Rebecca," Ellen claimed. Since she could imagine no more horrid fate than accompanying Lydia as she shopped for a wedding gown, she diplomatically added, "I'd hardly do much better with your own grand occasion."

"You'll assist me," Lydia declared, "as you have my sister, so you can rid yourself of this silly notion that you're leaving. I won't hear of it, and I won't have you pestering me." She waved toward the door and the loud party in progress down the hall. "Be gone."

Ellen couldn't give up, but she was treading a fine line. She hoped to split on decent terms so that she had a letter of recommendation as she went, but she was growing desperate and would go no matter what.

Knowing Lydia's parsimonious habits, Ellen tried another avenue. "It's such a waste of money to keep me on."

"Oh, it is, is it?" Lydia snidely questioned. "It's my money, and if I choose to spend it on you, I will. Now, Rebecca may need you, so I suggest you get back to work."

Ellen couldn't linger at Rebecca's side. The engagement would be announced at midnight, and the house was overrun with guests who'd come to witness the spectacle of the matrimonial noose tightening for Alex Marshall.

As events played out, Ellen couldn't bear to watch. The past week had been a nightmare as she'd hidden and avoided Rebecca, but complete evasion hadn't been possible.

Rebecca had constantly sought her out, wanting her opinion on every detail from floral arrangements to buffet menus. Ellen had struggled to be gracious, to comport herself as if their relationship were proceeding as it always had, but the charade was excruciating.

She'd told Alex that she'd wait indefinitely, and when they'd been snuggled in her bed she'd meant every word, but with distance and separation sanity had returned, and the folly of her actions was so blatant.

Though she had no clue as to when it had happened, she was in love with Alex Marshall. She couldn't fathom what had caused the dangerous attachment to develop, but whatever the basis, she had to put a stop to it, had to cut off her connection in a single swipe, as one would a festering limb. It was the only answer.

Over the next few days, he and Rebecca would be feted around the city, so it would be easy to slip away unnoticed.

She was a coward and had no intention of saying good-bye to either of them. She'd already penned farewell notes, which provided vague, impersonal explanations for her departure.

"I'm sorry, Lydia"—she braced herself and lied—"but I've accepted another position."

"You what?"

"I've taken another job."

"You're joking."

"No. With my post here about to end, I've been searching for a new place, and I found one. They need me immediately."

Lydia stared and stared, then she began to tremble with wrath, and she rose and stomped over. She wasn't as tall as Ellen, but Ellen was seated, so Lydia looked huge and downright menacing.

"How dare you!" Lydia hissed. "Haven't I been kind to you?"

"Yes," Ellen fibbed.

"Haven't I been generous?"

"Yes," she repeated.

"Yet you have the audacity to assume you can tot off, without so much as a by-your-leave!"

"I thought it would be best."

"You did, did you?" Lydia sneered. "You know, Ellen, I deem your worst trait to be the fact that you think too much."

How was she to respond to such a barb?

She apologized again. "I'm sorry."

"Who is it?" Lydia demanded. "Tell me who has had the gall to lure you away, and I will speak to them at once."

Ellen couldn't believe how she'd blundered. In uttering the falsehood it had never occurred to her that Lydia would ask after the identity of the new employer. On the spur of the moment, Ellen couldn't invent a name, especially when Lydia would track down any likely candidate.

"It doesn't matter," she mumbled. "I'll write and advise them that I won't be able to start after all."

"A wise decision. In the meantime, we'll pretend that this discussion never transpired. You may be about your duties."

Lydia moved away, and Ellen was overcome by the strongest feeling that if she'd pressed the issue, Lydia might have struck her, which was absurd. Ellen was a modern-day lady's companion, not some medieval scullery maid, but she couldn't shake the perception that she was lucky to have proffered a suitable reply.

She stood and straightened her skirt. "I'll locate Rebecca and see if she needs anything."

Her mind racing, her heart heavy, she rushed out, wondering what to do next.

Lydia paced the library, trying to rein in her temper.

She was enraged over Ellen's treachery. She'd hired Ellen with Ellen's having scarcely any experience or character references, when she'd been desperate and willing to work for pennies.

There had to be a reason behind her abrupt desire to quit, and Lydia strove to remember what had recently changed.

Naught had been altered except . . . except . . . Lydia was engaged! She halted in her tracks.

Did the pretty vixen have her eye on Nicholas? Could it be?

Lydia pondered, then discounted the prospect.

Nicholas wouldn't risk a liaison with Ellen, but might he with another? Lydia was no fool, and she grasped her limitations and Nicholas's. She couldn't expect him to be in love with her, but she absolutely would not allow him to be in love with someone else. She'd murder him before she'd permit it, and she'd get away with it, too—as she had with her father.

Her anger under control, she left the library, but she refused to head for the crowded section of the mansion. The throngs were present to gush over Rebecca and Alex, and Lydia burned with fury.

Though her own betrothal had been printed in the papers and her wedding was approaching much quicker than Rebecca's, she had yet to stumble on a well-wisher. Whenever the event was mentioned, she was greeted with gaping jaws, incredulity, and the occasional snicker.

Well, she would show them all. She would have Nicholas for her husband, would be a respected, married lady, *and* she would keep all of her fortune. She would have the last laugh.

She went to the door that led on to the verandah, and as she stepped into the cool night air she was surprised to spot Nicholas and Alex down in the garden.

They were arguing, and she was dying to discover why. There was a bench in the shadows, pushed against the balustrade. She sneaked to it and sat down so that the two men were huddled directly below her.

"You've read some of the documents Lydia's had drawn up," Nicholas whined. "When am I to receive some funds?"

"I have no idea," Alex said.

"But I must have cash this week!"

"For Suzette DuBois?"

"Yes! She's chosen the house I've promised to buy her. I have to make a down payment, and I have to arrange her trust account. I can't dawdle."

Alex gave a derisive snort. "What you're doing is so wrong, Nick. Have you any concept of how wrong it is?"

"Why would you say so? I'm about to be the happiest man alive. My every dream is about to come true, and all I have to do is marry Lydia."

"Yes, but your first act with your wife's money will be to set up your mistress! Isn't that a bit tawdry? Even by your low standards?"

"No, Mr. High-and-Mighty." Nicholas sounded smug. "You can't suppose that I seduced Lydia because I was swept away by . . . by passion!" He chuckled cruelly. "It was vile, but I forced myself through it, and I won't apologize. The homely bat was practically begging to have a man between her legs, and I obliged her. Now I want my reward, and you must ascertain when I'm to collect it!"

Alex muttered something else, and Nicholas responded, but Lydia had heard enough. She crept away, entered the mansion, and climbed the rear stairs to her bedchamber. She stared out the window, her mouth a grim, determined line.

Suzette DuBois . . . Suzette DuBois . . . The exotic name pulsed in the silence, matching the tempo of her heartbeat.

Stupidly, she'd presumed that Nicholas had ravaged her because he had gambling debts, or had overspent his quarterly income. She'd never contemplated the possibility of his having a more sinister motive.

He coveted her fortune, all right, so that he could fritter it away on his paramour!

She'd never been so livid! A loud ringing deafened her ears, and her vision grew a hazy red color. In such a provoked state, there was no telling what revenge she might seek.

Nicholas assumed he understood Lydia, but he didn't

really. No one did. No one had a clue as to how she would lash out when spurned. She'd had decades to practice on her father, decades to learn how to wheedle and manipulate, how to retaliate and wound.

She rippled with malevolence. She didn't know who Suzette DuBois was, but she was about to find out.

"James! What on earth are you doing here?"

James whipped around, and he was face-to-face with his sister.

The large residence was packed to the rafters. What were the odds that they'd have crossed paths?

"I came to watch the grand announcement—as has half of London." He managed a smile.

She studied him, then frowned. "You're lying. What mischief are you instigating?"

"Why would you automatically suspect I'm up to no good?"

Her gaze anxious, she rested a hand on his arm. "Let it go, James. Whatever your scheme, don't pursue it. Please."

"After what Stanton and his chums did to our family, don't you think he deserves some misery in return?"

"It wasn't him," she staunchly declared. "He was merely *there,* like so many others. He had naught to do with what happened to us."

"How can you be so sure?"

"I've met him," she said. "He's not anything like I imagined he'd be."

"Have you become an expert on identifying villainous traits in a man? If so, how many have you perceived in me?"

"James!" she admonished, and he was instantly chastised.

He hadn't intended to be short with her, but it galled him that she was lodged in Stanton's house, that she was eating his food and enjoying his company. He hated Stanton and was keen to have her share his dislike, but when she had to maneuver in Stanton's world it was probably asking too much.

"I'm sorry to bark at you," he told her. "It's been a while since I've had anyone care enough to scold me."

"I do care about you, so will you listen? Go away, and don't come back. You're only courting disaster."

"I can't. Not yet."

"But why? What are you hoping to accomplish?"

"I simply want to look at Stanton," he asserted, which was partially true. "I won't cause any trouble, if that's what has you worried."

As a younger, more naïve man, he'd briefly socialized with Stanton, and he was curious to discern if Stanton was still the pompous prig James remembered him to be. But mostly, James wanted to see Rebecca, and he wanted *her* to see him.

After his failed seduction, she hadn't contacted him, and he'd been positive she would. He'd misplayed that hand, had bet all the wrong cards. He never should have allowed her to scurry home to Stanton, and why he had was a mystery. His blunder had to be corrected, and it would be much more destructive and satisfying to abscond with her after she was engaged, rather than before.

Ellen was badgering him. "Swear to me that you'll let it go and move on."

"As I'm the one who suffered most horridly, I can't

blithely *move on*—as others obviously can—and it's contemptible of you to expect it of me."

At the stinging rebuke, tears filled her eyes, and he wanted to kick himself. It was the second occasion he'd spoken to her in ten years, and all he could do was belittle and berate. He recollected Stanton as being a despicable creature, but who was the real ass?

"Oh, Ellen . . ." He patted her shoulder, not concerned over who might observe their conversation. There were so many people squeezing past that no one so much as glanced in their direction.

"Could I come and live with you?" she suddenly pleaded, and, as if he'd denied her request, she hastily added, "For a bit. I wouldn't stay forever."

"Of course you could." He wondered what the hell he'd do with her. While his apartment was suitable, it was in a section of town where she couldn't safely set foot out the door, and if she bumped into any of his associates, or caught an inkling of how he earned his income, she'd be mortified.

"I need to leave here"—a deluge of weeping threatened to overwhelm her—"but I don't have any money, and I don't have anywhere to go."

"Has something bad happened? Has someone hurt you?"

His heart constricted with dismay. He paid others to keep tabs on her, and their reports—along with her infrequent letters—made it seem as if she was tended and sheltered. Had it been a façade? Had he failed her again?

"No," she contended, "no one's done anything. I'm just so unhappy."

"Then come with me now. We'll flee this very minute. You needn't even pack a bag."

"I don't know. . . ." Confused and distraught, she rubbed her temples. "I can't decide what's best."

"Let's be off, and we'll figure it out later."

Her attention was diverted by activity down the corridor. She appeared fearful, and she stepped away from him.

"I couldn't go without my things. I have the last of Mother's possessions at Miss Burton's house in the country. If I left without a notice, I couldn't ever retrieve them."

"Ellen, don't remain over a few trinkets."

"They're not *trinkets*! They're the final pieces I have of Mother!"

"But they're still chattels."

Necessity had taught him to shed his attachment to objects, but she bristled at the suggestion.

"I'll give them some warning," she said, "as I ought; then I'll prepare myself. I'll send you a note when I'm ready."

"Promise that you will."

"I promise."

Before he could stop her, she whipped away, and the crowd swallowed her up. He rose on tiptoe, trying to locate her, but she'd vanished. He had no idea where she might have gone, or how to look for her. It wasn't as if he could dash to the upper floors and search.

He whirled around, anxious to ascertain what had prompted her speedy exit, when he espied Alex Marshall meandering through the guests.

Why would Ellen rush off at sighting Stanton? Had Stanton offended her? Or had he perpetrated more ominous behavior?

James's blood ran cold. If Stanton had harmed Ellen,

he would die a slow, painful death, and James would be the eager fellow to bring it about.

But first, Stanton would lose his fiancée—and all of London would know of his disgrace.

James walked to the stage that had been erected near the orchestra. It was almost midnight, almost time for the announcement of Rebecca's betrothal. When she climbed up with Stanton, James planned to be front and center.

Rebecca dawdled in the dark hall, working up the courage to enter Alex's bedchamber, but she couldn't seem to find it.

She wore only a thin, summery nightgown, and she shivered. The temperature was chilly, her bare feet freezing, yet she continued to loiter, minute after agonizing minute. She had to proceed or depart, and she couldn't slither away without learning the truth.

She took a deep breath, then spun the knob. The deed was commenced and she'd forge on to the dastardly conclusion—despite how humiliating or dreadful it ended up being.

Alex was across the way, his back to her. He was attired in a blue robe, and she was positive he had nothing on underneath. She gulped with trepidation, questioning whether this had been such a wise strategy, after all. She had an inkling of what men and women did when they were alone, James having furnished a few hints.

Would Alex, given the privacy of the moment, be inclined to the same sort of naughty conduct? Had he any attraction to her? Was there any basis for the wedding to progress, besides the fact that they were cousins and their fathers had both wanted it?

In for a penny, in for a pound. The phrase darted past, and she heralded her arrival by shutting the door with a loud click.

"Is that you, El—" He twirled around and, on seeing her, cut off whatever his comment would have been.

"Hello, Alex."

"Rebecca?"

They stared, an awkward silence ensuing. Several emotions swept over him—astonishment, worry, shock— and she was tickled by his perplexity. He was always in control and unflappable, and she liked having confounded him.

"What are you doing here?" he eventually asked.

"We need to talk."

She forced herself to march over to him, and she gazed into his handsome face. Her pulse should have been fluttering with excitement, but it wasn't.

She tried not to compare, but she couldn't help thinking of James and how different it was when she was with him. Though she couldn't imagine why, he'd been downstairs during the party. She'd fought not to glance at him, but his hot focus had landed on her like a brand.

Bizarre as it sounded, he made her feel as if she was cheating on him by marrying Alex. She was besieged by baffling cravings and furious over his demands that she balk.

"Are you all right?" Alex queried. "Is it Lydia?"

"I'm fine! Lydia is fine! Forget about Lydia!"

What would it take to pry a reaction out of him? How could she gain the personal response she was desperate to receive?

Bravely, she let her attention travel down his body. The lapels of his robe were open, and she could see his chest, the matting of hair in the middle, and the spectacle—once again—conjured visions of James, as she pondered what his chest was like, if it would be coated with hair, too.

She chased the shameless reflection away.

With her scrutiny, Alex realized that he was scarcely dressed, and he tugged at fabric, concealing himself from her view. "You shouldn't have visited," he claimed. "Let's get you to your room—before you're discovered."

"I don't wish to go."

"But you must."

She strode forward so that her torso connected with his. She waited for the sizzle to erupt, as occurred when she was with James, but nothing out of the ordinary transpired, and Alex gawked at her as if she were deranged.

She was making a fool of herself, but she couldn't desist. She placed her hand on his chest, but she had no idea what to do with it, so it lay there like a stone. He saved her from herself by reaching out and drawing it away. At the rebuff, her cheeks reddened with embarrassment, but she refused to halt or retreat.

"I want you to make passionate love to me," she stated.

"You what?" he sputtered.

Nervously, she licked her lips, terrified that he might consent. "There's no one to know, and we're to be married soon, anyway. Show me what happens."

"Rebecca, what's come over you?"

"Nothing."

"You're acting so oddly. From one instant to the next I can't predict what outrageous remark will pop out of your mouth."

"Why won't you agree?" she challenged. "Is the notion of bedding me distasteful?"

He studied her, his exasperation obvious. "When a man and woman join together in bed, they can create a babe."

"I know that! I'm not stupid."

"I'm not saying you are, but the wedding is six months away, so a pregnancy would be difficult to explain."

"Then let's move up the date. Let's marry immediately."

At the suggestion she was surprised he didn't faint. His knees buckled, and he appeared horrified.

"You've always dreamed of a big wedding," he pointed out. "Since you were a little girl, you've wanted to walk down the aisle at the Cathedral, in a fabulous gown from Paris, with the organ blaring, and the choir singing. If we have it in a few days, you can't have any of those things."

"Maybe I've changed my mind. Maybe I don't need all the folderol."

He sighed. "Rebecca—"

"Kiss me."

"What?" he gasped.

"You heard me, Alex. Don't pretend you didn't."

"No."

"Why won't you?"

"It's not fitting for us to be lingering in the dark and carrying on."

"You do it with other women all the time."

"I do not, and I'm offended that you would level such a despicable charge."

"You have paramours crawling out of the woodwork—people delight in keeping me apprised—so if you can philander with every loose hussy in the kingdom, why not me?"

"You've gone stark raving mad, and I'm wondering if I shouldn't have your sister call for a physician."

"For God's sake, Alex!" She stamped her foot like a toddler having a tantrum, so angry that she yearned to grab a chunk of his hair and yank it out by the roots. "I just want a simple kiss. Is that too much to ask? We're not strangers; we haven't stumbled into each other on the street; I'm not some sixteen-year-old child who can be ruined. We've been betrothed my entire life! So kiss me—this very second—or I swear I will cry off, and I will tell everyone it was because you . . . you . . . like men instead of women!"

She'd managed to rattle the appropriate cage. The slur to his manhood was more than he could abide. He bristled with temper, but she stood her ground as he hemmed and hawed.

Ultimately, he did as she'd demanded. He kissed her.

It was very sweet, it was very innocent, it was very dull, and it confirmed each and every one of her suspicions.

He pulled away and, discouraged and saddened, she evaluated him; then she murmured, "You don't love me, do you? You never loved me."

"Oh, Rebecca . . ."

"Do you?"

"We'll develop deep feelings with the passage of time," he maintained, "with association and familiarity."

It's been twenty-two years! she longed to scream, but she didn't. Resignation washed over her, and she was relieved to have the issue out in the open. If he didn't love her, so be it, but she would enter into the union with no illusions, with her heart steeled against disappointment.

When the end result was so meaningless, she couldn't

see any reason to go to all the trouble and expense of a
fancy wedding.

"I want a Special License," she said. "We'll have a
small ceremony, next week, in the downstairs parlor."

He hesitated, trying to decide if he should talk her out
of it, if he should flat-out decline, but what excuse could
he give? What did it matter if they finished it tomorrow
or next month or next year? The outcome would be the
same.

He shrugged. "As you wish."

Without another word, she turned and left.

~ 13 ~

Ellen heard Alex stomping down the hall, but she ignored him to fold her undergarments and tuck them into
her portmanteau.

He tried the knob and, on finding the door locked, he
let out a vicious curse and kicked it so hard that her window rattled.

"Let me in," he hissed.

"No."

"Dammit, Ellen! Let me in this minute."

She didn't respond but took a final look around,
searching for any item she might have forgotten, though
she shouldn't have fretted. She had so few possessions
that she scarcely needed a satchel in which to carry them.

Her deck of cards lay on the dresser, and she decided
to leave them for the next occupant. They had given her
comfort during many lonely hours, but now they simply
and painfully reminded her of Alex.

"Ellen!" he barked, and he pounded on the wood.

He was growing more irritated, his voice much too

loud. As usual, it was the middle of the night, and if he kept on, he'd wake the whole house.

"Go! Away!" she quietly said.

With a sigh of resignation, she set her bag on the rug, then lay on the bed and gazed at the ceiling. She'd dispatched a note to James, begging him to come for her, and the moment he arrived on the morrow, she'd be ready.

If he didn't appear, she wasn't sure what she'd do. She had a bit of cash, but it wouldn't support her for more than a few days on the streets of London.

The prospects for disaster were great, yet she couldn't stay. News of Rebecca's rapid nuptials had raced through the mansion like a wildfire, sending the staff into hysterics of preparation.

Ellen didn't know why Rebecca had chosen to wed so fast, or why Alex had acquiesced, and she didn't want to know. There was one reason a bridal couple had to hurry—that being a babe on the way—and if Ellen learned that pregnancy was the cause, she truly thought her heart might quit beating.

She felt as if she were the last person left on earth, a shipwrecked survivor on a deserted island. A candle burned on the dresser. It flickered with each strike of his fist, and she closed her eyes against his rage, eager just to sleep, to sleep forever.

Suddenly there was a thunderous crack, then another, and the door burst as he rent it open. He stormed in, a veritable wave of temper billowing out ahead of him.

She should have realized that she couldn't keep him out. He was like a force of nature, a hurricane or blizzard that was relentless in its approach, that was impossible to halt or divert.

Silent and morose, she sat up as he assessed her packed bag, the emptied wardrobe. He rippled with fury.

"What in the hell are you doing?"

"If you're determined to fight with me," she said, "stop shouting. I won't have your servants tromping down to listen."

For once, he actually heeded her. He went to the ruined door and balanced a chair against it, bracing it as much as he could; then he whipped around. Hands on his hips, feet spread wide, he resembled an infantry captain about to question a prisoner, and she didn't know whether to laugh or hit him.

What right had he to be angry? What right had he to barge in, to bellow and rant?

"I had to be informed by Lydia," he snarled, "that you've resigned your post."

"Yes, I have."

"You told me you wouldn't."

She shrugged. "I guess I changed my mind."

He marched across the floor and towered over her. "I won't let you go."

"It's not up to you."

"We'll see about that!"

"You don't own me. You can't keep me here against my will."

He was so irate that he yearned to lash out, and if she hadn't known him better, she might have worried he'd strike her.

"How could you do this to me?" he demanded.

"To you!" Her own temper ignited, and she leapt to her feet. "You have an incredible amount of gall to ask."

"You're everything to me." He grabbed her arms and shook her. "You're my life, my soul, my . . . my . . ."

"I am not." She shoved him away. "How dare you claim otherwise."

At her assessment he was aghast. "You're my entire world."

"I'm a trifle for you!" She was shouting, too, having lost the ability of discretion. If they were overheard, she couldn't help it. She'd never been so incensed. "I'm a dalliance. You sneak into my bed, because you're bored, because you're lonely, or I amuse you—I'm not certain why—but you insult me by pretending our relationship has any more significance than that to you."

"Is that what you really think?"

"It's what I know."

"After all we've shared, how could you leave?" He gestured to her portmanteau. "You weren't even planning to say good-bye."

"You're marrying next week!" she wailed. "I won't watch it happen. You can't make me. I swear I'd kill you first."

"My marriage doesn't have anything to do with us."

"Are you insane? It has everything to do with us!"

"The situation is between Rebecca and me. It doesn't involve you."

"Only someone who was completely deranged would agree with you."

"I won't go through with it," he impulsively stated. "I can't. I'll cry off, and you and I will run away together. I'll marry you instead."

Her breath hitched. "Marry me? Why would you?"

"Because I . . . I . . . love you."

She chuckled, her voice cracking with indignation and mirth. "That's the most preposterous comment ever uttered in my presence. You don't love me. You don't love anyone but yourself."

"I do love you!"

"Oh, shut up! Please! You're embarrassing both of us."

He'd had plenty of chances to profess elevated devotion, and she supposed he probably did like her more than some of his other lovers. But he was like a spoiled child, who always got his way. She was ready to walk out, before he was ready for her to go, and he couldn't abide that she had the audacity to oppose him.

If he'd admitted a week earlier—even an hour earlier—how much he cared, she might have believed him. At this hideous juncture, he couldn't convince her that he was sincere. His words were like leaves blowing in the wind.

At having his declaration discounted, his bluster faded, and he studied her as if he'd stumbled into the wrong room, as if he wasn't sure who she was.

"Maybe I was mistaken," he said, "but I was positive that there was a special bond between us."

"There was," she concurred. "You're a handsome, tenacious man, who enjoys seducing women. I was a naïve, gullible female, who assumed she could romp without consequence. I did, even though it was terribly wicked of me, but it's over. You're moving on, and I am, too."

"I meant nothing to you then?"

He gazed at her as if he truly wished to know. He seemed to be sad and distressed—or perhaps betrayed—by her lack of empathy, though she couldn't figure out why.

His destiny was to marry Rebecca. There would be

no other outcome, and it was absurd for him to carry on as if they could forge a different ending. It wounded her to be taunted with dreams of what could never be.

What did he want from her? What did he expect? When he was finished, there'd be naught left.

"No," she fibbed. "You didn't mean anything to me. How could you have?"

As if she'd stabbed him with her remark, he sagged with despair, and she suffered from the strongest urge to reach out, to soothe and embrace, but she stopped herself. She refused to expend any energy pondering how much of his affection had been real and how much had been feigned.

Even if he'd been genuinely fond of her, he couldn't act on it. The only role she could ever play was that of mistress, and she would jump off a cliff before she'd accept such a shameful position.

"Do you recollect when we first met?" she queried, wanting to hurt him, wanting him to depart and never come back. "I told you that I'd been acquainted with you previously."

"Yes, but I didn't recall the circumstances."

"It was at a summer house party, a decade ago, when you were twenty and you were visiting friends in Surrey. Lady Barrington's ring was stolen."

"Yes, I remember it. She raised a huge ruckus."

"There was a boy from the neighborhood who was accused and arrested."

He nodded. "A local miscreant. He was hanged for the crime."

"No, he wasn't. He was transported to the penal colonies."

"And you're informing me because . . . ?"

"Because that *miscreant,* as you so blithely put it, was my brother, James."

She had to give him credit. He appeared stricken, though whether from compassion or guilt she couldn't decide.

"Oh, Ellen, I'm so sorry."

"I've always detested you for not saving my brother."

"How could I have helped him? I knew nothing about the incident. I was out riding when the theft occurred."

"Did you steal that ring?"

"Me? My God, how could you level such a charge?"

"Did you?" she pressed. "I've often wondered if you were the man who destroyed my family."

He was stunned. "I never could have."

"So you see, Alex—excuse me, I should say *Lord* Stanton—there never was any actual amour between us. Over the years, I've speculated as to what kind of person you are deep down, and I let you close so that I could satisfy my curiosity, but that's all it ever was for me."

He evaluated her, and she kept her expression carefully blank, not wanting to furnish him with a hint of her agony. Short of making him hate her, she had no idea how else to force a split, how to create such a breach that it could never be healed. She had to push him away.

"You're lying," he eventually murmured. "I can see it in your eyes, though for the life of me, I can't fathom why you are. Why don't I yank out my heart and toss it on the floor so you can stomp on it?"

"You're to be wed in seven days, Alex! It doesn't matter why I'm doing anything."

"It matters to me!" He clenched his fist and tapped it to the center of his chest.

The look on his face was excruciating, and she

couldn't stand it. She spun away to stare out the window
into the black sky, and he caressed her cheek, his knuckles brushing her skin. She ached to have him hold her.
She was afraid, afraid of what the morrow would bring,
afraid of what would become of her. She needed consoling and comfort, but he wasn't the one to whom she
could turn.

When they'd commenced their affair, she'd presumed herself sophisticated, that she could merrily philander, then emerge wiser but mostly unscathed. She
hadn't realized that the conclusion would be so devas-
tating, that she would feel as if her very bones might
break with the sorrow of their separation.

"Don't go," he begged.

"I have to."

"I must marry Rebecca, but I can't! It's so wrong.
She and I will both be so miserable, and I'm so confused! Tell me what to do!"

"Don't ask me. I can't advise you."

He pulled her into his arms. "I thought I had six more
months with you, six months to say good-bye and walk
away with no regrets. This is happening too fast."

If he'd wanted to spend more time with her, why had
he moved up the wedding date? She was dying to inquire but didn't.

She wouldn't try to decipher his motives. By probing
for details she'd merely be torturing herself. He'd chosen
his path, had made his bed, and he could lie in it. She had
no sympathy to offer, no commiseration to share, and she
wouldn't ease his conscience or smooth over his options
so they were more palatable.

He was rubbing her back, stroking his hands up and

down, up and down. The motion was soothing, and it had her recollecting how much she loved him, why she'd elected to do what she'd done.

She'd been attracted to him as she'd never be to anyone else. When she peered down the road—as a poverty-stricken spinster, as a woman with no family and no place to call her own—it was such a forlorn picture.

He was the bright star in her dull universe. She'd never meet another like him, would never know the joy and abandon he'd bestowed. There was simply no finer feeling in the world than to gaze into Alex Marshall's blue eyes and see the desire and affection written there.

Without him, she'd be adrift and the quiet years stretching ahead didn't bear contemplating.

While she doubted the depth of his fondness for her, her own sentiments were true and everlasting. She loved him, and she couldn't imagine how she would continue on without him.

They'd had such a brief association that she had no souvenirs of the magical interval, no locket with his portrait hidden inside, no flower tucked into the pages of a book. When she departed, she would have no evidence to take with her that she—plain, boring Ellen Drake—had once captivated dashing, dynamic Lord Stanton.

Only memories would remain, and if she dared, she could build a few more before dawn broke.

She hugged him tight and rose up on tiptoe so that he could kiss her. As if he was worried about his reception, he began tentatively, his mouth hardly touching hers, but she couldn't have him hesitant or restrained.

On this, their final rendezvous, she craved heat and fire, danger and recklessness. There were so many things he'd never shown her, and she was eager to experience them all. Before she left, she had to be filled to overflowing with reminiscence.

"Stay with me tonight," she said. "Remind me of how wonderful it's been, so that I will never forget."

Alex linked their fingers and led her to the bed. He lay down and drew her down with him.

He couldn't believe she'd consider deserting him. How could she?

She was correct that she had to leave, but where she was concerned he couldn't think rationally. He didn't want to marry Rebecca, but when she'd demanded an earlier wedding there hadn't been a single reason to delay, except that it meant he would lose Ellen.

His behavior toward both women was disgusting. He was furious with Rebecca for pushing the issue, was angry with Ellen for opting to go, and his life was in such disarray that he could scarcely function.

In a way, he was glad for the swift ending. If he hadn't been frantic, he would never have found the courage to confess that he loved her. If she hadn't thrown down the gauntlet, he might not have recognized the intensity of his emotions.

He was on top of her and pressing her down into the mattress. Her body rippled with pleasure, with the knowledge of what was coming. They both understood the gravity of what they were about. There would be this tryst, and just this one, then no more. He was as keen as she to build a store of memories.

He tugged her robe off her shoulders, then lowered the straps of her nightgown, baring her breasts to his questing hands. He dipped down and suckled her, biting at her nipple so that she squirmed and writhed, so that she fought to escape but pull him nearer, too. This was what he needed, this heedless spiral to ecstasy, where nothing mattered, where there was no hasty wedding, no morning after, no sins and omissions that were so glaring and bothersome.

He jerked her nightgown over her hips, her thighs, and she kicked it away. Whatever he required, he could have. Whatever he asked of her, she would provide. There would be no holding back, no limits.

She was so titillated, and she wanted him in the same impatient condition. She rolled them so that she was in control, so that she could pet and fondle, massage and excite.

With shaky fingers, she tried to unbutton his shirt, but she couldn't manage the chore, so she grabbed the lapels and ripped it down the center, the pieces of fabric falling away. She bent down and rooted across his chest, to his nipple, nibbling and teasing as he'd done to her.

She moved down, and lest she tear his trousers, too, he made quick work of the buttons, flicking them free so that the material was loose. She yanked them off; then she traveled down his stomach. His cock was rigid, the appendage extending out to her, begging to be stroked.

"Should I take you in my mouth?" She was licking and playing, driving him wild.

"Yes . . . yes . . ." he ground out.

"When? Now?"

"Please . . ."

She relished her carnal skill, how she could spur him to such a precipice. She opened wide, and he glanced down, planning to enjoy the spectacle, but the sight of her ruby lips wrapped around him was more than he could abide. His lust soared, and in an instant he almost spilled himself.

He lurched away, dragging her up and over so that she was beneath him, once more.

"Make love to me," she pleaded.

He arched a brow. "I believe I am."

"You know what I mean. I want to feel you inside me. I want to learn what it's like."

"No."

"Why?"

"We've had this discussion many, many times. As far as I can determine, naught has changed."

"Except that—after tonight—I'll never see you again."

"I can't do it. Especially if you're set on this crazed idea of leaving. Who can predict what awaits you? I won't have your circumstances any more dire than they already are."

"Alex!" She spread her legs, urging him on, bringing him so close to paradise. "Take me!"

"No!" he repeated, though his resolve was weakening, and he groaned in frustration.

Why not? a voice rang in his head. Why not be done with it? She'd given him everything else, and there was so little left of her chastity. It would be so easy to journey that last inch. With the merest thrust, he could finish it.

He leaned in and tormented himself by rubbing his cock across her cleft. She was so wet, so willing, and he wanted her so desperately.

Why not?

He shifted and pushed the blunt crown in just the smallest bit. His body trembled with restraint. He yearned to be joined with her, and he was perched on the edge of an abyss, feeling as though—whatever he chose—he was about to leap into free fall.

Should she remain a virgin? Should she not? Should he copulate with her? Should he not?

The answers eluded him, the question of *right* and *wrong* beyond his ability to factor. Desire won out. He couldn't decide the best course, couldn't select better behavior. He had to be in her or die.

"Promise me one thing," he entreated.

"What?"

"Promise that you'll never regret this."

She smiled. "No, I'll never regret it."

"Promise that you won't hate me later on."

"Hate you? Why would I? I want this; I want *you*."

"Swear to me!"

"I could never hate you. I swear it."

He gripped her thighs, his phallus an insistent rod, and she stirred with the beginnings of alarm. Her virginal state rose to the fore, and instinctively she tried to skitter away.

He pinned her down and commanded, "Hold still!"

"I can't. I'm afraid."

"It will be over very soon." He wedged himself in even farther.

"Alex!" she implored, but he was beyond the point where he could listen.

"Be silent."

"I can't be. You're too big . . . it's too . . . too . . ."

"No regrets, Ellen, remember?"

He kissed her, and he flexed once, twice, and he burst through her maidenhead. There was a tear, the rush of her woman's blood, and she arched up and cried out. Every muscle in suspended agony, he froze as she acclimated, and the instant she started to relax, he commenced again.

He was past the spot where he could be gentle, and he rode her hard, his actions propelling them across the bed, until she was knocking up against the frame, and she had to reach out to steady herself.

It was heaven, being inside her, and he kept on much too long. Finally, his seed surged to the tip, and he exploded in a fiery wave that flooded her womb. Vaguely, he realized that he should have pulled out, that he should have had more sense. If he'd impregnated her, both their situations would be more complicated, but the notion was swept away on a tide of pleasure.

It seemed so fitting that they end it in this fashion, and he wondered if he didn't secretly hope that she *did* become pregnant. If there was a babe, they'd have reasons for continuing contact. She couldn't simply vanish.

The spiral peaked and waned, and he collapsed onto her; then he withdrew and snuggled himself to her. She winced with discomfort, and while he knew he should be sorry for using her badly, he felt no remorse.

He was still so aroused that if he'd thought she could tolerate another go-around, he'd have mounted her again. Would his lust for her ever be sated?

"Have I hurt you?" he asked.

"I'll mend."

"I didn't mean to be so rough."

"You weren't."

"You drive me beyond my limit."

"I'm glad."

"You'll be sore for a day or two."

"I'm fine now."

"I could order up a hot bath, to ease the ache."

"Don't you dare."

"It won't bother you the next time," he offered as a meager consolation, though he detested speculating over when her *next* time would be. Would he be her partner? Most likely not.

Looking anxious, she stroked her abdomen. "Could we have—"

"No." He hadn't the faintest idea if pregnancy could occur from a woman's first sexual experience, but he wasn't about to panic her. There would be plenty of subsequent opportunity to worry about the consequences of his rash conduct.

For the moment, he intended to revel in the precious solitude, and he refused to let pesky details such as children or fatherhood interfere.

"Might we . . . we . . ." She blushed a delightful shade of pink.

"What?"

"Might we do it again?"

"Most definitely, my dearest, Ellen." He grinned. "We most definitely can."

As he rolled onto her, the strangest noise brought him up short. It sounded like a gasp or a wheeze, and it hadn't emanated from himself or Ellen.

He frowned and glanced to the door that he'd shattered during his temper tantrum. He'd braced it shut as best he could, but it wasn't shut now. It had been flung wide, and Lydia was standing on the threshold, her mobcap bouncing, her nightgown billowing, a lamp swinging from her fingers.

A group of servants was loitering behind her, and they were on tiptoe and straining to see the raucous spectacle inside the room.

"Oh no!" he grumbled.

What the hell was Lydia doing, roaming the halls and dragging the housekeeper and a cadre of footmen with her?

This was an unmitigated disaster! There'd be no explaining or justifying. He'd never be able to make this right for anyone concerned.

The men were leering at Ellen, and he grabbed a blanket to cover her, as she squealed with mortification and ducked under it.

"We heard some loud banging," Lydia informed them, and she chuckled maliciously. "We were afraid it was burglars, but I guess it wasn't. I'll speak with the two of you downstairs in the library. In ten minutes. Were I you, I wouldn't be late."

She spun away and shooed the others out, waddling along behind them like a mother duck. As their footsteps receded, Ellen peeked out and inquired, "What will Lydia do?"

"I don't know," he replied, "but whatever it is, it won't be good."

~ 14 ~

"Explain yourselves."

Lydia glared from Ellen to Alex, then back to Ellen again, but they stared at the rug, neither able to look at her.

They'd slinked in like a pair of whipped dogs and, with clothes scarcely on, lapels askew, buttons crooked, they resembled the malefactors they were. She rapped a paperweight on the desk.

"Well? I'm waiting."

She was trying to appear livid, but in reality, she was delighted by her shocking discovery. Ever since Rebecca had moved up her wedding date, Lydia had been furious. Despite Rebecca's protestations to the contrary, Lydia was positive that Rebecca's scheme was a wicked ploy to ruin Lydia's own wedding.

By demanding an immediate ceremony—one that would occur before Lydia's—Rebecca was diverting attention to herself, rather than letting Lydia enjoy her own wedding preparations. It was typical of the snooty, cosseted girl to behave so selfishly, and Lydia was tickled to return the favor.

With her witnessing Alex's heinous peccadillo, she had the perfect excuse to thwart the nuptials. After all, how could Lydia—in good conscience—let her baby sister marry such a villain? He was philandering with Rebecca's friend and companion, while Rebecca slept just down the hall.

His gross misconduct gave Lydia the right to cancel the proceedings. Not only would they be terminated, but Lydia would guarantee that Rebecca was humiliated.

"It was all my doing," Alex started.

Lydia scoffed. "A likely story."

"It was!" he maintained.

"I'm sure Ellen was a saint through the entire affair."

Ellen fidgeted, blushing with disgrace, as she murmured, "I'm sorry."

"You're *sorry*?" Lydia mocked. "You accept my money as wages, you reside under my roof and dine at my table, yet you have the gall to commit this . . . this treachery? Rebecca was kind to you, and you've repaid her with deceit!"

"I didn't mean for it to happen."

"You didn't?" Lydia trembled with a convincing wrath. "I never liked you, Ellen. I never should have hired you, but Rebecca insisted. Do you know why I didn't want to hire you? Have you any idea?"

"No."

"Because you're coarse and you're common, and I anticipated that we'd have naught but trouble from you. You've exceeded even my low expectations."

"Lydia, please," Alex interjected, "there's no call for insults."

"Shut up, Alex." She pretended to contemplate their fate when she already had it planned. If she'd scripted a melodrama, she couldn't have plotted a more satisfying revenge. "Your engagement to Rebecca is off."

"What?" Surprisingly, Ellen was the one to complain. "Rebecca will be crushed. You can't do such a terrible thing to her. I won't let you."

"It's not up to you, Ellen, and you have an incredible amount of temerity to presume that your opinion holds any sway in this conversation. Be silent."

Alex piped up. "Ellen's correct, though, Lydia. Let's not make hasty decisions that will hurt Rebecca."

Lydia stifled a smile. The couple's reluctance to harm Rebecca hardened her resolve. If they were so dead set against halting the betrothal, then Lydia was absolutely determined to press on.

"Alex, you were much too busy copulating to count heads," Lydia chided, "but there were a half dozen of your employees watching you dishonor yourself."

"Dammit!" he muttered.

"Do you think your liaison is still a secret? Are you supposing they haven't told anyone? The sun is nearly risen. Even as we speak, the news is being disseminated from house to house, through the back doors. By noon, it will be all around the city. After this perfidy, can you furnish me with a single reason why I should let you have Rebecca?"

Alex yearned to throttle her, while Ellen looked ill, her hands shaking, her cheeks pale, and Lydia toyed with various scenarios of how Rebecca should be apprised.

How would her sister be most devastated? Should Lydia have a blunt chat with her? Should Ellen confess? Should Alex? Should they be forced to confront Rebecca together? Each prospect had its advantages.

"The engagement is off," Lydia reiterated. "Alex will

obtain a Special License, and the two of you will marry later this morning."

"Marry! You're not serious." The ultimatum jolted Ellen out of her stupor, and Lydia sneered at her naïveté.

"You can't have assumed you could fornicate like a slattern, but there would be no price to pay."

"But . . . but . . . marriage!"

"Have you some quarrel with the condition?"

Alex found the courage to butt in. "Lydia, you're acting outrageously. Ellen is of age, and you are neither her mother nor her guardian. You haven't the standing to order her to do anything."

"Perhaps not," Lydia concurred, "but if she doesn't marry, and quickly, what will become of her?" She scrutinized Ellen, her loathing unveiled. "After this squalid tale slithers around, you won't be able to acquire work as a ragpicker. Where will you go? What will you do? Will you live on the streets?"

The threat hit home. Ellen had no kin, no friends, no savings to tide her over, and she couldn't conceal her fear over such a dreadful conclusion.

"Honestly, Lydia," Alex scolded, "you're scaring her, and you're annoying me."

"I don't care if you're *annoyed.*" She waved at him, indicating his eminent self. "I would hear a marriage proposal from you. This very second!"

"Ellen doesn't wish to marry me. I'm not even certain she *likes* me."

"She relinquished her options when she spread her legs."

"I won't tolerate another crude word from you," he warned. "If we can't have a civil discussion, then this meeting is over."

"Don't you dare take that tone with me, Alex Marshall," she snapped. "You may be the patriarch of this family, and you may believe you can wallow in any gutter you choose, but I am part of this family, too, and I'm about to be your sister-in-law."

"If you imagine your new status bestows the privilege of running my life for me, you've tipped off your rocker."

"You despicable libertine!" she taunted. "Have you considered that you may have planted a babe? Are you content to have her trotting around town, shaming us with no ring on her finger and her belly swelled out to here?" She made a vulgar gesture over her stomach. "I will not have you besmirching our reputation with your foul deeds. You'll do right by this woman, and you'll do it now!"

Her mentioning of a babe riveted their attention. They glanced at each other; then Alex went to the window and gazed outside. Ellen observed him, then she turned to Lydia.

"I can't marry him, Lydia," she stated.

"Then you should have reflected on the ramifications before beginning."

"Listen to me, would you?"

"About what?"

"There was an incident, years ago."

"What sort of *incident*?"

"My brother, James, was convicted of stealing a valuable ring from Lord Barrington's wife, and he was transported to the penal colonies."

Lydia smirked. "Your brother is a felon?"

"Yes, so you see, I can't join my name with the Marshalls'. It wouldn't be fitting."

"His situation definitely explains your base bloodlines,

but it makes no difference whatsoever." She glared at Alex. "What's it to be, Cousin Alex?"

After a lengthy pause, he spun toward them. "I apologize, Ellen."

"I'm an adult," she asserted, "and I'm responsible for my actions. You did nothing to me."

"You're wrong," he said, "and I have to agree with Lydia: I behaved contemptibly. Will you marry me?"

"You have no desire to marry me."

"I'll learn to like it."

"It will kill Rebecca."

"She'll get over it."

Ellen pondered, delaying; then she pleaded, "Don't do this, Alex. We'll both be miserable for the rest of our lives."

"It won't be as bad as all that," he gently replied. "We'll find common ground."

Ellen stewed, but no answer was forthcoming, so Lydia stood and pronounced, "Ellen accepts your generous offer."

"I do not!" Ellen insisted.

"It's out of your hands," Lydia said.

"No . . . no . . . someone is coming for me. I'm leaving."

"Who? Who is coming?"

"Well . . ." On the spur of the moment, Ellen couldn't invent anybody.

"When will this mysterious person arrive?"

"Ah . . . probably later today."

"Probably?" Lydia rolled her eyes. "If you suppose that a white knight is about to ride up and rescue you, you're mad. We'll reconvene in a few hours, once Rebecca has risen, so that you can tell her what you've done."

Ellen blanched. "You must spare me that humiliation."

"Coward," Lydia reproached. "You claim you're a grown woman. At least have the decency to admit your sins."

"I won't do it," she mutinously declared.

"Then I shall inform her myself, and I will be more than happy to give her my own version of events. Directly after, she and I will retire to the country. If we're lucky, we won't have to see either of you again for a very, very long time."

Dawn was just breaking on the horizon, and she'd already accomplished so much. She grinned and strolled out.

Nicholas stumbled down the hall. He'd reveled all night, had drunk too much and gambled away a small fortune he didn't have—yet!—and he was desperate to fall into bed.

The money . . . the money . . . the money . . .

The funds he deserved for sacrificing himself on Lydia's altar were about to start flowing, and he couldn't count how he would spend every pound. Life was so sweet!

He tiptoed by Lydia's room. At all costs, he avoided her, so he didn't want to risk waking her and having to chat. She kept imploring him to escort her to social functions, and there were only so many ways a fellow could politely decline.

He slipped through his door, stripped off his coat and cravat, and he was about to lie down when a noise emanated from his dressing room. He whipped around and frowned. Someone was inside, and it seemed as if a hot bath had been delivered. At such an ungodly hour, who the hell could it be?

He stomped over to peek in, and he gulped with dismay. Was he hallucinating?

"Lydia?"

"Hello, Nicky."

He never permitted anyone to call him *Nicky*, but he was too disconcerted to chastise her. "What are you doing?"

"I thought you might like a bath."

"A bath?"

"Yes. I'm going to wash your back for you."

At the suggestion, he fought down a shudder. He could envision nothing more repugnant.

She wore a robe that was loosely cinched at the waist, no clothing on underneath, and she leaned down and swished the water. Sounding very sly, she asked, "Where've you been? Why were you out so late?"

She stared as if she was aware of his precise routine, which was impossible unless she was having him followed. He nearly guffawed at the prospect. She wouldn't dare.

Yet suddenly he felt that he was tromping through a field filled with deep holes. One wrong remark and he'd topple in and never climb out.

His inebriation was waning, a hangover taking its place, and he wasn't about to match wits with her. He wanted her gone.

"You shouldn't be in here," he contended.

"Why not?"

"If someone saw you, there'd be a big ruckus."

"Oh pish-posh. Who would complain about the two of us? We've known each other so long that we're like an old married couple. No one will mind if we have a little time to ourselves."

She advanced toward him, and he wasn't positive what she planned, but she appeared as if she meant to undress him.

"Lydia, what's come over you?"

"That evening in the salon, you were so enamored of me, but since then, we've hardly spoken. I'm beginning to worry that your seduction was merely a sham so you could get your hands on my money."

"No," he scoffed. "I was swept away by passion. You heard me confessing to Alex."

"Yes, I did, so I can't figure out why you've been ignoring me."

She was unbuttoning his shirt, and he could scarcely keep from flinching. Everything about her repulsed him, but he couldn't let her suspect. There'd be plenty of opportunity after the wedding to notify her of his true opinions, but for the moment, with her riches just beyond his grasp, he had to play along.

"I decided," she advised, "that we should spice up our relationship before the wedding."

"I wouldn't want to sully you," he claimed.

"I'm having a conference with my solicitors," she mentioned. "There's a cash settlement due you—once I sign some papers."

"Really?" He feigned great surprise. "I had no idea."

"It's a small amount—a paltry gift, if you will—but you should have it straightaway."

"That's very kind of you."

His expression was guarded, but he had the eeriest feeling that she was threatening him, that if he didn't humor her, he wouldn't receive the funds. Could she be that devious?

The notion was absurd, and he pushed it away. She was too stupid to be cunning.

She yanked at his shirt, baring his upper body. "Have you talked to Alex since you arrived home?"

"No, why?"

"We had a bit of excitement."

"What?"

"You've met Rebecca's companion, haven't you?"

"Miss Drake?"

She was quiet and fetching in the unobtrusive manner he liked women to be, and if she'd had a penny to her name, he'd have ravaged her, instead of Lydia. He wished he'd chosen her anyway, despite her penury. Maybe he still would.

"Yes. I caught Alex in her bed."

"You what?"

"They were very involved. It was extremely sordid."

His brother? With Miss Drake? What was Alex thinking? Nicholas was eager to go to him, to ascertain the gory details for himself, but Lydia was fussing with his trousers.

"Lydia," he scolded, "I'm not disrobing for you."

"But the bath, Nicky. Remember?"

"You must stop." His words had no effect, and she continued on.

"The wedding to Rebecca is off, of course."

"Of course," he murmured, but why would it be cancelled? Alex had fucked the hired help. So what? Who cared? What relevance had it to Rebecca?

"He's to wed Miss Drake immediately. The staff is making preparations. Notices have been sent."

"I guess there'll be no backing out—for either of them."

Lord, what a mess! Where was Alex? Nicholas was anxious to parlay with him, and he tried to move away, but Lydia was firmly gripping his waistband, and she wouldn't release it. Short of wrestling with her, he couldn't escape.

"I'm quite resolved," she was babbling, "though Miss Drake whined about it being improper because she's Alex's inferior."

"Well, she is," Nicholas pointed out.

"It's not simply her birth status that makes her unsuitable. Her brother, James, is a dangerous felon who stole some jewelry from the Barringtons. So, not only is she lowborn; she's directly related to the criminal classes."

He rippled with unease. "What did you say his name was?"

"James Drake. Why? Are you acquainted?"

"No."

"Good, because I can't have you tarnished by a connection to him. I won't tolerate any further scandal."

"You're absolutely fixated on Alex and Miss Drake. Why does the situation matter so much?"

"When someone betrays me, I take it personally, and I expect compensation." She evaluated him, seeming menacing in a fashion he hadn't previously noted. "You wouldn't ever *betray* me, would you, Nicky?"

"What a peculiar question."

"If you did, I would be very upset. For example, if I learned that you'd done something you oughtn't, I would be unhappy."

A frisson of fear whispered down his spine. What

was she implying? Had she heard rumors about Suzette? Or was it other gossip? There had been a few incidents over the years, offenses of which he wasn't proud, but they were part and parcel of his history.

She wouldn't hold the past against him. Or would she?

His pants were loose around his hips, and he resisted the urge to clutch at them. Was he about to be ravished? Was she some type of sexual fiend? What if she was? What if—as his wife—she demanded regular servicing?

His stomach roiled.

"Poor Rebecca," he crooned.

"Yes, poor, poor Rebecca."

"She'll be devastated."

"She'll live."

For an elder sister, who'd raised Rebecca since she was a babe Lydia didn't sound very sincere, and her lack of concern had him even more disturbed. Did he know her, at all?

"I should probably go find Alex," he tossed out. "He might need me."

"We don't give two hoots about Alex."

"*You* may not, but I certainly do."

"A pretty speech, but you're about to be my husband, and I will require your support and assistance in my time of despair."

"What do you mean?"

"Rebecca and I are departing for the country at once, and you must escort us."

He was scheduled to tour Suzette's house. If he missed the appointment, there was no telling how she'd react.

"I . . . I . . . can't leave London this week."

"Why?"

"I'm a busy man. I can't tot off whenever you command it."

"What could be more important to you than helping me?" She narrowed her gaze, looking treacherous again, an adversary not to be crossed. "We'll go after I finish up with the lawyers. After I make the arrangements regarding your money."

Dammit! he cursed to himself. She had him trapped like a rabbit in a snare. If he declined to accompany her, he wouldn't get the cash. She might cancel the marriage altogether, and he'd never see a single farthing.

She'd always been an obnoxious hag. It would be just like her to entice him with the prospect of great wealth, then snatch it away. The witch!

She jerked at his trousers, and they plummeted to his ankles. His loins were exposed, and his balls clenched, his John Thomas shriveling to a tiny nub.

"I was told that these appendages were big on a man," she ridiculed. "What's wrong with yours?"

Without warning, she grabbed his phallus and clasped it tightly. He screeched in agony, but she was too thick to realize she was inflicting pain.

"Lydia, old girl—"

"I'm not your *girl*," she calmly retorted. "I'm not your anything—yet."

"Be a little more gentle, would you?"

He was genuinely fretting that she might rip the blasted thing off, and he had a terrifying image of himself standing there emasculated, his bloody cock dangling from her fingers.

"I want you to perform the marital act," she decreed.

"I most assuredly will not."

"Isn't it how a babe is created?"

"Well . . . yes."

"It recently dawned on me that—since I'm more mature—it might take a while for me to become pregnant, and I'm eager for us to have a family. We should get an early start."

"A family?" He felt as if he might retch.

"I can't wait for us to have children."

She went to the dresser, and he dawdled like an imbecile, his boots on, his pants wrapped around his feet and positioned to trip him should he attempt to waddle out. She returned with a jar of cream and knelt down. His cock shrunk even more.

"You seem to have trouble with manly functioning," she derided. "I hope this isn't evidence of your constant condition."

"Gad, Lydia. Be silent."

"I've heard that lotion can work wonders when a man can't manage on his own."

She scooped up a daub and slathered it all over his phallus; then she made a fist and pumped him. Of its own accord, the brainless rod swelled under her manipulation.

He was aghast. How had she learned the carnal deed? From where had her knowledge been obtained? When he'd initially seduced her, she was purportedly a virgin!

At her success with his erection she smirked, and she walked to a chair and bent over it, her fat ass sticking out. She lifted her robe and wadded it up, so that he had a disgusting and unimpeded view of her backside. He was sickened by the sight but too paralyzed to move.

"Come!" she barked. "Mount me! Do your job."

Sweet Jesu! She couldn't expect him to pant after her like a stallion to a mare. He wouldn't *rise* to the occasion simply because she nagged. She was mad as a hatter, and he swallowed down the insults he longed to hurl.

The money . . . Suzette . . . the money . . . Suzette . . .

The chant rang through his head. Both were about to be his. He couldn't refuse.

He took a faltering step, then another, stumbling over his pants, but he wouldn't stop to shed them, for it would seem as if he were complicit in the copulation, which he most categorically was not!

He clutched her hips, and his cock located the route all by itself. The cream she'd applied made it an easy entry, and he thrust and thrust, but he couldn't stay hard. The balm was so slippery, and he was so uninterested, that he wasn't able to generate any friction.

"Have you already worn out your shaft tonight?" she suddenly queried. "Have you been furnishing to another what you should be saving for me?"

"Lydia!"

"I have to tell you, Nicky, that if I found out you'd been unfaithful, I'd be very angry."

"I've been with no one."

"Then why are you so flaccid? Were you born with a limp noodle?"

"Good Christ, woman! Shut your mouth!"

"Why should I? I have every right to inquire as to your obvious problem. Will you keep *up* your end of the marital bargain?"

His temper soared, and he yearned to seize her by the throat and squeeze until he choked the life out of her, which he couldn't do. Not till after the wedding anyway. He tamped down his fury, directing it into his nether regions, where it provided the necessary impetus.

He grew rigid as stone and abruptly spurted into her,

a trickle dribbling out, the sensation of orgasm scarcely noted.

Revolted over her behavior and his own, he retreated from her and had his trousers straightened before she could drop her robe and spin around.

She assessed him as if he were a pet dog, as if she'd trained him to sit up and beg, and he nearly slapped her homely face.

"Will that be all?" he snarled.

"You haven't had your bath."

"I don't need one."

"But I insist." She grasped his waistband and held tight. "Kick off your boots."

They engaged in a tug-of-war he couldn't win. He gnashed his teeth but complied, and she yanked off the remainder of his clothes. He stood before her naked, his cock shriveling again. She strolled around him in a slow circle, studying him as if he were a bull she was considering purchasing.

"Are you finished?"

"I believe I am." She gestured to the tub. "You may get in."

He climbed in and sank down, thankful for the covering the water supplied. He felt defiled, and he was glad to have the chance to wash.

Lydia leaned over, her smile grim. "I've been thinking."

"About what?"

"Once we're married, we'll forgo separate bedchambers. We'll share the same room. Each and every night."

She dipped the soap and rubbed up a lather.

~ 15 ~

"But you don't want to marry me!" Ellen shouted. "And I don't want to marry you! Why didn't you tell Lydia to leave us alone?"

"I couldn't get a word in edgewise," Alex grumbled.

"You allowed her to bully us as if we were children."

"Are you actually supposing I could have shut her up?"

"Yes! Get us out of this mess."

She sounded like a deranged shrew, but she couldn't stop herself. As if she'd fallen in a raging river, the events of the night had swept her along, and she couldn't slow the torrent on which she was riding.

"What would you have me do?" Alex asked, as irate as she. "Should I parade about on the street, screaming to all of London that I've ruined you and I'll take no action to rectify my offense?"

"The only people who saw us were Lydia and a few of your servants. You like to brag about the fact that you're an earl. Use some of your power. Summon them! Order them to be silent."

"She's already sent out messengers, proclaiming that

the engagement to Rebecca is broken by me, that the marriage to you is on. The liquor's been spilled out of the bottle, and we can't scoop it up and pour it back in."

"I'm the hired help!" she grimly pointed out. "Your friends don't care if you behaved badly toward me."

"They're gentlemen. They'll understand why I had to propose."

"Hah! Nary a one would raise a brow over your seducing me. They'll all wonder why there's been such a fuss."

"Has it occurred to you that perhaps my feelings are genuine, and I'm perfectly happy to wed you?"

"A few hours ago, you were prepared to walk down the aisle with Rebecca. Now, with hardly any thought, you claim you're eager to do the same with me, so pardon me if I consider you to be a tad fickle in your choices."

"Better fickle than cold as a fish!"

She rippled with fury and whipped around to stare out the window into the manicured garden. Morning dew dappled the roses, birds sang in the trees, but she scarcely noted the beauty. She was in turmoil, careening from dread to joy to dread again, and she couldn't make sense of what she wanted.

Her body was aching, her head throbbing, and she yearned to lie down and rest, then take a hot bath. She needed to catch her breath, to steady her thinking and her nerves. In her chaotic condition, she couldn't be expected to make major life decisions.

She was filled with mixed emotions, and she couldn't determine if she was glad for what had transpired or if she wished she'd never met Alex. At the moment, he seemed to be a stranger, a hulking, angry fellow who was yelling and delivering ultimatums.

How could she marry him? While she was certain he hadn't had any connection to James's catastrophe, if she proceeded she'd be betraying James and her father. James would never forgive her, yet what alternative did she have?

If she didn't wed Alex, her reputation would be shredded, and she wouldn't be able to find a job. James had invited her to live with him, but what would that entail? Had he suitable lodgings where she could stay? For how long? Which brought about the old questions: What if he was captured by the authorities? What would happen?

Alex was laboring under the mistaken notion that James was out of the country. What if he learned that James was home? What might he do?

With Nicholas marrying Lydia, they'd all be related, though Rebecca was the spurned fiancée. Oh, the recipes for disaster didn't bear contemplation!

"It's over, Ellen," he murmured from behind her. "It's done. We have to move forward."

"*Forward,* is it?" She spun around. "What does that mean to you?"

"It means we'll marry today, as Lydia has demanded, and—"

"Lydia! Lydia!" She waved in a theatrical gesture. "I'm sick to death of her. If you mention her name in my presence ever again, I'm not sure what I'll do."

"She's the one who stumbled on us and—"

"Shut up!" she bellowed. "I will not discuss her! Why is she so set on this marriage? Why is she pushing us into it?"

"I haven't the faintest idea, but she's correct to press for a wedding. You have no father to speak for you, and you should be grateful that she was concerned enough to insist."

"Grateful? Are you daft? She's coercing me into a position I deem to be completely detestable." She wasn't referring to him personally, but she was too bewildered to be circumspect. He handled the comment as poorly as she might have predicted.

"So I'm *detestable,* am I? Well, you're not such a spectacular catch yourself. If I'd been aware of your temper and sour attitude, I would never have climbed into your bed in the first place, I can guarantee you!"

"You arrogant prig!"

There was a candlestick on the table next to her, and she grabbed it and hurled it at him, though he was too far away for it to inflict any damage. It clunked on the rug, so she didn't even receive the satisfaction of a loud bang.

Chests heaving, hearts pounding, they glared, the expanse separating them so vast that it might have been an ocean.

Oh, Alex . . . she cried on the inside. She couldn't figure out why they were fighting. She needed him to counsel and advise, to talk and listen, but she was too distressed, so lucid conversation was beyond her.

She was terrified of marrying him. From the fringe of his society she'd watched the calculated, cruel world he inhabited, and she didn't want to reside there. She'd been reared in a close, loving family, and if she was to be offered the gift of another, she was keen to restore the one she'd lost. She craved camaraderie and constancy, but she was positive that Alex was incapable of giving her a commitment.

Her tossing of the candlestick halted their bickering.

They had to calm down, had to quit going round and round in circles with no decisions made and no plans generated.

"I apologize," he bit out.

"Accepted," she responded, just as tersely.

"It's been a long night"—that was putting it mildly!—"and we're both exhausted. It's causing us to say things we'll regret later on. Why don't you go upstairs and rest before the ceremony?"

How could he presume they should proceed? Why couldn't he appreciate her reservations?

Yet what choice had she but to follow through? She couldn't *not* wed him. Wicked behavior required penance. Illicit fornication required marriage. There were no other options. If she didn't become a married lady, and soon, she'd be branded a harlot and cast out onto the streets.

"Have you thought about this, at all?" she asked.

"Not really."

"One woman is the same as the next?"

"Hardly." His torrid gaze traveled down her torso. "I imagine I'll be able to tell it's you in my bed as opposed to someone else."

She disregarded the gibe. "What type of relationship have you visualized for us?"

"I expect we'll carry on—as any married couple would."

"*Carry on* how?"

She'd finally exasperated him. He threw up his hands in defeat. "What do you want me to say, Ellen?"

"Will you be a true and reliable husband to me?"

"Of course I will be."

"Will you practice fidelity?"

"Fidelity?" He appeared as though he didn't comprehend the word.

"Don't be so shocked. Considering how we met, I can't help but inquire."

He sputtered and fussed, blushed and fumed. "Yes, I fully intend to be faithful. How about you? In view of how *easy* you were to seduce, should I worry that you'll be sneaking off with every fellow who glances in your direction?"

She realized that the insult was warranted, that she had no moral leg to stand on, no basis to suffer hurt or outrage, but she did.

What kind of wife was he getting?

She'd never given him a single reason to picture her in a favorable light. She knew right from wrong but had never once exhibited ethical conduct in his presence. If he assumed her to be a slattern, when had she ever acted any differently?

Yet his taunts wounded her. What a demeaning opinion for her new spouse to have. If they were to marry, shouldn't their association be built on mutual respect and esteem? With such awful feelings festering, how could a union ever work?

How had her great affection for him led to such a pitiful juncture? How could so much joy and happiness have metamorphosed into such despair?

He was scowling, mentally accusing her of the misdeeds he anticipated she'd perpetrate down the road. The thick oaf! Did he actually believe she was the sort who could philander? Who would take paramours and gad about London, shaming her husband and herself?

Her temper sparked. After the arduous night she'd

endured, she wanted to lash out, to blame somebody—besides herself!—for her dilemma.

"Oh yes," she replied, "I plan to have dozens of lovers. I'll keep one hidden in every alcove in the city. You'll never guess who I'll trifle with next."

"As I suspected." He smirked. "I'd hoped we could find common ground, but it won't be possible. You're determined to start on a bad note. So be it. I'll be in my library at eleven with the vicar. Come or don't. I don't care what you decide."

He stomped off, and suddenly her capricious self was reeling over his departure. He was her only ally in the large mansion, in the entire world. He couldn't abandon her. "Where are you going?"

He stopped and stared over his shoulder. "My chores aren't finished. I'm off to locate Rebecca. I'm anxious to speak with her before Lydia does. Would you like to join me?"

She vigorously declined the dubious honor, and he left her alone to brood and stew, the wedding—if there was to be one—looming like the Apocalypse.

"We need to talk."

"About what?"

Alex ushered Rebecca into a secluded parlor and shut the door. He'd rehearsed what he'd say, but with them face-to-face he had no clue how to begin. She was studying him as if he had two heads, as if she'd like naught more than to clout him on the ear, and he sighed with resignation.

He couldn't figure out what had happened between

them. They'd lumped along, without incident, for decades. Yet over the past weeks she'd changed. She was churning with an anger and resentment he couldn't fathom, was a veritable pot of umbrage about to boil over.

He wasn't sure how she'd take the news about Ellen, but he was fairly certain she'd be furious. Then again, with her current antipathy toward him, maybe she'd be relieved. Maybe the cause of her recent discontentment was her own recognition that they were a hideous match.

"Shall we sit down?" he queried, stalling for time.

"I can see in your eyes that you're about to confess something horrid, so I prefer to stand."

"Have you chatted with your sister this morning?"

"No."

Good! The last thing he'd needed was to have Lydia explaining the debacle.

Rebecca frowned, her toe impatiently tapping on the rug, and when he couldn't commence, she prodded, "Well . . . ?"

"Lydia and I . . . that is . . . we . . ."

"For pity's sake, Alex, I'm not a child. Spit it out before you choke on it."

He took a breath and said in a rush, "Our engagement is terminated."

"It most definitely is not! Whatever game you're playing, whatever you'd rather do than marry me, I'm not about to let you off the hook. So if you'll excuse me, I'm off to breakfast."

She whipped around to leave, and he reached out and pulled her to a halt.

"Rebecca, wait."

"Release my arm before I break your hand."

"We must discuss this."

"If you think you can weasel out of your commitment to me, you're mad."

"The deed is done."

"What do you mean?" she growled.

"Lydia won't permit you to marry me."

"She is not my mother, and she has no business butting her nose into this situation"—she yanked away from him—"so I suggest you hie yourself down to the tailor to be fitted for your wedding suit."

"It's true, Rebecca. Lydia called it off, but I agreed it was for the best."

"I'll just bet you did, you despicable swine."

"I wanted to tell you that I'm sorry."

"You're *sorry*! You're crying off, and that's supposed to be the end of it?"

"I don't know what else to say."

"How about if you admit what's behind this charade?"

"Well, I've done something . . . something . . . that will create quite a scandal."

"Why am I not surprised?"

"Lydia and I simply felt that it would be better for you if we split, if you left London while matters resolve."

"Isn't it grand"—she oozed sarcasm—"how you and Lydia always have my interests at heart?"

Their bond was a frivolous one that had flitted on the surface, so he had no idea how to have a frank conversation with her. He was mucking it up, but he couldn't seem to articulate the appropriate remarks.

What was the *right* comment anyway? Was there any decent method by which to conclude it? If there was, it was beyond him.

He shrugged. "I wish I could fix this, but I don't know how."

"Fix it!" she scoffed. "Have you any notion of what my life has been like?"

"I can't imagine."

"Year after accursed year, I've dawdled in the country, twiddling my thumbs, while you wavered and delayed. People laughed at me, they made crude jokes at my expense, and I weathered it all with a bland smile upon my face."

"I didn't realize that's how it was."

"Of course you didn't. Why would you spend a second of your precious energy wondering about poor little Rebecca?"

"It was cruel of me."

"I defended you at every turn, I rationalized, I lied to myself, and now here I sit—a woman far past her prime—and you have the gall to advise me I'm about to become a spinster on the shelf!"

Numerous consoling statements sprang to mind—about how she was very pretty, about how any man would be glad to have her, about how she wasn't that *old!*—but none of them could be uttered. Any observation would be placating and insulting and would increase her animosity.

He leaned against the wall, bracing himself, needing the support it offered, as he tried to devise a reply but couldn't. She stared him down, condemning, accusing, and a blistering silence ensued. It was full of recrimination and culpability, humiliation and disgrace, but he wasn't man enough to fall on his sword.

"Who is it?" she demanded.

"What?"

"Who is the woman to blame for all this trouble?"

"Why would you automatically assume it's a woman?"

"I'm not stupid, Alex. Who is she?"

"Why must you torture yourself with knowing? Isn't it enough to acknowledge what transpired and move on?"

"Who is she?" When he couldn't respond, she roared, "Tell me this instant!"

He gazed at the floor, struggling to recollect how he'd arrived at this vile spot. He'd never intended to harm anyone. He'd merely wanted . . . wanted . . . What had it been?

Happiness, a voice whispered, and he recognized that it was the only thing he'd ever truly wanted but had never really had. He'd never been happy.

"It's Ellen," he murmured.

She gasped. "Ellen Drake?"

"Yes."

She trembled with wrath, and his disgust with himself was excruciating. He was a dog, a beast. She was so lucky to be shed of him. But how he pitied Ellen! About to be saddled with him forever.

"She was my friend," Rebecca hissed.

"I know."

"You were carrying on with her? Here in the house while I was down the hall?"

He couldn't divulge what she was desperate to learn. He'd been so enamored of Ellen that their liaison hadn't seemed wrong, but it was fruitless to justify his obsession. He could never adequately explain that he'd had to be with Ellen, and everyone else be damned.

"Leave it be, Rebecca. There's no need to parlay over the tawdry details."

"Maybe I'm a glutton for punishment."

"I won't hurt you more than I already have."

She was growing more irate by the second. "What now?"

"Ellen and I will wed—if she'll have me."

"Is there some doubt?"

"She doesn't think I'm much of a catch."

"She's bloody right!"

"Lydia wants to take you home at once. So that you're far away when we . . . when we . . ." He cut off, too mortified to continue. The phrase *when we marry* was stuck in his throat like a piece of tough meat.

"Answer one question for me."

"If I'm able."

"What did you see in her that you obviously didn't see in me?" Tears welled into her eyes, and he yearned to vanish into thin air.

"Nothing."

"Liar. I deserve to know!"

He couldn't clarify the differences, couldn't elucidate what had lit a spark with Ellen but had never burned with Rebecca. If he'd had an eternity, he couldn't have described why it had occurred. It had been like the pull of the moon on the tide: relentless and impossible to stop.

"She's just . . . Ellen," he ultimately said.

She stepped closer, until they were toe-to-toe, and she pointed a finger in his chest, jabbing at him with each furious word.

"I waited and waited and waited. I hoped and dreamed, prayed and trusted. I made so many excuses for you; I invented so many stories. And this—*this!*—is how you repay me."

"I'm sorry," he repeated.

"Bastard!"

She reeled back and slapped him so forcefully that

his ears rang, his bones creaked, and he stumbled to the side. As he was groping about and regaining his footing, she ran out and slammed the door so hard that the windows rattled.

Then, she was racing up the stairs to her room and shouting, "Lydia! Lydia! Where are you? I need you!"

Rubbing his cheek, he stood frozen in place. He felt ill, his stomach queasy, his knees weak, and facetiously he muttered, "I'd say that went rather well."

It had been a hell of a day, and it wasn't even eight o'clock. In a handful of minutes he'd lost one fiancée and obtained another. They both loathed him. He'd spent his adult life avoiding matrimony, and when he'd finally resolved to proceed, he wasn't sure his bride would show up for the ceremony.

He couldn't blame her. What sane female would have him? If she walked out, he wouldn't chase after her, wouldn't attempt to find or dissuade her.

Sighing, he tiptoed out. He was too embarrassed to meet up with any of his servants, and if he bumped into Ellen or Rebecca, he'd die of shame. He slinked to his bedchamber, lurking along like the cur he was.

He locked himself in, fetched a bottle of his strongest liquor, and started drinking. In a few hours, he'd be married or he wouldn't be, and he'd need fortification either way.

~ 16 ~

"Why are you here?"

"I had to see you."

"I repeat: Why are you here?"

Rebecca stared at James. He was seated behind his desk, but he hadn't invited her to sit, too. He was irked by her arrival, and she dawdled, feeling awkward and embarrassed.

In the stark shadows of his office, tucked into the corner of a large, cold warehouse, he didn't resemble the prosperous gentleman she'd met out in society. He was attired as a workingman, tan shirt, brown breeches, no jacket or cravat. With a knife strapped to his belt and a pistol within reach, he looked like a brigand. The scar on his cheek was more pronounced, his broad physique more menacing.

She knew she should explain herself, but she couldn't. What woman would freely admit to being tossed aside? To being the second choice? After hearing Alex's appalling confession, she'd tarried in her fancy bedroom, in his stuffy, pretentious mansion, and she'd been suffocating with hurt and fury. She'd had to escape, so with only the clothes on her back, she'd sneaked out to find James.

The address he'd provided had led her to a tavern, and at another period in her life she might have been too timid to set foot inside. But with shame and disgrace motivating her, any wild conduct was likely. She'd gone in to inquire about him, and after a lengthy wait his blond footman had appeared. Without a word, he'd escorted her through several winding lanes to James's place of business, but she seemed to have made a terrible blunder.

She'd believed James when he'd claimed to be smitten. Had she miscalculated?

He was glaring at her, and her heart sank. If he wouldn't let her stay, where would she go?

She couldn't return to Lydia, wouldn't resume her position in the family as Alex married Ellen. She refused to carry on as though nothing had happened, which is what would be expected of her once the scandal had settled.

She had no other options, so she mustered her courage and forged ahead. "You asked me to run off with you."

"Yes, I did."

"Were you serious?"

"At the time."

"But no longer?"

Cool with disdain, he studied her. "You were very clear in your sentiments, Miss Burton. I'm neither a fool nor a dreamer. I've moved on, so you should scurry off to your precious fiancé."

"But I've decided to take you up on your offer."

"You are too late."

"Please?"

"No."

She saw no evidence of the sweet lover who'd been

so enamored of her. Had any of his dear flatteries been true? Or was it all part of some horrid game he'd been playing? If so, why would he?

Perhaps he was a libertine who reveled in the chase. Perhaps he regularly seduced women and she'd merely been one of many. The prospect that she'd further humiliated herself by seeking him out was the ultimate infamy.

To her mortification, tears welled. She couldn't stop them. The day had been so awful, the calamity so abrupt. She felt as if the earth were spinning too fast, that if she didn't latch on to something or someone, she might be flung off into the sky.

"If you think," he started angrily, "that you can shed a few tears to gain my sympathy, you're mistaken. Whatever your paltry troubles, they are no concern of mine."

"I thought you cared about me. I thought you meant all those things you said."

"I meant them," he maintained, "but you weren't interested."

"I am . . . I was . . . it's . . . it's—"

"You're naught but a silly girl," he interrupted. "You have the body of an adult, but on the inside, you're a spoiled child."

"I am not!"

"You have no idea what you want. Right this minute, you want me, but the instant I agree, you'll dart off like a frightened foal."

"I won't leave," she declared.

"A likely story."

He stood and went to the door, and he opened it and called out. "Willie, come here, would you? I need you to drive Miss Burton home, and don't bring her back ever again. Even if she pays you. Even if she begs."

At being thrown out she was stunned. She hadn't considered that he wouldn't welcome her. As disaster had pummeled her earlier, he'd seemed like a shining beacon, a safe harbor, and she'd raced to him immediately, positive that he'd help her, that he'd make everything better.

She scrutinized him, searching for a hint of the fondness he'd once had for her, but she couldn't detect a trace. Where was that romantic, dashing fellow? Why had he vanished?

She peered at the footman. "Willie, is it?"

"Yes, miss."

"I must speak with Mr. Duncan alone. Would you excuse us?"

"Certainly." He shrugged and added, "By the way, Mr. *Duncan,* you received a letter—from your sister."

"I'll have to read it later," James responded.

"As you wish, *sir.* Let me know if you need anything. I can't wait to be of service."

They shared an odd glance, then Willie walked away, and Rebecca shut the door. James watched her but had no comment. She stepped toward him, boldly nearing until they were touching. Sparks flew, the air charged with energy.

He noticed the agitation, and he wasn't unaffected. The color of his eyes deepened, his gaze growing rapt and piercing.

"I'll do whatever you ask," she said. "Just don't send me away."

"You haven't a clue as to what you'd have to do to change my mind."

"It doesn't matter what it is."

She wrapped her arms around him, relishing how solid he was, how real. The rest of her world had been shattered into tiny pieces, but he was tangible and constant.

"What about your bloody Alex Marshall?"

"Don't worry about him."

"And why shouldn't I? If you stay, I'll have to incessantly peek over my shoulder in case he learns that I've got you. I'm not too keen on having him hunt me down."

"He won't look for me."

He smirked. "So it's like that, is it?"

"Yes, it's just like that."

She rose up on tiptoe and kissed him on the mouth, and he joined in, but with none of the fervor he'd previously exhibited.

He evaluated her, taking stock, judging. Finally, he advised, "You can't scamper home tomorrow."

"I won't."

"If you try, I'll prevent you."

"You won't have to."

"I'll keep you against your will."

"Fine."

"If you say *yes* to me, it's forever. Do you understand?"

"Yes, I understand."

She felt as if she were perched on a cliff that was so high she couldn't see the bottom. She was ready to jump, her heart pounding with equal parts excitement and dread. The notion of falling free, of shucking off all that she was, suddenly seemed exactly right.

She'd always followed the rules, had done what she was told. Where had it landed her? She was out on her own, for the first time ever, with no funds, no clothes, no place to which she could return. If she cast her lot with him, she could become someone new, someone different.

When he was finished, what would she be? *Who* would she be?

"Come with me," he ordered.

"Where?"

"To my apartment upstairs."

"Why?"

"I'm about to guarantee that you can't ever leave."

She slipped her hand into his and led him into the hall.

Foolish girl! James mused, as he rippled with triumph. She was stupid to trust him. He could do anything to her—could murder her and dump her corpse in the Thames—and never be suspected or caught.

A terrible event must have transpired, though he declined to ponder what it might have been. She presumed it was over with Stanton, but James didn't believe it. The oaf was too vain to let her go, so James would proceed according to plan.

When his tryst with her was ended, Stanton wouldn't want her—no man would—but James refused to feel sorry for her. She had a perfect and wonderful life, and she was tossing it all away. For him! How ludicrous! How hysterical!

Was she daft? Was she mad? Or was she simply naïve beyond imagining? It had never occurred to her that James might have ulterior motives, that his intentions might be less than honorable, but she was about to find out how despicable a man could be.

They reached his quarters, and he locked them in, not because he was worried someone might enter behind them but because he was determined to have her realize she was confined, that she couldn't go unless he permitted it.

He escorted her through the parlor and straight to his bedchamber, and he closed and locked that door, too. It was dark inside, with no window to allow in any sunshine, and he lit a candle, wanting to see her, wanting to see everything.

She was struggling to appear brave. Her pulse raced, a vein fluttering in her throat like a trapped bird. In his office she'd promised much, but now that the moment was upon them, would she deliver?

"Why did you bring me in here?" she managed in a voice that was slightly breathless.

"As I already informed you, it's all or nothing with me."

"But I don't know what you mean."

"I'll show you."

"Are we to act as a . . . as a man and wife would?"

"Yes."

"Why must we?"

"It's the only way I can keep you." He guided her to the bed. "You contend that Lord Stanton won't search for you, but what if you're wrong?"

"I'm not."

"But what if he does? Or what if it's your family?"

As if this was a more viable prospect, she frowned. "My sister would raise a huge ruckus."

"If you're ruined beyond redemption, they won't want you, so you'll belong to me. They won't have any claim on you."

"Will you marry me after we . . . we . . ."

James stared at her and lied with ease. "We'll go to Scotland tomorrow. In my fastest carriage."

She studied him, probing for equivocation, for treachery, and though his expression was blank, he was positive she recognized his deceit but would continue on anyway.

"Swear to me," she implored, "that you'll be as kind as you're able. That you'll never beat me or—"

"For pity's sake, Rebecca! What sort of monster have you deemed me to be?"

"There's the rub, isn't it, James? I know so very little about you."

"Nor I about you."

"Are you sure this is what you want?" she inquired.

"I've wished for it from the very first."

"You couldn't have."

"I did. How about you? Are you certain? From this moment on, there's no going back."

"No going back," she echoed.

He untied her cloak, and it dropped to the floor and pooled at her feet; then he clasped her hand, inched off her gloves, and pitched them away.

"Turn around," he commanded.

"Why?"

"I want to fix your hair."

"My hair?"

"I like it hanging down, remember?"

He spun her and nestled himself to her, and he was deluged by a surge of expectation. He tugged at her combs, throwing them on the floor, and the lengthy mass swished down in a silky, luxurious wave. He riffled his fingers through it; then he leaned in and nuzzled her nape.

"I have to unbutton your dress, so I can remove it."

She gulped with trepidation. "Do you think you ought?"

"Absolutely." He nibbled across a patch of exposed skin. "Don't be afraid."

"I'm not."

"It's more pleasant if we take off our clothes."

"Will you . . ." Not having the vocabulary for salacious discussion, she blushed bright red.

"Yes, I'll take off mine, too, and we'll snuggle."

"I'd like that."

"So would I."

He continued till she was attired only in her chemise, and he paused to assess her, admiring how curvaceous she was. He cradled her to him, and he could peer over her shoulder, could see her shapely breasts, the nipples puckered against the fabric.

"You're very beautiful, Rebecca." *Too beautiful*, he thought. He couldn't let himself be captivated by her! He had to keep his distance, had to be about his business and conclude it as rapidly as possible.

"Do you mean it?" she shyly asked.

"Oh yes." He lifted the covers. "Lie down for me."

Without a fuss, she complied. He gazed down at her, much more enticed than he should have been by how grand it was to have her in his bed.

"We'll simply kiss and cuddle," he explained as he drew his shirt over his head. "It will feel marvelous."

"You have hair on your chest," she noted, sounding surprised.

"Most men do."

He'd never made love to a virgin before, and he was charmed by her comment. His sexual partners had always been lonely, desperate women, so her innocence was refreshing.

He gripped her wrist and rested her palm on his chest, demonstrating how she should rub in slow circles. "You can touch me—whenever and however you like. I enjoy it."

She smiled. "It's so soft. It tickles."

"There are many differences between us, more intimate ones." He started unbuttoning his trousers. "Close your eyes."

She obeyed, her lashes drifting down. She appeared so young, so pristine, and he hesitated, his dormant conscience stirring to life.

How could he do this to her? *Why* would he do this to her? In the prior decade, he'd endured many torments, but none of them were her fault. Why was he blaming her? Why vent his anger on her? Once, he'd have mustered some restraint, but time and circumstance had altered him into a bitter, resentful person.

He pushed any scruples away, jerked off his boots and pants; then he slipped under the blankets. His naked body connected to hers all the way down, just her thin chemise separating them.

"May I open my eyes now?" she queried.

He chuckled. "Yes."

"I wanted to see what you look like. Why wouldn't you let me watch?"

"You'll have plenty of chances."

He was in no hurry to have her discover the flogging scars on his back. He wasn't sure who she presumed him to be, but an ordinary fellow wouldn't have such disfiguring marks, and he was determined to maintain a pretense with her for as long as he could.

He urged her nearer, their loins pressed together, and a savage, dangerous desire swept over him. He yearned to jump on her like a wild beast, to take and take and take until she had nothing left to give.

The ferocity of his need scared him, had him wondering of what recklessness he might be capable, and he breathed deeply to calm himself. He was a ruthless bastard, but he wasn't so despicable that he'd ruin her initial carnal encounter.

He began kissing her, and she eagerly participated. She relaxed, and he draped a leg over her thigh, pinning her to him, as he worked her chemise down and off. Eventually, she was as naked as he, but she was so absorbed that she scarcely noticed.

He stroked and petted, whispering words of support, and finally, he was massaging her breast, fondling the plump mound, and squeezing the nipple. She was extremely sensitive and reacted to his slightest manipulation.

"Oh my!" she murmured. "That feels very good."

"It gets better."

"How could it?"

"Let me show you."

He rolled onto her, and he blazed a trail down her bosom to suck a nipple into his mouth. He toyed and played, as she writhed beneath him, each fidget wreaking havoc with his cock. He was so anxious to be inside her!

"Your skin is so warm," she said. "I didn't know it would be like this."

"I told you it keeps getting better."

"I didn't believe you."

"Scamp."

"I heard some women gossiping once. They claimed this would hurt."

"They were wrong." It was a small fib, but it reassured her.

She gazed at him in an adoring fashion, as if he'd hung the moon, and his silly heart skipped a beat. He caught himself thinking how fabulous it would be if she really were his wife, and the fact that he was pondering such a foolish notion had him worried.

He was aware of how sex encouraged emotions that had no correlation with the physical act, and he had to remember his purpose. He was hoping to taunt Alex Marshall, to repay the earl—in at least a minor way—for the agony he and his friends had imposed on James's family.

Any affection he had for Rebecca was idiotic, and he had to be cautious lest he develop a fondness for her. Come the dawn, she'd be in a carriage that would deliver her to Marshall's house.

He commenced the spiral again, until she was riveted in the experience; then his hand glided down, across her stomach, her abdomen, to her crotch. He cupped her, then eased a finger into her.

She arched up. "What are you doing?"

"I'm touching you in a special manner—as a man touches his wife."

"Are you positive this is what married couples do?"

"Completely positive."

He caressed in a lazy rhythm, and her hips instantly adopted the tempo. Very quickly, she grew agitated.

"What's happening to me?" she panted.

"It's pleasure, darling. Let it carry you away."

With scant effort, he sent her hurling into the inferno. She embraced the sensation, wallowing in it, and he grinned. He was thrilled by her lusty nature, by how she'd gifted him with such a private piece of herself.

As her orgasm waned, he settled himself between her

legs, his phallus at her center. She was so wet, so ready, that it wouldn't take much to commit the ultimate sin against her.

Her mouth was curved in a fetching moue of amazement and delight. "Was that the secret of the marital bed?"

"One of them."

"Can we do it again?"

"As often as you like."

"You'll kill me with ecstasy."

"I don't suppose anyone's died from it—yet!"

She rippled with laughter; then, as she noted his serious expression, she sobered. He widened her thighs and wedged himself in, and she squirmed with fear, trying to dislodge him, but he held her in place. His anatomy was screaming to proceed, and it was all he could do to keep from ramming into her like a sledgehammer.

"It's my turn now," he advised her.

"For what?"

"We'll join our bodies. Here." He stroked her sheath.

"I don't understand."

"You will." He pushed in a tad farther.

"This doesn't feel right."

"It will."

"James, I'm afraid."

"Hush," he soothed. "You're frightened because you've never done it before."

"It's not as I envisioned it would be."

"I know, but you trust me, don't you?"

"With my life."

The comment rattled him, had him questioning his motives and hating himself for who he'd become, but he shoved away the disturbing reflection. He refused to second-guess, to doubt or admonish. He was who he was.

"Put your arms around me."

"Like that?"

"Yes, exactly like that." He buried his face at her nape, as he increased the pressure, flexing, flexing again.

"James!"

He burst through, his cock sliding in all the way. She was so tight, so hot, the rush of her woman's blood goading some primal portion of his being that had him frantic to mate. It took every ounce of fortitude he possessed not to spill himself then and there.

She was rigid with tension, and she gave a cry of alarm, her fingernails digging into his skin.

"You said it wouldn't hurt," she accused.

"That was the worst of it."

"Am I . . . am I . . . still a virgin?"

"No."

"Do I look different?"

"Only prettier."

He couldn't delay, couldn't chat. His torso was quaking with restraint, begging him to finish.

"Let's be done with it," he murmured.

He was too near the edge, too aroused, and he had to continue. He gritted his teeth and slowed, being as gentle as he could, but he was overwhelmed by how remarkable he felt. They shared an affinity, so he'd never had to feign interest or desire. She simply called to him on a physical plane as few other women ever would.

With hardly any endeavor on his part, his seed gushed to the tip, and an unusual elation billowed through him as he emptied himself in her womb. He'd intended to pull out, but at the last, he couldn't resist, and he was stunned by his stupidity.

He was to have deflowered her, then sent her away. The prospect of a babe had never entered into his plans.

Was he mad? What if he'd gotten her pregnant? If there was a chance she was carrying his child, how could he let her go?

He rocked himself to a halt, and he was so satisfied, so very, very pleased.

After such a long, long journey, I've finally come home . . .

The peculiar thought slithered through his mind, and he frowned, curious as to why he was so maudlin. He was acting every bit as emotional as an untried female. What was wrong with him?

He retreated from her and dared to ask, "Was it awful for you?"

"No. It was very sweet."

"There at the beginning, I couldn't help but cause you pain. Women are created so that it's uncomfortable the first time. From now on, it won't bother you, at all."

"Good." She traced a finger across his lips, and his heart lurched with more of the same joy that kept popping up when he least expected it.

"We're united," she said, "before God, aren't we?"

"I imagine we are."

"Even if we never spoke any vows, we're *one flesh.* This is what the Bible means, isn't it?"

"Yes."

"I've always wondered." She snuggled herself closer. "Don't ever leave me. Promise me that you won't. I couldn't bear it."

"I won't," he lied, and he rolled onto his back.

Her cheek rested on his chest, her palm on his tummy, her torso half-draped across his. It was the most precious interlude of his life, and he stared at the ceiling, never wanting it to end.

What the hell was he going to do?

~ 17 ~

"He's here," Suzette hissed. "Hurry up."

"Arrogant sod," Peg grumbled. "Why can't he make up his mind?"

"I've almost got him," Suzette explained. "He's marrying a rich cousin in a few weeks, so we're off today to tour the house he's buying me."

"He'd better come up to snuff," Peg protested. "I'm tired of this."

"Then let's give him a show. Convince him I'm worth the price, eh?"

It was mid-morning, and an hour when she hated to be awake, so she was cranky and out-of-sorts, but duty called. He'd sent an urgent note, needing to speak with her, so she'd advised him to stop by the theater. There was no way in hell she'd have met him at her apartment. She wasn't about to have him learn her address, for she couldn't bear to have the annoying boor loitering on her stoop.

She stepped into her sister's arms, and they began to

kiss, tongues in mouths, hands on breasts. They'd already shed their camisoles, so they were half-naked. Out in the hall, she could hear Nick approaching, could feel his hungry gaze as he leered like a reprobate through the crack in the door.

Peg nibbled down to suck on her nipples, and Suzette moaned and writhed, displaying an exaggerated amount of carnal ecstasy. After witnessing a few more of their indecent exhibitions, Nick would realize that he enjoyed observing her with Peg, and he would let Peg live with Suzette so that the three of them could fornicate together. How could he spurn the chance for a regular *ménage à trois*? It simply wasn't in the male nature to forgo the naughty pleasure.

Such an arrangement would have numerous advantages. Peg would have a safe haven, and Suzette would have Peg's company, both during the day and at night. Peg knew what she was about under the blankets, while Nick—Suzette was positive—would be an inept lover who'd fumble and blunder. At least if Peg was in the bed, Suzette would have a bit of fun before she had to endure the masculine end of things.

"You're at it again, Suzette," he barked as he charged in. "I ordered you to desist."

"And I told you, *mon ami,* that I can't resist my darling Peg. I won't abandon her. I need her with me in my beautiful new home."

"Not bloody likely."

"You must allow it, *cher!*" Suzette rubbed his chest. "If you agree, I will . . . I will . . . make love to her whenever you demand it. You will watch us; then you will join in. It will be very *erotique, non?*"

Peg was quaking with feigned fear as Nick studied her with definite interest. He cupped Peg's breast, gauging weight and size.

"Please, sir," Peg implored, "I can't do what she wants. I'm not that kind of girl."

"For you, Nicholas," Suzette chimed in. "Only for you."

"We'll see." He shoved Peg away. "Be gone, you little harlot."

"Yes, yes," Peg wailed, stumbling out scarcely dressed, "whatever you say."

As she went, Nick evaluated her departing ass, envisioning the three of them doing the deed, and Suzette tamped down a smirk.

So soon! she mused. *So very, very soon!* Everything she'd ever craved was about to be hers.

As Peg's strides retreated, Nick whipped around, his greedy focus on her exposed bosom, but he wouldn't try any nonsense. He knew better. She would torment and tease, would give him a taste, but he understood—in no uncertain terms—that he didn't get to sample the fruits until he paid for them.

"Peg arouses me so much," she taunted. "After I've been with her, I'm all quivery, as if I'm about to explode."

She reached down to fondle her crotch, but before she could, he yanked her hand away and pushed her to the wall, trapping her with his large body.

"Your puss is mine," he claimed. "No one touches it but me."

"It is *not* yours. Not yet."

"I'm coming into some money this morning, so I'll sign the contract for the property this afternoon. You can move in tomorrow."

"Are you serious?"

"Yes."

"After all this time! I can't believe it!" She hugged him, their loins connecting, and she clutched his hips and ground herself against him. "I'm aching, Nick—on the inside. Make it go away."

She pulled down her drawers, baring her shaved privates, and she gripped his hand and placed it where it ought to be. He groped around, and she wondered if he had any idea how to proceed, but he finally managed to ram two uncouth fingers into her.

"Get down on your knees, Nick. Lick me and ease my pain."

"I won't debase myself as if I'm one of your Sappho friends."

"You must!" she begged, egging him on. "I'm desperate to feel you there."

He was convinced she had perverted tastes, and he was determined to cure her of them. "I'll show you how a man does it," he boasted. "After I'm through, you won't need a woman in your bed."

He slumped down and seized her flanks, but she figured he'd require assistance, so she spread her nether lips, granting him his first view of her pink center. He bent forward and tongued her, stroking over her clit in a rough fashion that did naught to titillate, but she was an actress, after all, and she played her part well.

She offered him embellished sighs and moans; then she put on the performance of her life by providing him with the most dynamic orgasm any female had ever faked.

He preened with satisfaction and wiped his lips on a towel, as she drooled over him, insisting he was the most superb lover in the world. Like the fool he was, he swallowed every word.

"I'm in a hurry," he said, "so let's be off. We'll visit the house you've selected, so I can be sure it's suitable; then I must leave town for a few days."

"Leave!" she pouted, though she was terribly thankful that he wouldn't be hovering about and sniping at her over where to situate the furniture or hang the paintings. "You can't go. Not now! Not when our dreams are about to come true."

"It's family business," he contended. "It can't be helped."

He waited in the hall while she donned her fanciest green gown, her matching shoes and gloves. She pinned on a jaunty hat, a feather trailing behind, a lace shawl draped across her shoulders. Her magnificent hair was down, swishing across her back. She appeared exotic and foreign, so out of the ordinary that people would gasp with amazement and delight as she passed by.

"Perfect," he murmured as she joined him. He took a box from his jacket, and he opened it, gifting her with a strand of pearls. "This should go nicely."

"Oh, Nick," she gushed, for once not having to affect gratitude, "they're splendid."

"There'll be plenty more where those came from."

She spun so he could clasp them around her neck. Through the door to her dressing room she could see herself in the mirror. She smiled with approval, then led him out to the street and his sporty yellow gig, with its dashing red wheels. Just as he would have lifted her up, someone called to them from down the walk. It was a woman, with a nasal, irritating voice.

"Nicky!" she bellowed, waving a kerchief to draw their notice. "Oh, Nicky!"

Nick froze; then he dropped Suzette's arm and

lurched away, putting several feet of distance between them.

"Dammit," he cursed, and he actually shuddered.

"Who on earth is that?" Suzette whispered as she assessed the ugly hag.

"My cousin."

"Your cousin?"

"Yes."

Realization dawned. "Good God, Nick, she's not your . . . your . . . fiancée, is she? Tell me she's not."

His cheeks flushed as he admitted, "She's rich as Croesus."

"But still . . ."

Suzette reveled with triumph. If he would marry such a horrid individual, he had to be smitten beyond sanity, and she saw years of manipulating him to beneficial effect.

The harridan advanced on them, her fat thighs squishing together. "Nicky, there you are." She was breathless from her race to catch up with them. "I've been searching everywhere."

"What is it, Lydia?"

Lydia? Suzette watched as Nick groveled. What strange behaviors money could induce!

"I can't find Rebecca," Lydia said.

"I'm sure she's about somewhere," he replied. "Keep looking. She'll turn up."

"You misunderstand. She's vanished without a trace."

"Oh, hell," he muttered. "Isn't there enough turmoil at the house?"

"Well, now there's more. You must accompany me at once, so we can discover if she's fled to the country on her own. Come!" Lydia started dragging him away.

Suzette was impatient to be off, and irked that the busybody hadn't so much as glanced at her. She was even more infuriated that Nick hadn't introduced her, that he was pretending she was invisible.

"Nick," she interjected, "aren't you forgetting something?"

"Oh yes," he mumbled. "Lydia, I can't attend you. I have a previous engagement."

"It's cancelled," Lydia decreed.

Obviously, Lydia wasn't a person whose edicts were ever countermanded, and Suzette wondered if Nick fathomed the catastrophe he was setting in motion.

Had he a clue as to how domineering Lydia was? Suzette could practically smell Lydia's obstinate character, and the recognition had her uneasy. She'd assumed Nick was marrying a simpering debutante, not a mature, independent female.

Should she be provoked, Suzette had no doubt, Lydia would be a dangerous adversary, but enemy or no, Suzette was tired of being ignored.

"Lydia, is it?" she inquired. "Nick has had an appointment with me for some time. Whatever is bothering you will have to wait. Let's go, Nick."

"Who is this interloper, Nicky?" Lydia demanded, her scornful gaze roving up and down Suzette's fabulous attire, her sneer indicating that she wasn't impressed.

Nick handled the awkward moment with more composure than Suzette might have predicted. "Lydia, may I present an acquaintance of mine, Miss Suzette DuBois, esteemed star of the London stage."

Suzette pulled herself up to her full height, giving the podgy shrew an imposing glimpse of what she was up against. Suzette was a great beauty, stunningly outfitted, her hair and eyes aflame in the bright sunshine.

To Suzette's shock and chagrin, Lydia scoffed. "An actress, Nicky? Honestly, you should be more careful about the company you keep. What would people say if they learned that you were wont to consort with someone so lowborn?"

With that deftly delivered snub, Lydia guided Nick away, and the hapless man hadn't the fortitude to so much as peek over his shoulder in farewell.

Enraged, fuming, Suzette tarried next to his abandoned gig, curious if he expected her to tend it like a humble servant.

She was more insulted than she'd ever been. The nerve of the witch! Deeming herself to be so bloody superior! Well, she might have a bank account crammed with money, but Suzette would have Nick, and all the cash in the world wouldn't alter that fact.

Suzette plotted her revenge. It would be fast, it would be beastly, it would be amusing, and she was eager to commence.

Rebecca stirred and reached for James, but he wasn't there. His absence brought her completely awake, and she peered around in the dark. Through the door to the outer parlor she could see a candle flickering, could see him leaning on the windowsill and staring out into the night sky.

He was naked, moonlight wafting in to starkly accentuate his torso, casting odd shadows on his skin. His back appeared striped, with peculiar crisscrossed lines moving in all directions. His legs were rugged and powerful, his bottom rounded and . . . and . . . cute! There was no other word to describe it, and she grinned, not having comprehended that a woman could take pleasure from viewing a nude man.

As she recollected the things he'd done to her, her stomach tickled. If she'd had a hundred years to ponder, she couldn't have devised such decadent, incredible acts. He'd been so patient, tender and loving one minute, then firm and insistent the next. She ached in spots she'd never noted before—even her inner thighs had been abraded by the scratch of his whiskers!—and when she thought about how he'd kissed her there, she burned with excitement.

She'd liked it! And she wanted to begin again as soon as she could lure him to the bed, but the relish with which she'd wallowed in the endeavor worried her. While she wasn't overly schooled in carnal affairs, she didn't suppose she should have enjoyed it quite so much. But she'd never tell another soul how glorious it had been! It would be her wicked, marvelous secret with James!

He seemed so sad and pensive, as if a heavy burden rested on his shoulders. She could sense his tension and concern, and she wished she had some idea of how to soothe him. A wife ought to know how to calm and console, but it was increasingly clear that many details had been omitted in the bridal preparation she'd received from Lydia.

She'd figure it out, though. By coming to James she'd made the correct choice. Everything felt so right, as if her destiny had clicked in place like the pieces of a difficult puzzle.

She crept off the mattress and, not as comfortable as

he with nudity, she wrapped a sheet around herself. She went to him, but he was so engrossed in his rumination that he didn't notice her until she was a few feet away.

He didn't speak but raised his arm in welcome, and she snuggled under it. The window was open, the cool air causing her to shiver, and he cradled her to him, his body's heat rapidly warming her.

After a lengthy silence, he asked, "Were you aware that in the Southern Hemisphere the stars are different?"

"No, I wasn't."

"When even the stars have changed, you feel so far from home—as if you know in your heart you'll never get back to where you truly belong."

He was so melancholy, and his woe had her afraid. Was he already regretting their decision?

"Have you traveled the Seven Seas?"

"I've been to many exotic lands."

It was the first real comment he'd shared about his past, the first reference to a personal event, and she was thrilled.

Gently, she prodded, "Have you found your way home?"

"I don't think I ever will." Glum and dejected, he gazed outside again.

"What is it, James? You can confide in me. I'm your wife now. Perhaps I can help."

He muttered a curse, and she couldn't deduce which portion of her remark had him scoffing. The part about being his wife? About helping?

He brooded, as she rippled with dismay. Whatever he was about to confess, she didn't want to hear it.

"I've done a terrible thing," he finally claimed.

Murder? Mayhem? What? What? The questions

screamed through her head, but she smiled and stated, "You're the sweetest man I know. What mischief could you possibly have perpetrated that would qualify as *terrible*?"

"Sweet? Gad!" He chuckled with derision. "I've been called many names in my life, but *sweet* has never been one of them." He hugged her; then he said the most dreaded words of all: "Sit down. We need to talk."

He led her to the table, and he held out a chair; then he pulled up another so that he was facing her, their knees intertwined.

"For the last ten years," he asserted, "I've hated Lord Stanton."

The admission confused her. She'd thought he and Alex were acquaintances, maybe even friends. "You hated Alex?"

"Yes. I've been consumed with how I could hurt him." He stopped and studied her, cataloguing her features as if he was anxious to memorize them, as if this was farewell. "Instead, I've hurt you."

"You haven't done anything to me." Frantic to touch him, she took his hands in her own. "I'm fine."

"I was determined to find what mattered most to him and wreck it."

"You assumed it was me?" How absurd. She'd been so insignificant to Alex that he probably hadn't yet realized that she'd left.

"I sought you out on purpose," he contended. "I seduced you so that I could ruin Stanton's marriage, so that I could send you to him sullied and defiled."

"He never wanted me, James."

"Then he's a fool." He caressed her cheek. "Let's get you dressed, and I'll have Willie drive you home."

"I'm not leaving. We're going to Scotland to be married. You promised."

"I was lying." Ashamed, he glanced away. "I'm sorry."

"You're *sorry*? That's all you have to say?"

"Yes."

"It was a game? Is that what you're telling me? You've had your petty revenge on Alex, so you're eager to be shed of me. Is that it?"

"I don't care about Stanton anymore, but you can't stay with me. It would be wrong."

"Why would it be wrong?"

"Have you any notion of who I am?"

"A . . . a merchant?" She'd been an idiot for never having inquired. Why had she—the epitome of caution and prudence—been so willing to race to perdition without pausing to obtain information that was so important?

"That's hilarious." He laughed, but it was a wrenching, awful sound. "I guess I have a knack for fabrication."

"Who are you James? *What* are you?"

"I'm a criminal, Rebecca."

"You are not!" she vehemently declared.

"I am."

"I don't believe you."

"It's true. A decade ago, I was accused of stealing some jewelry from one of Stanton's chums."

"You'd never do such a thing. Which imbecile blamed you?"

"Everyone pointed a finger at me. I didn't stand a chance."

"But you couldn't have been more than a boy!"

"I was sixteen."

"Oh, James . . ."

"I was convicted and transported to Australia. I was

supposed to remain there for the rest of my days, but I ran off and sneaked into England. I'm an escaped felon, and I'm wanted by the law. If I'm caught, I'll be hanged."

She could perceive his anger and humiliation, his disgrace and dishonor, and a wave of indignation swept through her.

He was a kind man, a good man, and he had a tender heart. She knew it to the very marrow of her bones. Whatever horrid stories others had spewed, whatever spurious charges they'd raised, were false. She had no doubt.

"Are you actually expecting that any of this matters to me?" she asked.

"It has to. What if you cast your lot with me and I'm arrested? I can't imagine what would happen to you. In the meantime, how am I to support you? I won't deign to hint at how I earn my living. My situation is so precarious, and I would never thrust you into the middle of it." As if she were a child, he patted her wrist. "Now, let's get you out of here before this charade gets any worse."

A spark of temper ignited, and it grew into a raging inferno. All her life, she'd been told what to do and when to do it, and she'd serenely complied. She was so sick of having others make her decisions, of being quiet and unobtrusive.

How dare he assume he had all the answers! How dare he assume she'd scurry away at the merest sign of trouble!

"Listen to me, Mr. Duncan—"

He shook his head in disgust. "My surname isn't Duncan! That's how badly I've behaved. You don't even know my real name!"

"Well, I know mine, and it's Burton. I'm a member

of a powerful family. I am cousin to Alex Marshall, Lord Stanton, one of the wealthiest, most influential personages in the kingdom."

"Don't remind me!"

"I'm rich, too, in my own right, and I don't give a hoot about how you earn your money, for you won't have to ever work if you don't wish it. So if you think I'll sit idly by and have this injustice continue, you can just think again."

"You can't help me!" he bellowed. "If you speak a word of this to anyone, I'll be taken into custody. If I'm not immediately executed, I'll be sent back! I won't go, I tell you. I'd kill myself first!"

"James, oh, James, my dear man."

She scooted off her chair and onto his lap. It was odd how the simple fact of meeting him had so thoroughly transformed her. She felt as if she'd always been with him, as if every step had been gradually propelling her to her spot at his side, and she couldn't envision being anywhere else.

"I'm not leaving you," she murmured.

"Yes, you are! You have to."

"We're off to Scotland—as we planned. We'll start out as soon as it's light enough to travel."

"Let me be more clear: *I* won't permit you to stay here."

"And let *me* be more clear: I love you, James whoever-you-are."

"You can't love me," he insisted bleakly, "for there's nothing to love!"

"*One flesh*, James, remember? We're not two separate people anymore. We're one. You and God made it so, and I wouldn't have it any other way."

"Rebecca"—he was weary, disconsolate, and he rubbed his hand over his face—"you don't know what you're saying. You're acting crazy."

"I've never been more lucid." She stood and urged him to his feet. "Come to bed. I consider this to be my wedding night, and I have a few more hours to revel before the dawn. I have every intention of being pregnant when we return from Scotland, so you need to get busy."

"You're mad," he grumbled.

"Yes, I am," she agreed, feeling wild and more than a little dangerous. "I'm *mad* for you."

She led him to the other room, lay down, and drew him down beside her.

~ 18 ~

"Where are you, you blasted man!"

Ellen downed her wine and slammed the goblet on her dresser as she glanced at the clock. One thirty in the morning. The time taunted her with how late it was, with how long she'd paced, waiting for him to arrive so they could consummate their marriage.

The cavernous countess's suite was intimidating, the slightest noise echoing off the ceiling to emphasize how she was more alone than she'd ever been. She tiptoed to the door that separated her bedchamber from Alex's, and she pressed her ear to the wood, hearing only silence on the other side.

He still wasn't home, the knave! Apparently, he couldn't be bothered to see matters through to the hideous end.

Oh, why had she gone through with it? She should have refused, should have thrown his pathetic, disingenuous offer in his face and stormed out of his house and out of his life. That's what she should have done! That's what she *would* have done if she'd had any sense, if she'd had more than a few pounds in her empty purse.

She was such a coward! Such a timid twit!

She'd been too ashamed to bump into Rebecca, too mortified to meet up with any of the servants, so hour after hour she'd huddled in disgrace in her room until the housekeeper had knocked to advise that Alex and the vicar were ready in the library.

If she'd retained any hope that James would ultimately come for her, she might have reached a different decision, but he hadn't appeared. Without thought, without conviction, she'd marched down the stairs to her wedding, had spoken the vows like an automaton, letting others tell her where to stand, what to say.

The vicar was no fool. Immediately after the ceremony, he'd left, as had the purportedly *happy* bridegroom. The second the final *I do* had been uttered, Alex had fled, not to be seen again.

She had no idea where he went, when he'd be back—if he'd be back! Perhaps the notion of being married to her was so repugnant that he'd raced for the docks and boarded the next ship set to sail. Perhaps he'd drowned himself in the Thames. Perhaps he was seeking solace in a brothel, or with a mistress—of whom she was certain he had many.

What a fraud! What a travesty! The trying day had been a sham, had made a mockery of every fine thing that holy matrimony was supposed to be, yet ninny that she was, she kept expecting he'd return, that they'd work through the calamity.

Soon, the entire staff would know that he hadn't stayed with her on his wedding night. She'd never forgive him for the appalling snub.

The grand clock down in the entry foyer chimed the

quarter hour, taunting her with how fast dawn was approaching.

Well, she'd had her fill of cowering and cringing, of feeling sorry for herself. She was now a countess and wife to a very wealthy man. In the morning, she'd leave with her bag packed and her head high. She'd embarrass *him* by checking into a hotel, and she would inform anyone who asked exactly why she was there.

To arrange her affairs and negotiate an allowance she'd hire a solicitor, and she'd charge the cost to her husband! Hah! That would show him! Then she'd move into seclusion in the country where he'd never find her.

He, and his enormous pride, and his bachelor's existence, and his bevy of paramours, could all go hang!

She wrenched off her robe and stomped to the bed, cursing as she scrambled onto the gigantic mattress. Why . . . she practically needed a ladder to climb onto the stupid piece of furniture!

What sort of extravagant, wasteful person owned such a monstrosity? Its size and opulence underscored how out of her element she was, how much she didn't belong in the mess where she'd landed. She had no clue how to be an earl's wife.

She was mad! Stark raving, cackling, howling mad!

In a temper, she punched at the pillows, striving to relax, but there was no comfort to be had. Her mind was too chaotic, her body too tense.

Her torso stiff with fury, she peered up at the ceiling, when suddenly the door from Alex's room burst open.

At the racket she rose up to observe him looming on the threshold. A ripple of gladness surged through her—he wanted her, after all!—but she tamped it down.

He was staring as if he didn't recall who she was or why she was in the countess's bed. He was angry, even more irate than she, and his wrath billowed out in waves, seeming to pummel her like bricks falling from a wall.

His neck cloth was missing, his jacket off, his shirt unbuttoned, and the sleeves rolled back to reveal his muscular arms. He stalked toward her, reeking of tobacco, alcohol, and cheap perfume, and she was awhirl with images of where he'd been and what he'd probably been doing.

She was terribly hurt, though she couldn't comprehend why she would be. He didn't care about her, and she didn't care about him. They were two strangers, thrown together in abhorrent circumstances, like survivors tossed about in a carriage accident.

What was it to her if he'd been off fornicating with another on their wedding night? What was it to her if he'd humiliated her to all of London? She was about to depart, and if she was very lucky, she'd never see him again.

"Go away," she said.

"No."

His obstinacy wasn't surprising. In their twisted relationship, he was always barging in where he wasn't wanted. There was no middle ground for them, no easy rhythm. There were only huge swings of emotion, great battles of will and determination. She was exhausted by the energy it took merely to be in his presence. If she were stupid enough to remain—which she wasn't!—she'd grow old before her time, would drop dead of fatigue from dealing with the passion the two of them generated.

"You're drunk," she snapped, sounding like a nagging fishwife.

"So I am."

"You smell like a brothel."

"When a man's recently been in one, it's impossible to smell any other way."

She gasped with outrage, even as her dismay spiraled, and she demanded, "Get out of here!"

"No."

Looking dark and dangerous, he frowned but didn't budge, and his cool demeanor incensed her further. "Get out! Or I swear to God, I will start screaming and I will continue until the glass in the windows begins to break."

"No one will rush to your aid. You're mine. I can do whatever I wish. There's no one to prevent me."

On any other occasion, she'd have discounted the remark as so much bluster. She'd never felt threatened by him, but his menacing mood was frightening.

She was fairly positive that he'd come to claim his marital rights, but if he assumed he could force her after he'd admitted to being in a brothel, she'd kill him. She'd tarry till he fell asleep, then she'd sneak down and fetch one of the fancy pistols he kept in his library, and she'd shoot him through his black heart.

When they executed her, she'd march to the gallows with a smile on her face!

He reached down and gripped her throat, his large hand making her realize how vulnerable she was. He could strangle her, but who would know? Who would fret?

She pushed him away, declining to be bullied, and resolved not to let him ascertain how he was scaring her.

"I'm not afraid of you," she maintained, but the quiver in her voice belied her bravado.

"You should be." He yanked at the covers, his fiery gaze meandering down her body. "Take off your nightgown."

"You can't think I'll permit you to have sex with me."

"I don't *think* I'm going to have sex with you. I know I am."

"You abandoned the privilege fifteen hours ago when you walked out after the ceremony. When you're sober and capable of courtesy, you may return."

"You will not refuse me. Not now, not ever." He grabbed the front of her gown and ripped it from bodice to hem.

She was so stunned that she hadn't an instant to react before he stretched out on top of her. Resistance was futile, but she skirmished with him anyway, though she wasn't sure why. Hadn't she wanted him to come to her? Hadn't she been waiting for this very moment?

They were only compatible in bed. The outside world and their petty problems faded away, so if they were to mend their differences, to achieve a truce, it would be when they were dallying.

Still, she was upset, and she needed him to be a friend before he was anything else. Instead, he was being an insufferable, overbearing beast. He seemed destined to act badly, while she seemed destined to complain about it.

Why couldn't they ever meet somewhere in the bland middle?

"Get off me!" she insisted.

"Not till we've finished this farce."

"I will not participate when you're behaving like such

a churl." She clopped him alongside the head, pleased when she delivered a hefty blow.

"Stop it!"

"No."

"Why must everything be a battle with you?"

"With me? You're the one who stormed in like a lunatic!"

She increased her wrestling, and he responded by leaping to the floor and retrieving her robe. He tugged the belt free, and while he was occupied she scurried away, but before she could escape he seized her ankles, dragging her onto the mattress and pinning her down. He straddled her, and though she persisted with her grappling, it was all for naught. She couldn't pitch him off.

A malicious gleam in his eye, he bent down, and to her utter shock, he clasped her wrists and wrapped the belt around them; then he knotted the other end to the headboard. She was shackled like a criminal in a torture chamber, and she jerked and pulled at the restraint, but to no avail.

"Let me go!" she commanded.

He surveyed his handiwork. "No. I believe I like you just as you are."

"What are you intending?"

"Is there any doubt?"

"I'm not doing this with you! Not when you've shamed me on my wedding day! Not when you've been to a brothel!"

"My, my, aren't we in a snit?"

"You loathsome swine!"

"Be silent, or I'll gag you, too."

"You . . . you . . ."

He kissed her, capturing her mouth in a bruising embrace. He was brutal, clearly wanting there to be no question as to who was in charge, who would always be in control. He was a tyrant, her lord and master, her husband, and he would never let her forget it.

She'd planned to defy him, or at least ignore him, but her disloyal anatomy was eager for his clever caresses. There was something extremely wicked about being tied down, and the more she struggled, the more arousing it became.

She felt like a pirate's prisoner or a sultan's slave. She was the virgin about to be sacrificed, the daughter sold to marauders, the bride kidnapped by savages. The more adamant he was, the more she fought, and the higher the enjoyment spiraled.

Was she deranged? How could she revel in such abominable conduct?

He blazed a trail to her bosom, his treacherous lips on her nipples. Ruthless, relentless, he took his pleasure with no regard for her own, which enhanced the excitement.

He continued on, down her belly and lower, and he clutched her thighs so that she was splayed wide. She detested being so exposed, and she tried to close her legs, to buck him off, but she had no leverage.

His fingers were inside her, his tongue, too. He was merciless, and she had no defense against his skilled seduction. He could make her beg for what she wanted, what she was desperate to receive.

She was rigid with desire, her body weeping with her need for release, yet he moved away, declining to provide the conclusion she craved.

"Finish it!" she implored.

"No."

"Do it now!"

"When I'm ready," he maddeningly replied.

He was on his knees, huddled at her center, his fingers not ceasing their torment. He would lead her to the edge, then ease her away, over and over again, so that she was frantic with unfulfilled ardor. Her heart was pounding so ferociously that she worried it might simply burst.

"You're mine," he declared. "All mine."

"In your wildest dreams."

"Tell me that you love me," he ordered.

"That I what?"

"Tell me!" he repeated.

"Never in a thousand years."

"Say that you love me. Say it and mean it!"

Was he insane? Affection had never played a part in their relationship, and any feelings she harbored had to be hidden from him. If he ever discovered how much she cared, he'd have too many ways to hurt her.

"I don't love you," she claimed. "I never have."

"Liar," he hissed.

He gripped his cock and wedged it into her. Disgustingly, she squirmed and writhed, anxious to impale herself, and he laughed at her impatience. He bit her nipple, being much too rough, but she needed the vicious manipulation. Down below, his thumb carried on its dastardly provocation, finally flicking at her long enough that she could let go.

The sensation commenced in her nether regions, cascading out, and as she came, he penetrated her, driving deep at the first clenches of her orgasm. She sailed to ecstasy, the rapture so intense that she was blinded by it. As she flew up and up, she screamed with delight. With her hands fettered, it seemed as if she'd leapt off a cliff, but there was no bottom and no method to hold on. The bindings lent an extra amount of iniquity to the deed, making her feel more sinful, more decadent, than ever.

Through it all, he thrust, his hips ramming him into her like the pistons of a huge machine. He rode her hard, keeping on and on, as if he couldn't get enough of her, as if he might never be sated.

As she reached her peak, he did, too, his hot seed flooding her womb; then he shuddered and collapsed, but only for an instant. Then, as if he couldn't bear to touch her, he pulled out and rolled away, flopping onto his back. His pulse was thundering, his torso coated with perspiration, and he stared up at the ceiling, an arm flung over his eyes.

They lay in the aftermath, stunned by how erotic it had been, with neither of them having the faintest idea what to say or do next. After such a rowdy escapade, what could possibly be appropriate?

The moment grew strained, then awkward. Ultimately, he broke it by untying her wrists. Once she was free, she wrenched away and curled into a ball.

She'd hoped, with the exploit being over, that he'd leave, that he'd be chagrined and would slink out without a word, but she should have known better.

He chuckled, sounding much too proud of himself, and his mirth rekindled her fury. Why had she joined in with such relish? When he started in on her, why couldn't she muster any restraint? Had she a shred of dignity remaining?

"The whole house had to hear you screeching." He swatted her on the rear. "Good. They'll assume I beat you, which you'd thoroughly deserve for being such a shrew all day."

She rippled with ire. "Me?"

"Yes, *you*. Don't you dare deny it."

"You huffed out after the ceremony, you don't come home till it's almost dawn, you admit to being in a . . . a . . . brothel, but *I* am the shrew?"

"Bloody right."

His speech was slurred, reminding her of how much he'd had to drink, and it occurred to her that he'd viewed bedding her as a chore, so he'd required fortification. The realization had her near to weeping.

"I may be a shrew," she muttered, "but you're an absolute ass." She elbowed him in the ribs.

He grunted. "Stop fussing, or I'll tie you up again."

She glared over her shoulder. "Try it, and I'll murder you when you least expect it."

"You loved every second, you little strumpet."

"I hated it!" she felt honor bound to insist. For emphasis, she added, "I hate *you!*"

"No, you don't. You love me." He spooned himself around her, enfolding her in his arms. "Go to sleep, Countess."

"No, I plan to stay awake all night. Merely to spite you."

"It figures. You're the most stubborn woman I've ever met."

"I am not," she argued.

They were still, lost in thought, their respiration slowing, and he whispered, "Everything will be all right, Ellen."

She imagined it was as close to an apology as she'd ever get, that it was his initial attempt at a truce, and she answered, "I know."

"It will all work out. Give it some time."

"I will."

"I wasn't at a brothel," he said. "I was just trying to make you angry."

"You despicable lout."

"I like how your eyes flash when you're in a temper."

The candle sputtered out. He snored. She cried quiet tears.

❧ 19 ❧

"What are you doing?"

"I'm snooping through your belongings," Ellen called through the door to Alex's dressing chamber, "as any proper wife would."

"Let me know if you stumble on anything interesting."

"Believe me, I will."

He was bathing, and she'd boldly entered as if she had every right—which she supposed she did—and she was surprised by how normal it felt to carry on as if they were a real married couple. Perhaps there was some hope for them, after all.

"Ouch!" he barked.

"What happened?"

"My hands are a bit shaky. I cut myself shaving."

She giggled and retorted, "An excess of liquor has that effect on a person."

He muttered several indecipherable remarks, and she chuckled with satisfaction. He'd awakened with the worst hangover, which she deemed a suitable penalty for putting her through such anguish the previous evening.

Morning had brought an odd peace. Neither of them mentioned their awful wedding, or their dissolute wedding night, though the belt from her robe still dangled from the posts of her headboard. She blushed every time she glanced at it.

Her body was bruised and sore from their raucous coupling and, due to his overindulging, he was in a wretched state, so they'd both been too miserable to quarrel. They'd proceeded as if sleeping and rising together was their usual condition.

She was already dressed, her hair arranged, so her day was progressing a tad quicker than his. Though she was aghast to admit it, she'd agree to romp again, should he show the slightest inclination in that direction, but he was incredibly grumpy, so ardor was probably out of the question.

He'd ordered them a private breakfast to be served in his bedchamber, but their food hadn't yet been delivered, so she had the perfect excuse to explore while she waited. She'd taken advantage of the opportunity, riffling through shirts and trousers, counting shoes and boots.

At having the chance to poke around she suffered a possessive thrill. He was her husband now, and touching his things was deliciously romantic in a fashion she couldn't describe.

She shut the wardrobe and moved to a dresser. The top drawer was littered with jewelry. There were bracelets and rings, necklaces and chains, haphazardly tossed into bowls and boxes, and she was fascinated. The collection was gaudy, with heavy stones that she presumed to be genuine, and she was amazed by the fortune spread before her. If a burglar ever entered, he'd certainly be delighted! Why weren't the treasures secured in the family vault?

Obviously, the pieces were designed for women, and she refused to contemplate why he'd have so many, telling herself that they were definitely *not* an indicator of how often he gave expensive gifts to females.

She tried on a bracelet, liking how the gold encircled her wrist, when he spoke from across the room.

"Did you find something you like?"

She spun around, and she blushed, embarrassed at having been caught, but her flush deepened when she saw that he was leaned against the door frame and naked but for the towel swathing his loins. His shoulders were so wide, his waist so narrow. He was a fine specimen of a man, and she shivered with excitement. Whatever transpired between them, they could work through it—if she could eventually lure him back to her bed. With a spouse as attractive as he was, what else could possibly matter?

"Where did you get all these things?" she asked.

"People give me presents"—he shrugged as if receiving priceless artifacts were a common occurrence— "and I buy items that are beautiful. You can have the lot of it if you wish."

She understood that he was rich, that she was now rich, as well, but his wealth had seemed abstract. She was married to a man who had a drawer full of precious gems, who'd relinquish them with a smile and a wave, and she struggled to envision herself being so nonchalant about their fortune, but the image wouldn't gel.

It was a further sign of how she was an imposter, of how she'd stepped into shoes she could never fill.

"Where would I wear such a fancy trinket?"

"Anywhere you desire," he replied. "You're a countess. That type of conduct is permitted. Some would say it's necessary."

As if the entire situation was absurd, he grinned, and she grinned, too, praying that they could generate such levity throughout the day. It was better than fighting like cats and dogs.

"I don't want anything." She felt awkward, as if she'd been scrounging like a pauper on the side of the road.

"I insist," he declared in a lofty tone that demanded compliance.

She almost bristled at his arrogance. If they were to have any hope of marital harmony, he'd have to temper his domineering attitude, but for the moment she decided to make him happy. If she declined, they'd have a spat, and she was determined to get through breakfast without arguing.

Besides, it was the first gift he'd offered her, and she wasn't about to reject it.

"All right." She turned to search, sure that she could locate an appropriate bauble in the dazzling pile.

She sifted and sorted, and she could sense his hot gaze on her. He was curious, eager to see what she'd choose but too nervous to approach and watch.

Everything was too ornate for the modest individual she pictured herself to be, and finally she reached to the rear of the drawer and pulled out a ring. She deemed it too flashy, and she was about to pitch it into the jumble when she froze.

The ring had a gold band and an unusual setting of stones in the shape of a bluebird. It was an exact replica of the ring James displayed on his finger to flaunt his downfall, an exact copy of the drawing that had been distributed throughout her neighborhood shortly after the ring's exalted owner had reported it missing. .

Her heart began to pound, her ears to buzz.

"What have you found?" he queried. "Is it extraordinary?"

"Yes. Yes, it is."

She tipped it toward the window and peeked inside the band, knowing without looking that Lady Barrington's initials would be etched there. But still, when they became visible, she nearly collapsed to the floor in a shocked heap.

The ring! The accursed, dreadful ring—that had killed her father, ruined her brother, and destroyed her family—was casually thrown into a drawer in Alex's dresser.

How had it come to be there? How long had it lain, year after agonizing year, with no one daring to inquire?

The enormity of the discovery was too much to absorb, and her mind couldn't wrap itself around the facts. The ring was in her husband's drawer. In his drawer . . . in his drawer. . . .

It was such a hideous, bizarre conclusion that she couldn't deduce what her next move should be. He was behind her. Waiting . . . waiting . . .

Was he dangerous? He hadn't ever seemed to be, but if he'd stolen the ring, of what else might he be capable? If she interrogated him, what would happen?

She whirled to face him.

"This is an interesting piece." She held it out for him to view; then she clutched it in her fist, gripping it tightly so that she wouldn't drop it.

"I always thought so."

"You did?"

"Yes. It's very unique."

Even though her world was being smashed to bits, she sounded so calm, so composed. "Can you recall how you came by it?"

"I haven't the vaguest. I've had it for ages."

"Really? For ages?"

"What is it, Ellen?" He started toward her. "What's wrong?"

"I'm fine."

He was crossing toward her much too rapidly. With each step he took, she took one back, sidling toward her bedchamber, though what she intended when she arrived was anybody's guess.

"Ellen! What's the matter? Speak to me!"

"It's so peculiar."

"What is?" He halted, recognizing that he shouldn't try to touch her.

"Do you remember when I told you about my brother?"

"He'd gotten himself in some trouble over a theft."

"Not just any *theft*," she stated, "but of a very valuable ring."

"A ring?"

"Yes, and I'm positive it's an odd coincidence, but this is the same ring. It even has Lady Barrington's initials on the band. See?" She showed it to him, then snatched it away, before he had a true opportunity to study it.

"What are you implying?"

"Why is it in your dresser?"

He frowned, then gasped. "You can't think I stole it."

"I'm not sure what I think. I've merely posed a simple question, and I'd like a simple answer: What is it doing in your drawer?"

"How the hell should I know?"

"Yes," she murmured, "how the hell should you?"

"Give it to me, Ellen. Give it to me right now."

"No."

"I'm not asking you; I'm telling you."

He stuck out his palm, expecting her to meekly surrender it, but she couldn't. If she turned it over to him, she was convinced it would disappear. Her proof—that James had been innocent, all along—would vanish without a trace.

"This ring killed my father. Were you aware that's why he died?"

"No, I wasn't."

"He couldn't bear the shame of James being pronounced guilty, and all this time the ring was in your dresser."

"Ellen, let me explain—"

"Explain? Are you actually supposing you could *explain* this in any logical way?"

"Before you go off half-cocked, screaming about felonies and whatever else, listen to me, and listen good."

He advanced, and she retreated farther. "I need to confer with my brother."

"I thought your brother had been transported."

Too late, she realized her error, but she didn't care what he suspected. James was the only one who could help her, who could advise her as to what they should do.

"He's in London," she admitted, "and I mean to—"

Quick as a snake, he clasped her wrist and pried at her fingers. She struggled to free herself, and when she couldn't, she scratched the back of his hand, digging in with her nails so deeply that she drew blood.

He hissed with pain, and before he could recover,

she yanked away, then raced to her room to slam and lock the door. She sagged against it as he stormed to the other side and pounded with all his might.

"Ellen! Stop this nonsense! At once!"

His fist vibrated through the wood, and she staggered away, wondering if she'd ever really known him.

"Ellen!" he shouted again. "Open up!"

"I can't. I can't."

Tears streamed down her cheeks, so many that they blinded her, and she tried to swipe them away, but they kept coming. She couldn't believe he was the one—refused to believe he was the one!—yet she was holding the evidence.

He'd said that he'd had the ring forever, that he couldn't recollect from where it had originated, and he had so many trinkets. Had he stolen the others? Was he naught but a petty thief?

She'd heard of people who seemed perfectly normal but who were plagued by a horrendous compulsion to steal. Was he such a person? Had the strange impulse spurred him to take the ring? Was that all it had been?

If so, how sad that such a paltry act could have wreaked such havoc.

She ran to the hall and down the servants' stairs, desperate to be outside before he chased after her. He couldn't follow without his clothes, would have to dress before proceeding, so she had many minutes as a head start, but where—precisely—was she to go?

Nicholas left the mews and stomped toward the mansion, glad to be home and to have escaped Lydia's clutches.

Despite his plans with Suzette, Lydia had forced him

to escort her to the country. He'd accompanied her against his will, not giving two hoots about Rebecca or where the jilted girl might be hiding.

The instant Lydia's attention had been diverted, he'd sneaked away. He wasn't her slave, and he wouldn't be treated like one. Lydia had to learn that she could only push him so far. His courtesy had been exhausted, and fiancée or no, she would not control him.

He had his own problems—problems that were much more dire and pressing than Lydia and her annoying sister. Suzette had to be fuming, and he had to put out that fire, but first, he had to deal with his new sister-in-law.

The entire trip to Lydia's house, she'd harangued about Ellen and Alex. Typically, Nicholas would have ignored her, but for the fact that a name kept creeping into her rant: James Drake. Ellen Drake's brother.

Lydia had mentioned him once previously, but Nicholas had disregarded her comments, not comprehending the man's relevance. But Nicholas was swiftly growing uneasy.

After so much time, he'd forgotten about James Drake, but his suddenly being repeatedly thrust at Nicholas was like having a ghost walk over his grave.

He remembered the peculiar conversation he'd had with Lydia, when she'd quizzed him about earlier sins and had subtly threatened him over prior indiscretions.

As he was discovering, nothing was an accident with her, so there had to be a reason she'd alluded to his past. She could be a vindictive, spiteful shrew, and he couldn't let her ascertain his connection to James Drake. She might use the information as an excuse to withhold funds or—God forbid!—to decline to marry him, at all, and he couldn't risk such a calamity.

He was through the rear gate when, to his great astonishment, Ellen Drake rushed onto the verandah and careened across the yard, as if the hounds of hell were on her heels. What could have occurred? Alex was renowned for his sexual prowess, so her wedding night couldn't have been that bad!

She was so distraught that she nearly bumped into him. She was a fright, crying and mumbling, and she lurched to a halt.

"Oh . . . oh . . . Mr. Marshall. I didn't see you standing there."

"I'm your brother now, Ellen. You must call me Nicholas."

"Yes, yes . . . of course." She was confused and alarmed, and she continually glanced over her shoulder, as if she anticipated pursuit at any moment.

"What is it, dear? What's happened?"

She looked beyond the gate to his fast, sporty gig, the horse still hitched and not overly tired.

"Is that your carriage?" she inquired.

"Yes."

"Would you mind terribly if I imposed on you by asking for a ride?"

"Certainly, Ellen. We're family." He was teeming with curiosity. What was amiss? "What's mine is yours. Where is it you wish to go?"

"I need to speak with my brother immediately. I must visit an address down by the docks."

"Your brother?" His heart plummeted to his shoes. The criminal was supposed to be in Australia! What was he doing in England? "I didn't realize you had relatives in the city."

"He's lived in London for over a year."

Gad! Why hadn't he been apprised? What good was the law if they couldn't keep a dangerous felon from slipping in? "The docks, you say? It's not the best neighborhood."

"I know. It's quite a distance, too, but it's dreadfully important."

"Well, it must be vital." He took her arm and led her to the alley. "You're in a fine fettle. Why don't we get going, and you can tell me all about it on the way."

He helped her up, then climbed in beside her. As he did, he peeked at the house, and he was relieved to note that no one appeared to have seen her exit. He clicked the reins, and in a few seconds they were off.

Alex listened to Ellen's retreating footsteps, and he hammered his fist several more times, though she'd fled and wouldn't have answered even if she'd been there.

The only thing the pounding accomplished was to set his head spinning. His hangover roared to life with a vengeance, and he tottered to his dressing chamber and began yanking on his trousers.

He wasn't about to chase after her wearing just a towel around his privy parts. She'd already goaded him into behaving like a deranged lunatic on too many occasions, so he wasn't about to parade down the halls with his bare arse displayed for his employees.

He'd catch up with her soon. After all, how far could a woman travel on foot? He'd be on horseback, so he'd have no difficulty in overtaking her, and after she ran for a bit, perhaps she'd calm and return on her own. She had no money, so where did she assume she could go?

Her sole item of any value was the ring, which she

could sell for cash if she had an inkling as to how to locate a villain who'd buy it. Which she didn't.

He cursed with disgust. That bloody ring! Hadn't it caused enough trouble? Enough misery? Why hadn't he disposed of it as he'd always planned? What had he been thinking, having it lying about where anyone could stumble upon it?

Obviously, he hadn't been *thinking*. That was the problem.

"What a mess!" he grumbled.

He tugged on his jacket, then marched toward the stairs, calling for his horse to be saddled.

❧ 20 ❧

"Where are we?"

"Does it matter?"

"You said you'd take me to my brother."

"I lied."

Ellen tugged at the rope that bound her wrists, but she was tightly secured. She wasn't sure when Nicholas had tied her, but it had to have been shortly after he'd clouted her on the head. Once she'd realized they weren't proceeding to the docks but were racing out of town in the opposite direction, she'd begun to struggle, and she'd been stunned to learn that though he often looked and acted like a bumbling idiot, he was very, very strong.

She hadn't had a chance.

Up until that moment in her life, she'd never been hit, not so much as a swat on the bottom as a toddler, so she hadn't comprehended how painful a blow could be, or how thoroughly it could rattle the senses.

She'd threatened to jump out of the gig, and she recalled dangling a foot over the side, the highway flitting past below. They'd been speeding through the deserted countryside, so he was able to perpetrate his violence without fear of discovery. He'd jerked her away from the edge of the vehicle, had punched her hard enough that she saw stars, and next she knew, she'd awakened in a daze, trussed like a Christmas goose, and huddled in a ball at his feet.

She tried to figure out how long it had been since she'd exited the house, how far they were from London. Had anyone seen her leave the mansion or climb in the gig? She didn't think so.

Alex was aware that she'd run off, but he likely assumed she was having a tantrum and would come back after she cooled down. If she failed to return, he probably wouldn't even search. Why would he? They'd done naught but fight. No doubt, he was glad she'd gone.

She wouldn't be missed, and at the notion of how alone she was, how alone she'd always been, tears flooded her eyes. She'd lived for twenty-eight years and had made such a negligible mark that she might as well have been invisible.

The wind rushed around her, and as she hunkered down, it dawned on her that the ring—her precious evidence of James's innocence—wasn't in her hand. Had she dropped it? Had it plummeted onto the road when Nicholas had struck her? Had he taken it?

As the frantic questions swirled by, they slowed to travel down a narrow lane that ended at a country cottage. There was no one to greet them, not even a caretaker, and Nicholas leapt out to help her down, but she recoiled.

"Where are we?" she repeated.

"Can't you guess?" He gestured around the quiet yard. "We're at Alex's love nest. He brings his paramours here when he's eager for a lengthy tryst. He enjoys the privacy." He chuckled, but it was more like a witch's cackle. "It's the perfect spot for what I have in mind."

The hairs stood up on her neck. "What have you *in mind?*"

"I won't spoil the surprise by telling you."

He reached out to her, and when she declined his assistance, he grew irate. As if she were a sack of flour, he hauled her to the ground. It was quite a distance, and with her wrists shackled, she couldn't break the fall. The impact knocked the breath out of her, and she cried out with agony and alarm.

What was the matter with him? Why was he doing this?

Previously, she'd spoken with him on a few brief occasions, but it was sufficient to judge his character as polite, bored, and lazy. After he'd become engaged to Lydia, she'd added other traits to the list—fortune hunter and dunce—but she'd never pegged him as an aggressive individual, nor had there been stories about his being crazed.

He leaned over her, evincing no sympathy over the undignified tumble.

"You can walk inside," he said, "on your own two feet, or I can drag you. The choice is yours."

After numerous attempts to get her lungs working, she replied, "I'll walk."

He yanked her up, then guided her toward the cottage. As the threshold loomed, she was overcome by a powerful impression that if she went inside, she'd never come out. Trying to delay, she dug in her heels, but she couldn't halt their forward progress.

She screamed, but he merely laughed.

"Scream all you like. No one can hear. That's why Alex bought the property. His lovers can shriek or shout or beg, and there are no neighbors to complain."

"Alex is guilty of many sins, but he's never stooped to kidnapping."

"Not kidnapping, no. Not the sainted Alex Marshall, but as you mentioned, he's committed his share of sins. You wouldn't believe how many women he's entertained here, and what he's done with some of them. He's not called the *rogue* of London for nothing."

He pushed her, and she stumbled through the door and into a spacious parlor. The place was hedonistic, with red rugs and drapes, cushy sofas and chairs, and there were large pillows scattered on the floor as though a person could plop down just anywhere and get comfortable.

Her unease spiraled as she wondered if both brothers weren't mad.

What sort of man owned such an indecent abode? And what sort of fellow would want his new sister-in-law to see it? Why torment her with such disturbing information? She was barely acquainted with Nicholas. From where had his animosity sprung? Why was he so rabid?

"Why are we here?" she inquired.

"All in good time."

"I demand to know!"

"I liked you better when you were silent, so shut up, or I'll hit you again."

He had a vicious gleam in his eye, and she was terrified about what his next act would be. Torture? Murder? Any insane deed seemed imminent, and she refused to follow along like a lamb to the slaughter.

She flung herself at him, her entire bodily weight smacking into him. He hadn't been expecting any resistance, so he didn't block her or move out of the way. Her head crunched into his cheekbone, the collision cracking his jaws together so hard that he might have broken a tooth.

Howling and clutching at his injury, he lurched away. There was a deep gash, and blood dripped down, staining his white shirt. "You bitch! You bitch!"

With her hands tied, she wasn't capable of more. The lunge had thrown her off balance, and she'd collapsed to the floor. In her imagination, she pictured herself jumping up, beating him to a pulp, and running out, but the reality was that her skirt was tangled around her legs, and she had no leverage, so it was impossible to regain any momentum or scurry away.

He was on her immediately, his heavy torso pressing into her. His phallus was aroused from their skirmishing, and with sickening force, she realized what he intended.

Rape! Of all things!

Why would he? What was he hoping to achieve? Did he hate Alex? Did he hate her? She couldn't fathom how they'd garnered such enmity, and she had no idea how to stop him. How could one reason with a lunatic?

"Get off me!" she hissed, striving to sound tough and brave.

"I was simply going to talk to you," he claimed, "but I've changed my mind. I've decided to have some fun before we chat. Perhaps with the appropriate coaxing, you'll tell me what I wish to know."

"I'll tell you now. Ask me."

"No. It will be more amusing if I pry your responses out of you."

He scooped her to her feet, his fury giving him the strength of ten men, and he grabbed her around the waist and towed her toward the stairs.

"What is it you want from me?" She was wrestling with all her might but couldn't deter him.

"You're being awfully stupid. I shouldn't have to spell it out."

She blustered, "You'd better release me."

"Not bloody likely."

"You're in so much trouble already. How will you explain your shirt? Your face?"

"I won't have to explain. I *never* have to explain."

"Alex will kill you when he finds out what you've done to me."

"Alex will never know."

They arrived at the top of the stairs, and he lugged her down the corridor. As they went, she caught fleeting glimpses of the madhouse's decadent salons. Would she come out alive? Unless she could escape—and fast!—the answer was certainly *no*. He couldn't permit her to leave, for he couldn't risk that she would notify Alex.

He halted at the last room and pulled her inside; then he hauled her to the bed and heaved her onto the mattress. She made another feeble attempt to flee, but she was winded and battered, so her effort was as unsuccessful as the others had been.

Before she could prevent it, her wrists were trussed to the bedposts. She kicked at him, not able to inflict any damage, and she was rewarded by having her ankles fettered, too. In a thrice, she was stretched wide, and she shuddered with dread, as he reveled in her predicament.

"I always thought you were very pretty, Ellen."

Such a bizarre comment! Such a bizarre man! "Did you?"

"I'm curious as to what you saw in Alex."

"In Alex?"

"Yes. If you were so hot to be debauched, why turn to him? Why not me?"

Was that what this was about? Was he jealous of Alex?

He was growing more peculiar by the second.

"Alex was kind to me."

"Alex? Kind? How hilarious!" He waved toward a divan that was positioned in front of the hearth. "He really has a tawdry side to his personality, but I'd say he hid it from you rather well."

"I never noticed any bad conduct," she staunchly declared.

"If you'd chosen me instead of Alex, no scandal would have occurred. I know how to be discreet about my mistresses."

"*You* have mistresses?"

"Of course, and I'm adept at managing them. I especially don't philander with the hired help while my fiancée is down the hall. I'm smarter than that."

She couldn't argue the point. She and Alex had chased disaster with a reckless abandon, and when calamity had crashed down, she'd had no one to blame but herself.

"Love makes people behave in strange ways," she insisted.

"Love? You're assuming Alex *loves* you? My God, but you're naïve."

He left her and proceeded to a dresser, retrieved an object from the drawer, then displayed it for her.

It was a knife! A huge, shiny knife with a ferocious blade! It looked very sharp. Beads of perspiration popped out all over her body.

He approached and rested the cool metal against her neck, letting her feel it on her skin, letting her fear escalate.

"You're afraid," he casually remarked. "Good."

"Yes, I'm afraid," she admitted. "Whatever it is you're planning, whatever you want, just ask for it, and I'll give it to you. You don't have to . . . to . . ."

"I know I don't," he interrupted. "What happens next is up to you. Tell me about your brother and about this ring." He showed her that he'd slipped it onto his finger. "You can invent any story you like, or you can be truthful. If you're candid, I will rape you, then I'll take you home, and this morning's affair will remain our little secret."

As if her ravagement would be a massive burden, he sighed; then he continued. "However, if you're lying, I'll rape you, then I'll kill you. Very slowly. I'll leave you bound to the bed, and I'll send an anonymous note to the local magistrate so he can locate your corpse. I'll also advise him that a reliable witness—who's much too timid to come forward—saw Alex bring you here but depart without you."

Alex would be charged with the crime! She couldn't allow such an atrocity to transpire. Alex had done nothing! Nothing! If she was found dead in his private haven, he'd never be able to account for the circumstances.

"No one will believe that Alex murdered me."

"Why wouldn't they? The servants can all testify that the two of you fight constantly. You're a shrew—everyone at the house agrees. Why wouldn't he wish to be shed of you?"

"He loves me!" she contended, but if Nicholas was watching for prevarication, that was definitely a colossal falsehood. "He'll search. He'll find out."

"I know Alex extremely well. He won't bother to hunt for you, so don't get your hopes up." Lost in contemplation, he gazed out the window; then he murmured, "Yes, this is for the best. I should have done something similar years ago. I'll be the earl, and I'll have all the money. I won't need to marry Lydia."

"Alex is your brother!"

"A minor technicality, I assure you." He held up his hand. "Now, about this ring . . ."

"I stumbled on it in Alex's dresser. We quarreled."

"What is its significance to you?"

"A decade ago, it was stolen at a party in Surrey. My brother, James, was convicted of the crime, but he was innocent."

"How can you be certain it's the same ring?"

"A drawing of it was circulated. And the countess who owned it had her initials carved in the band."

He tugged it off and read the tiny letters. "So they are. When did your brother return to England?"

"At least a year ago. I'm not positive of the exact date."

"Where does he live?"

"I haven't a clue."

He scowled and leveled the knife, and he poked the blade under the skin at her nape. It stung and bled. "Remember: You can't lie."

"I'm not." She was trembling so violently that if she hadn't been secured to the bed, she might have shaken herself off the mattress. "I send him messages at the tavern I told you about. They're delivered to him, but I don't know how; then he contacts me with a reply."

He studied her, gauging credibility, and apparently, he was convinced of her veracity. "When you questioned Alex about the ring, what was his response?"

"He had no explanation."

"Ellen!" he warned.

"I swear it! He simply demanded that I give it to him, but he didn't offer any excuse as to why he had it, though the reason is obvious."

"It is?"

"He must have been the thief."

"So loyal, so faithful. So naïve." He tossed the knife on the floor. "I took it."

"You?"

"Yes."

"But why?"

"Why would you suppose? I needed some money. I received a pretty penny for it, too, though for the life of me, I can't figure out how Alex came to be in possession of it. Let's finish this, shall we?" He lay down, his weight crushing her, and he nudged a knee between her thighs, but she couldn't push him away.

"You let them blame my brother! You ruined my family!"

"Yes, I did," he concurred. "I was sorry about the uproar. I hadn't any idea there'd be such a ruckus."

"You killed my father!" she wailed.

"Don't be absurd. If your father perished, it was none of my doing."

"You killed him!" She started screaming and grappling in earnest.

"Shut up!" he ordered.

"I hate you! I curse you to hell for all eternity."

He slapped her, but she wouldn't be silent. She would bellow and chastise to the very end.

He clasped her chin and kissed her, his foul, deceitful tongue sliding into her mouth, and she bit down as hard as she could. Desperate to pull away, he reared back, and she felt skin tear, felt blood spurting. He reached inside her dress and pinched her nipple, squeezing and squeezing until she couldn't tolerate the pain, and she let go.

He stared her down, his malice rolling off him in waves, and he put his fingers on her throat, cutting off her air, making her squirm with anxiety.

"I like it when you resist," he said. "Let's see how tough you really are."

"Crazed bastard!" she hurled.

He gripped her dress and ripped it down the front, baring her to her navel. At the sight of her exposed breasts, he grinned evilly; then he punched her. She was rapidly losing consciousness, and soon she'd be incoherent, and she couldn't imagine what would happen then. Of course, if he murdered her while she was blacked out, maybe it would be for the best.

"Move away from her!" a male voice commanded. "Now!"

In her confused state, several seconds passed before she grasped that someone else had spoken. He'd entered without their noticing, and as Nicholas clutched his fist to dispense another blow, the man threatened, "My pistol is loaded and cocked. If you strike her again, the next breath you take will be your last."

They both froze, the words washing over them, invading the mysterious place of brutality and terror that they occupied.

She glanced to the side, wondering if he were an apparition, if she were hallucinating, but no . . . He'd truly arrived, though through the bright sunlight cascading in the window it was difficult to determine who it was. He took a step toward them, then another, his form gradually taking shape.

"Alex!"

She careened between puzzlement and incredulity. She'd been certain she'd never see him again, so her mind couldn't wrap itself around his opportune appearance. Yet he was actually standing there. He was holding a pistol, and it was pointed at Nicholas.

"Alex?" Nicholas said, too, but his exclamation was imbued with panic. He leapt away from her and off the bed.

"Are you all right, Ellen?" Alex queried without looking at her, his focus on his brother.

"He's hit me, but he hasn't had a chance to do any worse."

Nicholas was nervous and embarrassed and not nearly so brave as he'd been. The bully had vanished, and he switched to being the bumbling younger sibling.

"Alex," he sneered, "you wouldn't believe what a little slattern you've married. I ran into her out in the mews, and she was all over me. She told me she'd heard about this cottage, and she begged me to show it to her. She wouldn't let me refuse."

"That's a lie!" She was crying, struggling to loose the restraints. Surely Alex wouldn't presume her capable of such treachery! "I never did any such thing. I merely requested a ride in his gig, and he—"

"Hush!" Alex said. "When she left with you, Nick, I was watching from an upstairs window."

"Well"—Nicholas shifted with discomfort—"matters didn't get cooking until we were out of the city. She couldn't keep her hands off me."

"Really?" Alex mused with a deadly calm.

"Oh yes," Nicholas responded. "It's rather beneficial that I found out about her, wouldn't you agree? Saves you a lot of bother at the divorce and all that. I can be a witness as to her low character."

"How was your face injured?"

"I bumped into the door."

"And you tied her up because . . . ?"

"She insisted she likes it rough. You lucky dog. Must have been quite a wedding night, eh?"

Alex's expression was shielded. There was an awkward pause, both brothers glaring; then Alex raised his pistol and walloped Nicholas alongside the head. Nicholas lurched to the side, and Alex whacked him again, even harder. Nicholas fell to the floor, and Alex kicked him in the stomach. With the force of the impact, Nicholas's body lifted, his air rushing out in a loud whoosh, and he huddled on the rug, wheezing and heaving.

Alex stepped over him, retrieved a blanket, and draped it over her; then he freed her from her bindings. The instant the ropes dropped away, she curled up into a ball, her back to him, as she quietly wept. He hovered closer, as if he might cradle her in his arms, and with every fiber of her being she wished he would, but he didn't know how to cross the bridge that separated them. Or perhaps he couldn't bear to hold her. Perhaps he was sickened by seeing her stripped and at Nicholas's mercy.

In her distraught condition, his declining to touch her

seemed the most horrid moment of all, as if she'd relinquished everything precious.

"He'll never hurt you again," he murmured. "I swear it to you."

"Thank you."

"I'll have you out of here in a minute."

"Just do what you have to do." She was too ashamed to look at him, and she gazed at the far wall. Although none of the ordeal had been her fault, she felt to blame, as if some misbehavior had brought on the assault. "Can you . . . can you take him away? Please?"

"Yes. You rest. I'll return shortly. Will you be all right alone?"

"I'm fine," she asserted.

With the nightmare ended, she was shivering with shock, but she hid her anguish so that he wouldn't observe it, so that he wouldn't be obliged to offer solace that she was positive he'd find distasteful.

He spun away, and she yearned to shout, *Don't go! Don't leave me!* but she swallowed down any silly, weak words he wouldn't want to hear.

"Get up!" he snarled to Nicholas, and she listened as he nudged Nicholas with his boot.

"Bugger off!" Nicholas was huffing and spitting, and trying to catch his breath.

"You kidnapped my wife, you were about to rape her, and you have the audacity to disrespect me?"

"She's a whore," Nicholas maintained. "She asked for it."

"You know, Nick, the more I learn about you, the more inclined I am to think that the rumors about your parentage are true." Alex delivered another blow, though with his fist or his gun she couldn't tell, and he repeated, "Now, get up, and walk out like a man—instead of slithering out like the snake you are."

There was some scuffling and shuffling; then Nicholas stood, and he grumbled, "I hate you. I've always hated you."

"The truth finally comes out," Alex retorted.

"Mother said I should have been the earl, that I would have been better at it than you."

"I have no doubt that our dear mama felt that way. She loved you best, didn't she? She pampered you and cosseted you, lied for you and covered for you. Were you aware that she was called the Harlot of the *Ton?*"

"Be silent!"

"I wonder which of her lovers was your father?"

At the nasty exchange, Ellen gasped. What odious, grim comments! How long had their enmity festered? What part had she played in luring it to the surface?

Suddenly Alex ordered, "Put it down, you deranged fool! Haven't you caused enough trouble?"

At the strange remark she rolled over, and she was astonished to see that Nicholas had grabbed the knife and was wielding it with malicious intent.

"I should have killed you years ago," he threatened.

"Why haven't you tried?" Alex inquired. "Could it be cowardice?"

At the taunt Nicholas attacked so fast that Ellen didn't have time to react. Nor did Alex. The knife was plunged into his abdomen, and as Nicholas stumbled away, the handle was sticking out, blood oozing around it, and Alex casually yanked it out.

He seemed unconcerned, as if he'd expected nothing

more from his recalcitrant sibling. Nicholas was stunned, as Ellen frantically mumbled, "Oh my God . . . oh my God . . ."

"You idiot," Alex snapped, as he glanced down at the wound. "You've ruined a perfectly good shirt."

He aimed his pistol and fired at point-blank range. There was a loud bang, plenty of smoke, and Nicholas dropped like a stone.

～ 21 ～

Alex trudged up the stairs to the third floor of the hotel. He supposed he could have had the lawyers handle the conclusion, could have stayed at home and waited to be apprised when it was over, but that had seemed the cowardly route. This was one occasion when he had to act like a man, when he had to take control and clean up the mess he'd made.

His body ached from the mild physical exertion of climbing, and he fretted that he might never return to his prior vigor. He was so pathetically enfeebled, yet for the next few minutes he had to shield any infirmity.

As he reached the top step, he leaned against the wall, catching his breath, commanding his shaking legs to do their job and keep him on his feet. He was perspiring, his heart pounding, and he'd love to find a cushy sofa and lie down.

He'd been stabbed by his brother and had lived to tell about it, but over the past weeks there had been many moments when he wished he'd died. He'd always been a healthy person, had never had so much as a broken bone, so he hadn't realized that recovery could be so tedious. Or so painful.

A footman tromped after him, and from the man's concerned assessment it was obvious he was about to remark on Alex's dismal state, to offer assistance as if Alex were an ailing grandfather, so he pushed himself upright and walked on.

Of all the ignominies Nicholas's insanity had generated, Alex most hated being viewed as an invalid by his staff. During his recuperation, they'd been kind and solicitous, but he loathed their pitying glances, their veiled whispers about good and bad blood, about Cain and Abel. He yearned to forget the whole sordid episode.

When he'd espied Nick slinking off with Ellen, he'd suffered the worst sensation of disaster, so he'd gone after her. But he hadn't gone alone. He'd had two men travel with him, and the split-second decision had saved his sorry hide. The men were loyal servants, and they'd been composed throughout the crisis. They'd restrained Nick, had gotten both brothers medical care, and had brought in women to tend Ellen.

He'd been relieved to have their help, but by the time Nick had been taken away in chains—wounded but alive and complaining—too many people had observed the debacle. It was impossible to conceal the facts. The gossip mills were spinning at a frenzied pace.

He arrived at the door and knocked. He'd had a note delivered, requesting the appointment, so he was expected, and he hoped to resolve the matter quickly and be on his way. He'd never been adept at farewells, and this one would be the most difficult of all, but it had to be done and done as graciously as he could manage it.

He prayed that he could stumble through it without

making a fool of himself or blubbering like a babe. Lately, he'd been so accursedly sentimental. The least comment or memory would have him moping in an insidious depression for hours, and for once, he refused to be maudlin.

He'd been born and bred to obligation, and on this day of all days he'd do what he ought, would hold his head high and carry out his responsibilities.

The maid showed him into the outer parlor, then departed. There were two chairs, a table in between. No tea tray was provided as courtesy demanded, but he ignored the snub. This wasn't a social call, and there was no reason to pretend the meeting was anything but the final installment of an awkward and uncomfortable business transaction.

"Hello, Ellen." He sat across from her, making an extreme effort not to display any frailty.

"Alex," she replied coolly.

As if she was in mourning, she was dressed in black. She appeared frozen, icy as a marble statue, and so brittle that the slightest noise might crack her into tiny pieces.

Her pretty face, formerly so animated and alluring, had no expression whatsoever. Previously, he'd felt so close to her that he could read her mind, but no longer. He couldn't begin to guess what she thought.

After so much had occurred, was she glad he'd come? Was she weary? Was she angry? If she was experiencing any heightened emotion, he couldn't discern what it might be.

"How have you been?" he queried.

"Fine."

"I trust your accommodations have been suitable?"

"Certainly."

He halted, and a cumbersome silence festered, but he couldn't initiate any small talk. He hadn't seen her since the terrible morning in the country, and it was evident that she wasn't *fine*. She'd lost weight and might have been ill, but he had no idea how to probe for details that she would likely consider to be none of his affair.

Immediately after Nick's mayhem was ended, Alex had been too impaired for rationale reflection, and by the time he'd been sufficiently coherent to worry, she'd been ensconced at the hotel. As soon as his condition had improved, he'd deliberated over the wisdom of sending her a letter, had started and discarded a dozen, but he'd been too ashamed to contact her.

He might have begged her to come home, but he hadn't. If she'd wanted to be residing with him, she would have been—there was nothing keeping her away. Or he might have ordered her to return, but it was clear she preferred the sterile surroundings of a public inn, and he couldn't blame her.

When he'd created his private sanctuary for his mistresses, he'd never contemplated how reprehensible someone of a more decent character might find such a dwelling. It was horrid enough that she'd been violently whisked to the tawdry abode, but after what Nick had done to her there, Alex didn't feel he was in any position to direct her to do anything.

She hadn't wanted to marry him, but he was pompous and vain, and he never let anyone tell him *no*. When she'd spurned his proposal, his enormous pride had been dented, so he'd driven her to consent, but look where his coercion had landed her!

If he'd had a thousand years to atone, he never could.

"And how are you?" she asked, but she didn't seem genuinely curious.

"I've been better."

"I'm sure you have been."

The volley was an opening where she might have inquired as to his injuries, as to his recovery. When no further questions were forthcoming, he tamped down his hurt that she was so uninterested.

After all that had transpired, he couldn't suppose that any fondness remained, and if he'd been harboring some ludicrous, misguided hope that she still cared, he had to bury it. Nothing was to be gained by wishful thinking, by lamenting over what might have been.

They stared, a multitude of comments floating through the air, but neither of them could grab hold and utter one aloud.

"I have some papers with me," he murmured.

"Have you?"

He couldn't believe how hard it was to refer to them. He'd rehearsed what he would say, but none of his preparation had equipped him for how awful it would be, for how desperately he wouldn't want to proceed.

Yet he wouldn't humiliate himself by pleading for a second chance. He didn't deserve one, and if he could convince her to try again, he'd only fail her. It simply wasn't in his nature to behave as he should. He was a cad and a scoundrel—as she had learned to her peril.

"You'll need to sign your name in a few places." He dug in his satchel. "My solicitor, Mr. Thumberton, has marked the appropriate spots."

"That makes it easy, doesn't it? Everything nice and tidy."

"Yes."

He retrieved the documents and laid them on the table, then he searched for pen and ink, but he hadn't brought them, and he hid his irritation. Anymore, he was such a scatterbrain.

"I don't seem to have a pen," he lamely mentioned.

"I have one we can use."

"Oh. Perfect."

Just bloody perfect! he mused, incredibly irked that she was so unruffled. Would it have killed her to be fretting? To be nervous or hesitant?

She went across the room to fetch the required items, then she scrawled her signature wherever indicated, not bothering to read the terms, and his annoyance grew.

They were terminating their marriage. They were separating forever. After he left her suite, they'd never see each other again, yet she was acting so nonchalant that she might have been checking her maid's shopping list.

He forced down his aggravation. If she could be apathetic, so could he. If she could be indifferent, so could he. He'd never really wanted to marry—not her or anybody. He should be shouting in the streets that the wretched liaison could be severed so painlessly.

"It will take several months—perhaps more—for the annulment to be completed."

She studied him as if he were a stranger, as if he were expounding in a foreign language. "Are you positive this is what we should do?"

"Well . . . yes . . ." he stammered. "Thumberton says it's the best way."

"We wouldn't want to argue with Mr. Thumberton, would we?"

"He claims a divorce would be so messy." She was

scowling, though he couldn't figure out why. "Don't you agree?"

"Your attorney is the expert. Why wouldn't we defer to him?" He detected a hint of sarcasm in her words, but her face was impassive.

"I've purchased a house for you in Surrey."

"Marvelous."

"You can move in whenever you're ready. If you correspond with my secretary, he'll see to everything."

"I'm certain he's a very competent fellow."

There was that sarcasm again. Didn't she want a house? Didn't she want to be settled? If she was opposed to the plan, why didn't she speak up? "And I've arranged a trust—with Thumberton as the trustee."

"Thank you."

"You'll never want for anything." His voice shook with a fervor he hadn't intended, but he couldn't bear to imagine her struggling. The notion tormented him.

Her perplexing, impartial appraisal swept over him. "You don't have to, you know," she eventually said. "I'm fully capable of employment. If you'd give me a reference, I could find a job that would—"

"Ellen . . ." he scolded.

"What?"

"You're not working, and that's final."

She tipped her head in acknowledgment. "As you wish."

"I've taken steps to help your brother."

"I appreciate it."

"I've had the ring melted down, and I've sold the gems. He can have the money."

She shrugged. "It's a paltry gesture."

"I'll also transfer title to a farm called New Haven.

It belongs—belonged—to my ... my brother. It's an excellent property, with a steady income, so he'll be able to support himself."

"Any action is pointless if he's still a felon."

"I understand that, so I'll utilize my influence to have the charges expunged."

"I hope you succeed."

He sighed. Not even the discussion of her dear sibling affected her. She was so cold, so detached. What would it take to pierce the wall she'd erected to keep him at bay? Unfortunately, there was probably nothing he could do.

"You once confided that he's in England."

"Yes."

"He and I should converse about these matters. How might I contact him?"

She grabbed a piece of paper and scribbled the name of a tavern. "I always sent letters to him at this establishment, but he's vanished."

"Has something happened to him?"

"I haven't the foggiest."

At the admission she was unusually calm, while he had to stifle a shudder of dread. Mr. Drake could have been killed by a villain, conscripted into the navy, or caught by the law. He might already be hanged, and if he had been, it would be another sin the Marshall family had perpetrated upon her.

"I'll investigate," he offered.

"I'd be very grateful."

"I'll visit again, to let you know what I learn."

At the prospect he felt a flutter of excitement, but instantly she snuffed it out. "You needn't trouble yourself. I realize how busy you are. Your lawyer can write to me."

So ... she wasn't interested in an enduring connection. It was a bitter tonic to swallow, but he couldn't blame her for desiring a clean split. What purpose would be served by fraternization? Why torture himself? They were never meant to be together, and he had to remember that fact and come to grips with how their separate futures would evolve.

Another awkward silence ensued; then she said, "Before you go"—Gad! Was she so eager to be rid of him?—"might I ask you a question?"

"Yes. Anything."

"Why was the ring in your dresser?"

"My mother gave it to me, when she was in her final decline. She begged me to keep it and conceal it, though she never told me why."

"You didn't inquire?"

"She was a very theatrical female, so I assumed it might be any silly reason. She was mortally ill, so I didn't press. I threw it in a drawer and never thought about it again."

"You weren't aware of what it indicated?"

"No," he truthfully replied. "My mother doted on my brother—to excess. She spoiled him horridly, and I'm guessing she suspected his crime, that she covered it up for him."

"I see."

After that, there wasn't any other topic worth review. They stared and stared, an impossible gulf dividing them.

It was time to exit, and he recognized that he should rise and depart, but there were so many things he should explain, so many apologies to make, that he couldn't begin. He could talk to infinity and not adequately convey his sentiments.

He craved a different ending and yearned to have rendered a conclusion that didn't seem so wrong.

"This is farewell, then."

"Yes, it is."

"If you ever need anything, if there's ever anything I can—"

"I won't ever need anything from you," she interrupted.

If he'd had any doubts as to her opinion of him, they'd definitely been clarified, yet he hated to go on such a sour note. Once prior, he'd loved her so desperately, and he was certain she'd harbored some fondness for him, as well. Where had it all gone?

"Ellen . . . I'm sorry for . . ." he tried to start, but she leapt from her chair and went to the window, her back to him, her fingers fiddling with the drapes as she peered outside.

"Leave it be, Alex."

"But I want you to know that I—"

"Alex! Please! You're embarrassing me."

He stood and reached out, wanting to touch her, or that she would turn around. He was anxious to gaze into her beautiful blue eyes, to imprint every detail in his memory so he'd never forget, but she ignored him.

He dawdled as long as he dared; then he mumbled, "Good-bye."

"Good-bye," she answered.

His heart breaking, his world in disarray, he tarried another second; then he spun and left.

Ellen listened as he hobbled out the door, as his strides marched him down the hall and away from her. He was limping, his heels clicking in an odd cadence as the sound faded. He'd looked wretched—thin and pale and lost—and she could tell he was in pain, that his wound continued to plague him.

Eventually, he appeared on the street, a burly footman dogging his heels. He was too frail to climb into his carriage on his own, and with an eerie detachment she spied on him as his coachmen jumped to assist. Ultimately, the coach was prepared, and with a crack of the whip, the horses pulled him away forever.

She watched until he was out of sight, vehemently concentrating as if—through the force of her attention—she could persuade him to change his mind.

How could he abandon her? How could he walk away?

For weeks, she'd languished at the hotel, too uncomfortable with her shaky status as his unwanted bride, to show up on his stoop. Instead, she waited and waited, positive that he'd send for her as soon as he was able.

But he never had.

She'd ached to be at the mansion, but his staff had made it clear that her aid was neither wanted nor needed. She'd written several letters to him but had received courteous responses from the housekeeper, advising her of his improving condition.

Then, without any warning, his attorney had delivered notification that Alex was seeking an annulment. Alex hadn't asked her opinion, hadn't endeavored to learn what *she* might select. He'd simply forged ahead, which was so typical of him, and exactly what she'd expect from one as impervious as he.

But how could he cast her aside?

She pondered the property he'd bought her in the country, the quiet years without him. What sort of life would that be? How could he presume she would choose to be so alone?

Their relationship had never had a chance. They'd never had the opportunity to determine if they could have built a lasting foundation, and it was wrenching to admit that he didn't care to find out if they could have had a future.

Didn't he recall how fond they'd been of each other? Didn't he recollect how much passion and joy they'd shared? He'd claimed he loved her. Where had his affection gone? How could it have vanished so swiftly and so completely?

"Oh, Alex," she murmured, "how could you forsake me?"

She lingered at the window until her eyes were tired and her knees weak; then she went to the wardrobe and began packing her bag.

He'd said that her house was ready, and she couldn't conceive of a single reason to delay.

~ 22 ~

"Wait here for me." Rebecca gestured to a chair.

"I hate having you speak with Stanton alone," James complained.

"He doesn't bite."

"Not yet."

She chuckled. Where she was concerned, James fussed over the littlest thing. "Don't worry. I'll be fine."

"You can't be certain how he'll react."

"He's my cousin, James. Not some ogre." She kissed him, making him reach for her. "This will take but a second."

"I'll give you five minutes. Then I'm coming to fetch you—whether you're ready to go or not. I won't dawdle in this bastard's house."

"I understand."

"You couldn't possibly."

"Relax, would you?" She rested her palm on his cheek, knowing she could calm him, that she could get her way. There was one fact she'd learned without reservation:

He was putty in her hands, and he would do whatever she asked.

"Hurry" was his reply, and he smiled.

She smiled, too, and walked down the hall to the library. She'd entered the mansion without knocking, so her presence hadn't been announced, and she'd have the advantage of surprise. It was Tuesday, and it was two o'clock, so Alex would be at his desk and working on his business papers. He had many bad habits, but he was diligent about his estates and his intricate finances.

With a wink at her handsome husband, she opened the door and waltzed in. Alex was frowning over a large stack of bills, and not bothering to glance up, he said, "Jenkins, leave the tray on the table, then don't interrupt me again."

"It isn't Jenkins."

At hearing a female voice, the first word out of his mouth was "Ellen?"

He leapt up so quickly that his chair toppled over. On seeing that it wasn't Ellen but only herself, his joy faded, and he scowled, once more.

"So you're still lusting after Ellen, are you?" she chided. "Apparently, nothing changed while I was away."

"Rebecca? Where the devil have you been?"

"Why don't you just marry the poor woman, as you promised you would, and put yourself out of this misery?"

He rounded the desk and approached. "We've been frantic. Are you all right?"

"Why wouldn't I be?"

"Lydia has been beside herself."

"Oh, I'm sure she has been." She oozed sarcasm. Of all the eventualities that might have occurred while she was away, none of them would have involved Lydia fretting over Rebecca's plight.

"She's had people searching high and low," he contended.

"I doubt it," she responded. "Listen, I've constantly been apprised that I'm an heiress, that I have a substantial inheritance from my father. It should be around thirty thousand pounds."

"That's true."

"I want it, but I'll have to pry it away from my sister. I need you to help me wrest it from her." She arched a brow. "You owe me a favor."

"Of course I'll assist you. But you have to wed before you can have the money."

"I know." She grinned, so thrilled to be having the conversation, to be married but not to *him*!

He eyed her suspiciously. "Maybe you'd better tell me where you've been."

"Scotland."

"Scotland! Whatever for?"

"I eloped."

He choked on the news. "You . . . you what?"

"Elo-o-o-ped," she pronounced in an exaggerated fashion as if he were an imbecile. "You must be familiar with the term. It's when a person runs off and gets married in secret."

"I'm aware of what it means," he snapped. "Who would dare such an outrage with you?"

"*I* dared." She pointed a proud finger at her chest. "I realize you'll find this difficult to believe, but as opposed to you and your tepid regard, there has always been a man who loved me beyond imagining."

His jaw dropped. "You . . . had a . . . a beau? While you were engaged to *me*?"

"Hilarious, isn't it? Considering your horrid behavior, I call it tit for tat."

"Tit for tat!"

"I've forgiven you for tossing me over. You'd sworn I'd be wretched with you, and you were right. I'm much happier now."

She was having such fun, but he wasn't taking the news with the same merry humor. He appeared positively weak.

"Cousin Alex, should you sit down? You don't look well."

"Why didn't you say anything?"

"I couldn't."

"You're correct: I need to sit." He plopped into the nearest chair and let out a huge breath. "You're married?"

She dangled her fingers, showing off her wedding band. "Absolutely."

"Who is the lucky man? Anyone I know?"

"I don't think so."

"Who!"

"Mr. James Drake."

"James Drake!"

"Is there an echo in here?" She laughed, delighted that she had him so flustered.

"Would this Mr. Drake, by any slim chance, be Ellen's brother?"

"I told you it was hilarious. Actually, Ellen introduced us, though I hadn't any notion that he was her—" He held up a hand, and she halted in mid-sentence. "What?"

"Slow down, and let me catch up. I can't absorb all you're throwing at me."

"It sounds crazed, I'm sure."

"It's beyond crazed. You've wed a convicted felon, who is wanted by the law."

"And that's one of the reasons I stopped by to speak with you. He's not guilty. He was *never* guilty."

"I know."

"You *know*?"

"Yes."

She'd been prepared to argue and fight, to lie and cajole. With his easy concurrence, some of the wind went out of her sails. "We need to figure out a way to clear his name."

"I've already started."

"You have?"

"My attorney is working on it."

"My goodness" was the sole comment she could make.

"It may take a while."

"How long is that exactly?"

"I can't say."

"Is it safe for him to be in England with me?"

"I assume it is. As my wife's brother, and my cousin's husband, he's under my protection."

"So you married Ellen. I was wondering if you'd have the gumption."

"Rebecca! Despite your low opinion, I'm not a scoundrel."

"Hah! Time will tell, won't it? When I fled, I was very upset, but I've decided you both did me an enormous favor. I'm so glad she ended up with you! Better her than me!"

"I'm wounded by your insults," he claimed. "Why don't I just give you a knife so I can be stabbed all over again?"

"What on earth do you mean?"

He waved away the peculiar remark. "I'm blathering. Don't mind me."

"I've forgiven Ellen, too. Is she here? I'd like to chat with her."

"No, she's not." He blushed to high heaven.

"Where is she?"

"She's living in the country."

"But you two still qualify as newlyweds. Why aren't you together? How very odd. What's come over you? You don't seem yourself, at all."

"I've had a few trying weeks."

"You look like death warmed over. What happened while I was away?"

"Well . . ."

As he would have commenced his explanation, James stomped in. Pistol drawn, in a furious temper, he stared at Alex and snarled, "What have you done to my sister?"

"Mr. Drake, I presume?" Alex answered, unflappable as ever.

"James!" Rebecca scolded. "I warned you not to bring a gun into the house. Put it away this instant."

"I'll put it away," James replied, aiming more closely, "when I find out what he's done to Ellen. If he's hurt her, I'll shoot a bullet through his black heart."

At his threat, she scoffed. "You're being melodramatic, and I abhor this menacing side of your character. You must learn to rein it in when we're in polite company."

"Rebecca," Alex interjected, "you *do* realize that you've married a man who goes about armed?"

"Isn't it thrilling? He's so much more exciting than stuffy old you!"

Alex sighed. "Come in, Mr. Drake; come in. Obviously, we need to talk."

"This is your one and only option."

"Bugger off, Alex," Nicholas muttered.

As if Nicholas hadn't spoken, Alex continued. "Whether you choose to exercise it is totally up to you. I couldn't care less."

Nicholas glanced around his grim cell—he refused to call it a room—where he'd been detained. There was a bed, a writing desk, a pitcher and basin for washing, as well as an alcove where he could use the chamber pot, but the place was filthy, the smells nauseating, the noises terrifying.

Due to Alex's position, he'd been quartered in the private wing at Bedlam, rather than the public block at Newgate Prison. Nicholas supposed he should be grateful, but he was having trouble mustering any appreciation.

He glared at Alex, hating him more than ever. Why was it that Alex always landed on his feet? Nicholas had stabbed the knave in the belly, the knife entering to the hilt, yet as usual, he was alive and lording himself over everybody.

Why couldn't the bastard have died as any ordinary individual would have done? Didn't anything faze him?

"Go away," Nicholas grumbled, wanting to be left in peace.

"Not until you make your decision."

Nicholas nervously rubbed his wound, which occasionally festered. He'd had no contact with anyone on the outside, so he had no notion of what rumors were circulating. He'd been allowed no visitors, though his jailer—or nurse, or whatever the hell the fellow was purported to be—insisted he hadn't had any.

Where was Suzette? She had to be frantic with worry, and he had to depart the asylum and be with her, but he had no idea how.

He was kept under lock and key, and any release was up to Alex, who maintained that he'd been appointed Nicholas's guardian, but Nicholas couldn't imagine why. He wasn't insane! If Alex had marched into a court of law and alleged as much, how could anyone have believed him?

An eerie scream floated down the hall, and dozens of people took up the lament. The sounds of human agony wafted by, and Nicholas shuddered, relieved that Alex had had the money to separate him from the masses.

Gad! What if Alex hadn't been rich? What if Nicholas had been lodged with the general population? What then?

He had to escape, had to meet with Suzette, and he'd agree to any strategy to flee his confinement.

"What is it you want of me?" he asked.

"Lydia is still willing to marry you," Alex said.

"Lydia!" If he never heard of her again, it would be too soon. "You can jump off a cliff. She can join you."

"Are you positive that ought to be your response?"

"I'm weary of your harangue."

"Fine." Alex had brought a stack of papers with him, and he scooped them up, cramming them in a satchel. As he turned toward the door, Nicholas panicked.

"Where are you going?"

"Home."

"Take me with you."

"No."

Nicholas studied his sibling, searching for a hint of affection, of brotherly fondness. At the least, Alex should have felt bound by the ties of family, but Alex stared back as if Nicholas were a stranger.

Nicholas tried for a smile. "You can't intend to . . . to desert me?"

"Actually, I do."

"For how long?"

Alex shrugged. "Forever."

"Forever! And you contend that *I* am mad."

"I used to think that you were simply spoiled and stupid. However, of late, it's occurred to me that you're dangerous."

"Dangerous? Why . . . why . . . that's preposterous."

"You shouldn't be permitted to walk the streets. There's no predicting what mischief you might commit, and I won't risk that anyone else could be injured by you."

Nicholas bristled but tamped down his fury. He had to reason with Alex, had to make him grasp how perverse he was being. No harm had been done. Everyone involved was a bit bruised, but alive and carrying on. What was to be gained by harping?

"Look," he said, "if it's about that woman, Ellen Drake—"

"Her name is Ellen Marshall, and if you ever mention her again, I shall cut out your tongue, stuff it down your throat, then watch with joy as you strangle on it. In case you haven't noticed"—he stepped closer, as if he might begin the bloodletting at any moment—"there's no law in this facility. I can do whatever I wish to you and get away with it."

Nicholas recoiled. From Alex's livid frown it was clear he wasn't bluffing, that he might initiate a heinous attack. Perhaps he'd had feelings for the little harlot, after all. Who would have guessed?

Alex whirled away, and Nicholas was terrified. What if Alex went and never came back? What if—as he'd threatened—he left Nicholas to rot?

"Tell me about Lydia," he begged in a rush. "What is it I would be required to do?"

Alex stopped—thank God!—and spun around.

"You'll marry her. Right here. Right now."

"Now?"

"She's waiting outside with the vicar. Once you're wed, you'll travel to her house in Southampton. You'll reside there—with her—and you'll never show your sorry face in London again."

"And if I refuse?"

"Then you'll remain in this cell till you draw your last breath, which is more than you deserve. I should have had you hanged."

"Why didn't you?"

"Because I want it over. Ellen and her brother have suffered enough because of us. I won't put them through further anguish."

Ellen! Ellen! Ellen! He was so sick of her! Why should she be more important than everybody else? "I need a few days to consider. How about if we go home, and I'll clean up, and I'll—"

"No. This is a one-time offer. You may accept it or reject it, but I must have your answer immediately."

Nicholas fumed and stewed, having no doubt as to what his reply would be. There wasn't any other option. He'd have to marry Lydia, but he'd never known a woman he couldn't manipulate, his mother being the prime example.

Yes, he'd marry Lydia. He'd journey to Southampton, spend a week or two acting repentant; then he'd hightail it for London and Suzette.

"I suppose you've told her the entire sordid story."

"Yes."

"Then why is she amenable?"

"I haven't the vaguest idea."

Nicholas knew why: Lydia was smitten. The old crone always had been, and he chuckled to himself. If she was so besotted, it would be that much easier to control her.

"I'll do it." He nodded, more confident by the second. "You may bring her in."

"First, you must sign these papers." Alex retrieved some documents from his satchel and laid them, a pen, and a jar of ink on the desk.

"What are they?"

"You're relinquishing your ownership of New Haven."

It was his only legacy from his father, his only source of legitimate income. He couldn't surrender it! No one could make him!

"Like hell I am."

"You're giving it to James Drake," Alex declared, a cold gleam in his eye. "As reparation. We can never fully compensate him, but it's a start."

"I'd rather die in here."

"As I said, Nick: It's your choice."

They engaged in a staring match. Finally, Nicholas

grabbed the pen and scrawled his name at the bottom.

"A wise decision," Alex jeered.

"Shut up."

"By the way," Alex added, "I can see how your devious mind is spinning, conjuring up schemes to thwart
me. You should understand that I never intend to speak
with you again. Lydia has vowed that she'll be responsible for you, but if I learn that you've sneaked away, that
you've come to London to visit that witch Suzette
DuBois—or if you approach my wife or her brother—
all bets are off. I shall have you tried and executed for
attempted murder."

"Murder!"

Alex patted the satchel. "I have all the statements.
My solicitor has copies. So think twice, little brother.
Think twice."

He went to the door and shouted to a guard through
the small hole. Shortly, the key grated in the lock, and
Lydia waddled in, the vicar trudging behind. There was a
glee about her that sent a frisson of fear down Nicholas's
spine. He rippled with dismay.

"Hello, Nicky," she said. "Fancy meeting you here."

Suzette sat at her dressing table, listening as people filed
out of the theater, and she scowled at her reflection in
the mirror.

Where was Nick?

He'd bought the house, had given her the keys; then
he'd disappeared. She'd moved in, had hired servants, had
purchased furniture and a new wardrobe, but she hadn't
seen him. There'd been peculiar rumors about Nick
landing himself in a hideous predicament, but none of

her acquaintances could verify if they were true, and with each passing day she was growing more anxious.

The previous afternoon, a merchant had stopped by to inquire about a receipt she'd signed. He couldn't locate Nick, and his request for payment—delivered to Nick at his brother's mansion—had been returned unpaid. The merchant wanted his money, but it was an exorbitant amount, and Suzette hadn't the funds to square the debt.

In fact, she didn't have any cash. Nick was to have set up an account, but he hadn't.

Where was the blasted oaf?

Footsteps sounded in the hall and halted outside her room. There was some murmuring; then the door was opened without anyone knocking. In a temper over the discourtesy, Suzette whipped around and found herself face-to-face with Nick's fiancée.

The dismal woman had to have a reason for coming— a reason that included Nick—and whatever it was, she was in for a surprise. It was obvious that she was used to bullying others and, from her forbidding expression, she assumed she could push Suzette into a frightened swoon.

Well, Suzette was no wilting violet, and she wasn't about to scurry away.

"Who the hell are you?" Suzette demanded, seizing the initiative. "You've barged in without invitation! Have you any notion of who I am? Be gone at once, or I shall call for the stage manager and have you thrown out."

The woman didn't answer Suzette's taunt. Instead, she glanced over her shoulder at two burly men who'd accompanied her.

"That's her." She pointed a condemning finger at Suzette.

"Are you sure, Miss Burton?" one of the men queried; then he corrected himself. "Ah, I mean Mrs. Marshall."

"Yes, I'm *Mrs.* Marshall now, and don't you forget it. And I'm positive it's her. I have no doubt."

A quiver of alarm slithered down Suzette's spine, but she shook it away. The fat cow! Suzette wasn't about to be intimidated.

"Mrs. Marshall, is it?" Suzette sneered. "You may have married my dear friend Nicholas, but if you presume you have the right to—"

Suzette's comment was cut off when Marshall strutted in as if she owned the place. The two men followed, and suddenly the space was much too crowded.

"Of all the nerve!" Suzette blustered.

"Be silent, you impertinent hussy!" Mrs. Marshall barked.

"How dare you berate me!"

Marshall looked at the men. "As I explained, my husband and I had been in the country for several weeks, but imagine my shock when I returned, only to discover that this . . . this"—she gestured at Suzette—"interloper had been camping out in our house."

"*Your* house? That house is mine."

"She'd been apprised that we were away, so she must have thought she could take advantage without consequence. Have you ever heard of such gall?"

"You are completely deranged," Suzette said.

"Am I?" Marshall motioned toward Suzette's dressing table and urged one of her minions toward it. "There's her jewelry box. Why don't you have a peek inside?"

"I won't allow you to snoop through my things!" Suzette declared. "Get out. All of you."

"You have enough problems as it is," the lead man advised. "Don't make it any worse by resisting."

He marched over, lifted the lid on the box, and, to Suzette's horror, he extracted numerous gem-laden necklaces, rings, and bracelets that she'd never seen before. He held them up like a prize.

"My . . . my . . ." Marshall mused. "Who would have guessed that such a pretty, pretty girl was naught but a common thief."

"Thief!" Suzette huffed.

The other man retrieved a length of rope from his coat. He stalked toward her, apparently intending to bind Suzette's hands.

"What are you doing?" Suzette eased away, wondering if she could reach the hall and race off before he grabbed her.

"You're in a peck of trouble, Miss DuBois."

"Are you claiming I stole that jewelry?"

"Not *claiming,* miss," the man said. "Mrs. Marshall has sworn out an affidavit, and these items are hard evidence against you."

"But they're not mine! I have no clue how they came to be there."

"A likely story," Marshall derided, and she nodded at Suzette. "Seize her."

Both men lunged, and though Suzette fought and kicked, she was no match for their superior strength. In a thrice, they had her shackled, the rope digging into her wrists.

"I haven't done anything!" Suzette bellowed. "The old hag is simply jealous. Her husband doesn't love her! He loves me! He always has. I'm his mistress! She's trying to be rid of me."

"Please, Miss DuBois," one of them counseled, "there's no cause to insult Mrs. Marshall."

"When I get out of this, I'll do more than *insult* her. I'll kill her."

"An interesting wish, Miss DuBois," Marshall stated, "but you shouldn't count on being released any time soon. Those jewels are incredibly valuable, so you'll probably be transported to the penal colonies. You might even be hanged. This is the type of situation with which my husband is intimately familiar. He could tell you all about it."

"Where is Nick?" Suzette challenged. "I must talk with him!"

"With Nick?" Marshall snorted out an evil laugh. "I'm afraid you can't. Hasn't anyone told you? He's gone mad as a hatter."

Suzette ceased her struggling. "What did you say?"

"Nicky's crazed as a bedbug. His brother had him committed to Bedlam."

"I don't believe you," Suzette raged.

"It's true, though authority over him has been relinquished to me. *I* am Nicky's guardian, so you shouldn't plan on seeing him ever again." She waved toward the exit. "Take her away."

The two men hauled her out, and though she screamed for help and her coworkers gawked with dismay, not a person leapt to her aid. She was dragged to the alley and tossed in a carriage unimpeded. With her arms trussed, she couldn't ward off the fall, and she hit the floor with a thud. The door slammed shut, the driver clicked the reins, the horses pulled away, and she was swallowed up by the busy street, vanishing as quickly and easily as if she'd never been there, at all.

• • •

"You'll never be invited to Christmas dinner," Lydia cackled.

Nicholas stopped chewing and glared at her. After residing with her for eighteen torturous days, he hadn't learned how to fully ignore her. She was insane—he'd been forced to accept the fact—and the depth of her lunacy was startling. She entered his bedchamber at all hours, would wake him and order him to perform his marital obligations. Dread and loathing were making him ill.

He had to flee, without delay, but he had no funds, and it was clear that no nuptial stipend would be granted.

He'd been swindled by her, but he couldn't deduce how it had occurred. With his being so desperate to quit the asylum, he'd signed the marriage contract without reading it. He should have been able to trust Alex. He wouldn't have countenanced Nick's being destitute and totally dependent on Lydia. But had Alex known? Or had it been Lydia's deceit?

Nick would put nothing past her, had to constantly be on guard, and the strain was unbearable. He'd tried to escape, but the sole occasion he'd sneaked to the stables and demanded a horse the groom had refused to give him one. Then the impertinent boy had tattled to Lydia, and before Nicholas could react, he'd been locked in his room like a misbehaving child.

"About what are you blathering?" He glanced over to where she was perusing a letter.

"Rebecca's gone and wed Mr. James Drake. You remember him, don't you? He's Ellen Drake's brother, the man whose life you ruined."

He was aghast. Would the Drakes plague him forever? Why couldn't the accursed criminal have stayed
in Australia where he belonged? Instead, he was prancing about England! Marrying his betters! Flaunting his
freedom! If Nicholas had plotted more carefully, the
man would have been executed and none of the uproar
would have transpired.

"They've moved to your estate," she added, "the one
your beloved mama insisted you have. What was it
called? New Haven?"

"Why would you presume I give a bloody damn
about that paltry farm?"

He couldn't let her discern how much the property
had meant to him. She had a penchant for cruelty, and if
she had any notion that he'd enjoyed his ownership,
she'd flay him with the knowledge.

"Anyway, I was saying that you shouldn't plan on
visiting them over the holidays."

"As if I'd go."

"So, Nicky—"

"My name is not Nicky!"

"So *Nicky*, after being notified of your sordid business with Mr. Drake, I considered it prudent to ascertain
more about the fellow I married, so I've been delving
into your history."

"Have you?"

"You won't believe how much I've uncovered."

"Really?" He did a great job of affecting boredom.

"There's been so much to gather."

"And you're telling me this because . . . ?"

"No reason." She shrugged. "I merely find it curious
how people keep detailed, meticulous records of the
most trivial events. Were you aware of that?"

"No, I wasn't."

"I've purchased the most intriguing information."

He studied her, wishing he could open up her thick skull and see what was lurking inside her devious head. If he'd been feeling more himself, if he'd been more recuperated, he might have beat her into submission, but there was time enough for that later.

How difficult could it be to murder her in her sleep? He'd been wed to her for only a few weeks. Could he get away with it? Or—more likely—would he be an immediate suspect?

"Are you threatening me, Lydia?"

"Me? Threaten you?" She appeared so innocent. "Why, no. I'm simply advising you that the evidence has been assembled, and my solicitor has it. For safekeeping. In case I had an *accident*, I thought you might like to know where it is."

The bitch! Gad! He'd never be shed of her. She might as well have gotten out a rope and wrapped the noose around his neck, herself!

She went back to eating her breakfast and reading the London paper, when suddenly she clucked her tongue. "Do you recollect that actress you befriended? You introduced me to her when we were in London. Wasn't her name Suzette DuBois?"

His heart dropped to his shoes. "I'm acquainted with Miss DuBois. Why?"

Her gaze level and lethal, she slid the paper toward him. "There's a story about her. She was arrested. Why . . . they carried her out of the theater in shackles! Whatever could she have done?"

He forced himself to remain calm, to focus on the words on the page. The paper was over three weeks old,

so the legal system would already have swallowed her up.
She could be anywhere. Flogged and starving in Newgate
Prison. On a ship to Australia. Hanged!

Slowly, he raised his eyes to Lydia's. She was evaluating him over the rim of her teacup, a sly smile on her
lips, and he knew—he knew!—that she'd had her revenge, and she'd had it against Suzette.

A rage unlike any he'd ever experienced swept over
him. He yearned to grab her by the throat and press with
his fingers while she clawed for air and begged for
mercy. He'd do it, too. Just as soon as he figured out how
to accomplish it without being caught.

"I'll kill you for this," he vowed.

"I don't think so."

She stood and gestured toward the stairs. "Let's resume the sexual play we commenced last night."

"Go fuck yourself," he crudely said, "for I never will
again."

"There's a deed I'm eager to try," she prattled as if he
hadn't spoken. "I've heard that a man can place his
mouth on the woman's privates. He licks her there and
kisses her there, and it can be very stimulating. Let's
head upstairs so you can show me how it's done."

"I'd rather choke to death on this scone."

She marched to the hall, yelling for someone to attend her. Momentarily, the two male aides who'd accompanied them from Bedlam lumbered in.

"My husband is having an episode," she told them.
"I'm afraid he might hurt himself. When he loses control, the doctors directed me to restrain him."

"Yes, ma'am," the bigger one agreed.

"Take him upstairs, at once, and tie him to the bed so
that he can't injure himself or anyone else."

"We'll see to it right away."

Nick blanched. They assumed he was deranged? That he could be fettered—at her whim—like a dog on a leash?

The pair stomped around the table, and though he had nowhere to go, he ran. They were much faster than he, and the fight was ended before it had opportunity to begin.

❧ 23 ❧

Ellen strolled down the rutted road, the autumn leaves dangling from the trees. The scenery was brown and gray, the grass wilted from frost, and the drab colors of the landscape matched her mood perfectly.

For once, she had everything a person could possibly desire: a beautiful home, more money than she could spend, a staff of efficient servants, fine clothes, food on the table. Yet she was so unhappy.

There were so many hours to fill, so many quiet evenings to endure. Each agonizing minute ticked by, the clocks reminding her that she had nothing important to occupy her time, no one to look after, no duties to tend to. She was a woman of leisure, but the freedom was driving her mad.

London seemed far away, the events that had occurred a crazed dream. Had she actually married Alex? Had she been reunited with her brother, merely to have him vanish? Had Nicholas Marshall tried to kill her?

She couldn't make sense of any of it, and she wished

she had someone with whom she could discuss her ordeal. She couldn't turn to any of the neighbors she'd met. At a period when she desperately needed sympathy and consoling, she was naught but an oddity, a strange newcomer who had rumor and innuendo encircling her like a shroud.

She quit the lane and walked up the drive. Several carriages were parked in front of the house, and they belonged to various gentlemen visitors who were extremely persistent in their attentions. As she was soon to be rich and single, they viewed her as they would a divorcee: loose and trolling for a paramour. She was always polite to them, but she'd grown weary of their pathetic attempts to woo her.

Craving solitude, she skirted the entrance and headed for the rear door, hoping to slink in without encountering anyone. Her predicament rankled, and her aggravation with Alex surged anew.

She'd consented to his every demand, to his cold insistence that she scurry off to the country, to his blasted annulment. Since then, she hadn't received so much as a note, and his total disregard irked her to her limit.

Did he ever think of her? How could he cast her aside? Had his wedding vows no meaning to him, at all?

She pictured him in the city, surrounded by a harem of adoring women. While she was miserable with the conclusion, he was probably delighted. He was about to be shed of her, and he would carry on as the lusty bachelor he'd been before Ellen had stumbled into his life.

She simply had to accept his decision and move on, but it was so difficult! Her pride was battered, her confidence the lowest it had ever been.

If her own husband couldn't bear to live with her, who could? Lucky Alex! He'd been able to banish her, but Ellen could never escape her odious self.

She'd rounded the corner of the house, was ready to sneak inside, when her brother stepped out into the yard. She stopped in her tracks, the sight of him too disconcerting to be believed.

She'd thought him arrested, tortured, killed, yet here he was. He was so healthy and handsome. And so content.

My goodness! What had happened?

"Oh, James," she murmured.

"Hello, big sister," he greeted as he studied her. "You look dreadful."

"Why, thank you."

"Seriously. You've lost weight; you're pale as a ghost. Have you been ill?"

"I had a bad influenza."

"Really?"

"Really," she lied, "though I must confess that you don't seem any the worse for wear."

"I'm feeling more grand than I've ever been." He grinned. "Have you missed me?"

"Yes, you despicable vanishing rat! Where have you been?"

Then, they were running to each other, and she fell into his arms. He hugged her and scooped her off her feet, twirling her round and round until she was dizzy. When he set her down, she punched him in the chest.

"How dare you disappear without a word!" she chided. "How dare you make me worry myself sick!"

"I'm sorry."

"Have you any notion of how terrified I've been?"

"Well, how about you? I returned to London after a bit of a holiday, and you'd vanished, too. I was panicked."

"How did you find me?"

His scowl was dour. "I inquired of your husband."

Envisioning fisticuffs—or murder!—she gulped with dismay. "You spoke with . . . with . . . Lord Stanton?"

"You call him *Lord*? Was that his idea or yours?"

"I could refer to him as Alex—if I wanted to—but I don't. It wouldn't be proper."

"Gad, the oaf is your lawful spouse, so you're entitled to call him whatever you like. Even swine. Even cruel, conniving bastard."

"You didn't hurt him, did you?"

"No, but I should have. Why ever would you marry that ass? And please tell me it was for love, because if it was for some stupid reason—like reputation or honor—I can't predict what I might do."

"Of course I didn't marry him for . . . for love. I scarcely know him."

"That's not what I was told. In fact, I heard that you were *intimately* familiar with him."

"You heard wrong."

"Then why agree?"

"Because . . . because . . ."

Tears welled into her eyes. She couldn't explain why she'd done it. Alex had been her whole world, and deep down, she'd loved him beyond imagining, so she'd persuaded herself that marrying him was the correct choice. He'd pretended to care for her, too, but she'd since realized that his comments had been insincere drivel. At the first sign of adversity he'd tossed her over, had casually rid himself of her as if she were a mess on the floor his minions could sweep away.

"Because why?" James prodded when she couldn't continue. "If you want him to be a real husband to you, Ellen, just say so. I'll see that he does right by you."

"It doesn't matter what I want."

"And why doesn't it?"

"He . . . he . . . detests having me as his wife." She sucked in huge breaths, feeling as if there wasn't enough air in the entire sky. In all her hiding in the country, she hadn't had to admit her shame to anyone, and she was humiliated at having mentioned it aloud.

"How can you be positive?"

"He sent me here, without asking what I desired. He couldn't wait to wash his hands of me."

"That's not true," he claimed.

"It is."

"His life is in a state of complete chaos, as is yours." He gripped her shoulders and gave her a firm shake. "If you love him, Ellen, then fight for him. I'll help you. You know I will."

"I won't force myself on him. If he doesn't want me, so be it." She glanced around the trimmed garden. "And I'm happy. This is a good place for me."

He scoffed. "I bumped into some of your purported suitors in the parlor, and I chased them off. So don't tell me you're content to live like this. You shouldn't be on your own. It's his idiotic pride—and yours—that's keeping you apart. This shouldn't be your ending. Let me assist you in crafting a different one."

"I was awful to him, James. He has valid grounds to loathe me."

"He's a beast, so whatever your actions, I'm sure he deserved them."

"No. I was horrid, so don't try to change my mind. You can't."

For a long, charged interval, he evaluated her; then he sighed with resignation. "Have it your way. But if you ever decide that you'd like him to—"

"I won't," she interrupted.

She was too distressed to hear what he might propose, for she couldn't have him raising false hopes. Alex Marshall was who he was—a confirmed bachelor and rampant libertine—and despite how she might want him to be another sort of man, her wishing wouldn't make it so.

She could have gone to Alex on her own—she didn't need James to do it for her—and she could have begged him to take her back, but she hadn't.

If she went to him, if she bared her soul, but he refused to relent, she'd perish from mortification. She'd survived one rejection by him, and it had been too demeaning. She wouldn't put either of them in such an appalling position ever again.

She switched subjects. "Where have you been, and what have you been doing? I thought you were dead."

"They can't kill me," he said. "I'm too tough."

"I'm beginning to concur." He was full of energy and vigor, the rage and tension that had swirled around him having faded. The resentful, acrimonious man she'd met in London had ceased to exist.

"You won't believe what I did."

"Should I sit down?"

"By the time I've finished, you might need to."

A garden bench was nearby, and she walked to it and seated herself. "All right. I'm ready for anything."

Bubbling over with merriment, he laughed. "I ran off and got married."

"Married! That's . . . that's wonderful."

"Aren't you going to ask who I selected as my bride?"

"From how you're grinning, I'm almost scared to know."

"Guess," he urged.

"I haven't any idea."

He sobered and straightened. "It's Rebecca."

The news was such a surprise that it took several seconds for it to register. "You married Rebecca Burton? But when . . . how . . ."

"We eloped to Scotland. We just recently returned, or I would have come for you sooner."

"You married Rebecca. Rebecca!" It was too far-fetched to be true, yet apparently it was. "Is she . . . is she terribly angry with me?"

"No, not a bit. She wound up with *me,* instead of him. How could she be upset? You saved her from decades of agony." He gestured toward the house. "She's waiting inside. Will you speak to her?"

He held out his hand, and she clasped it and rose to her feet. "Yes, I will. I'd like that very, very much."

The carriage rattled to a halt, but James scarcely noticed. Rebecca was on his lap, her luscious lips pressed to his own. At such a delectable moment, how could a mortal man focus on the outside world?

"It appears that we've arrived," she murmured.

"I'd rather stay in here with you." He pulled the curtain aside and peeked out at Alex Marshall's mansion.

"Perhaps I shall. I have no desire to converse with my brother-in-law."

"Don't be too harsh on him," she counseled. "He got us all that money from Lydia and, my darling farmer"—she batted her pretty lashes—"don't forget that he wrenched New Haven away from Nicholas and gave it to you. He's atoned for a few of his sins."

"Not to Ellen."

"But maybe you can fix that situation, hmm?"

"Maybe," he agreed.

He couldn't quite trust in his sudden reversal of fortune: He'd gone from being a criminal with no future to being a member of a wealthy, aristocratic family. His record had been wiped clean, and he was a prosperous landowner, with a stable income, a rich and devoted wife, and his first babe on the way. He constantly worried that he might awaken to discover that he'd been dreaming.

Ellen was the only burr under his saddle. With Rebecca's help, he'd received many priceless boons, while Ellen had received nothing, at all. Yes, Stanton had supplied her with a large, drafty house and a pile of cash, but chattels could never replace the home and family she would have cherished in their stead.

She should have had people around her whom she could tend and mother. She needed a husband and children. What she *didn't* need was to be shuffled off to the country like a crazed relative or tiresome mistress.

If Stanton assumed he could be shed of Ellen so easily, he was in for a shock.

Ellen was in love with Alex Marshall. No matter how vociferously she denied it. She was miserable without him. Stanton was miserable, too. It was so obvious that they needed each other, and if James had his way, they would reconcile.

"I'd better go in," he said. "Are you sure you won't join me?"

"I'm not in the mood to see Alex. I'm anxious to proceed directly to our hotel—and our hotel room."

She flashed him a smile that had his pulse pounding and his cock stirring. "You'll be the death of me."

"I'll make it slow and painless."

"Promise?"

"Yes, now go. The sooner you're off, the sooner you can return." She licked her bottom lip in invitation. "I'll have a treat for you when you get back."

"Sweet Jesu," he groaned. "I'll hurry."

"Please do."

He jumped out and headed to the front door, and shortly he was being escorted to Stanton's library. As he walked behind the snooty butler, he gazed at the pretentious surroundings. How could Ellen ever fit in? Was it right to bring her and Stanton together? Was it for the best?

He was announced, and as he marched in, he decided to let Fate take its course. If this was their destiny, it would happen with very little intervention.

"Hello, Stanton," he greeted, stomping over to the desk.

"Hello, Mr. Drake, but as I previously advised, you might as well call me Alex."

"But such courtesy would give others the impression that I like you or that we're close. Considering what my wife and sister think of you, I won't have anyone presuming we're friends."

Stanton sighed. "Would you like a brandy?"

"No."

"Well, I'm dying for one." He stood and went to the sideboard, pouring himself a stiff dose and gulping it down.

"You look worse every time I see you," James mentioned, and he wasn't joking. Stanton had lost more weight, and he seemed confused and lonely, as Ellen was, herself. "You wouldn't—by any chance—be pining away for my sister?"

"Why would I be sulking over her?"

"Because you miss her?"

"I was stabbed, Mr. Drake, and I'm still recuperating. And I've . . . I've had an influenza." It was the same excuse Ellen had furnished for her waning health, and James wanted to laugh aloud.

What a pathetic pair! Both of them disconsolate and heartbroken! Why couldn't they see the resolution? It was so clear.

"Must have been a bad bug," James needled.

"It was." Stanton refilled his glass and downed the contents again.

"You're certainly drinking a lot these days. I wonder why?"

"Mr. Drake, if I thought my personal habits were any of your business—which I don't—I'd respond to your observation." He was plainly hankering for a third application, but he refused to imbibe with James watching, and reluctantly he moved back to the desk. "Why are you in town?"

"Rebecca and I are passing through. We're on our way to New Haven."

"I hope, this trip, you'll avail yourself of my hospitality. I have plenty of space."

He appeared so eager for company, and so morose,

that James almost felt sorry to disappoint him. "Rebecca would rather sleep in the street than stay here."

Stanton sighed again. "Mr. Drake, we'll be crossing paths on a regular basis. We're family, so contact can't be avoided. If you insist on being antagonistic at every meeting, we'll never accomplish anything. Must you be so hostile?"

"I enjoy harassing you, so I hate to stop, but I suppose you can call me James."

"I will—James. How is New Haven? I trust it's satisfactory?"

"It's fabulous, and I can't thank you enough. Nor can I thank you for retrieving Rebecca's money."

"Lydia is a dreadful miser. It was no small task, I assure you."

"That's what I've heard. I can't imagine how Ellen tolerated her. Speaking of Ellen . . ."

"What about her?" Stanton ventured.

"She wanted me to deliver these papers regarding the annulment." He opened his satchel and laid them on the desk. "She says she signed them, but there ought to be more than these."

"My solicitor dropped off the last ones this morning. I was about to put them in the post."

James was silent, letting the moment play out. Stanton was prickling with curiosity about Ellen, frantic for James to offer a few tidbits, but James was mum. Stanton could stew to a boil.

Just when he figured Stanton would reach over and squeeze some comments out of him, James prodded, "You can ask me about her."

"Why? What would I need to know? I've completely provided for her, so she couldn't want for anything."

"That's true. She's definitely not *wanting*."

James was intentionally suggestive, and Stanton leapt at the innuendo.

"What do you mean?" he demanded.

"I shouldn't have to tell you how it goes with a woman like Ellen."

"How it *goes*? I haven't the vaguest notion about what you're babbling."

"Ellen's very beautiful, as I'm sure you'd agree, or you wouldn't have been so quick to debauch her."

"James!" Stanton snapped. "I won't discuss the intimate details of my relationship with her."

"Good. I'd have to kill you if you tried."

He was quiet, letting Stanton grow more and more surly.

"So . . ." Stanton began, "what's she up to that you've felt it necessary to boast?"

James grinned. "She's pretty, and she's rich, and she's about to be divorced."

"I am *not* divorcing her," Stanton claimed, bristling. "We're simply correcting a mistake."

"Divorce. Annulment." James waved away the words. "The results to Ellen's reputation are the same. The men in her neighborhood can't wait for the process to be finalized."

"Her *male* neighbors? Why would her situation be of interest to them?"

"She's viewed as a loose, scandalous divorcée. They're practically drooling over her."

"Over Ellen?"

"Why wouldn't they be?"

"But she's married!" Stanton protested.

"Barely and not for long."

"Still, it's not fitting. I can't believe anyone would dare."

"It's not just any *one*. She has a steady flow of suitors."

"What?" Stanton nearly fell off his chair.

"She's constantly entertaining, and I have to admit that—once you're through with her—there are several who would be acceptable as her next husband."

"They're courting her?"

"Of course. With the fortune you've dumped on her, she's quite a catch."

"Is she encouraging their attention?" If Stanton's jaw dropped any farther, it would slide off his face.

"Why shouldn't she?"

"But . . . but . . . she's married."

"Merely a formality."

"Not to me!"

In a temper, he jumped up, and he was anxious to punch something—or someone, with James the only person in proximity.

"Why are you so upset?" James goaded. "It's not as if you have any feelings for her. Why would you care?"

"A man has his pride."

"Yes, he does."

"She could at least be discreet until our dealings are concluded."

"Ellen has always yearned for a home and a family, and she deserves to have a husband who loves her—as you obviously don't." He paused for effect. "I can't think of any reason for her to delay. Can you?"

Stanton was ready to explode, and he engaged in a desperate inner struggle, grappling with dozens of emotions that were too strong to name. Then, with great effort, he reined himself in.

"You're right," he ultimately said. "There's absolutely no reason for delay."

"I'll let you know when her next wedding is to be." James turned and started toward the door. At the last second, he spun around. "Would you like me to wrangle you an invitation?"

"To her wedding?" Stanton was so aghast that James wondered if he might faint.

"Ellen wouldn't mind. After all, you two were never close. By your presence, you could show the world that there is no lingering bitterness over your split."

"No . . . no . . . I wouldn't want to see it," Stanton hastily insisted, "but thanks for offering."

"You're welcome. I'll stop by next time we're in town."

"You do that," Stanton answered.

James strolled out, whistling as he went, and as he climbed into the carriage, Rebecca was rippling with impatience.

"How did it go?" she queried.

"Very well," he replied. "Very well indeed."

~ 24 ~

Alex dismounted and stared at Ellen's house. He'd bought it sight unseen, so he was happy to note that it was eminently suitable. It was a two-story affair, with white shutters and gray walls, shiny windows and pretty flower boxes. Ivy crawled up the sides, although it had browned with the change of the season.

A carriage sat out front, and his anger surged as he wondered to whom it belonged. No doubt, it was one of the audacious male neighbors described by James Drake.

The remarks about Ellen, about how men were vying for her favor, had him rattled, though he couldn't deduce why. As her brother had indicated, he didn't care about Ellen. If she chose to flaunt herself like a common trollop, it wasn't any of his business. Still, an absurd inclination had spurred him to view the spectacle for himself.

He had a valid reason for coming. The final contracts regarding their annulment had to be delivered. He could have mailed them, or hired a messenger, but after extensive deliberation, he'd brought them to her.

Throughout the journey, he'd tried to clarify exactly

why he was going to so much trouble, but he couldn't adequately justify his actions. He simply had to see her one last time, had to persuade himself—again!—that he was doing the right thing by setting her free. But with the documents in hand, their marital conclusion a pen's stroke away, his decision seemed wrong.

He was conflicted over their awkward appointment in her hotel suite. She'd obviously yearned to say something important, but he hadn't given her a chance. The prospect of what that comment might have been gnawed at him like an itchy scab.

He marched to the door and was about to bang the knocker when he glanced at the carriage that was so boldly parked in her drive. His temper sparked, and instead, he turned the knob and strolled in as if he owned the place, which he did.

In the vestibule, he dawdled, listening for voices or other—he wouldn't call them *incriminating*—sounds, but he heard nothing, so he proceeded into the parlor and, without being noticed, made himself at home.

The room was comfortable and bright, with vivid drapes and furnishings, and he was intrigued to observe how Ellen had decorated. Despite all the passion they'd shared, he really knew very little about her and had few notions as to such elemental details as her favorite colors or styles.

He examined the clock on the mantle, the plant in the corner, the painting on the wall. He wouldn't label it snooping; he was merely curious as to how she'd settled in.

There was a writing desk tucked in an alcove by the window, and he went to it. A deck of playing cards was scattered across it, the cards arranged in neat rows. Evidently, she'd been interrupted in the middle of a game of solitaire, and he traced his finger over one of the stacks.

Surprisingly, the motion tugged at sentiments hidden deep inside, and he was assailed by memories of when they'd met. She'd always had a deck of cards handy, had claimed she passed many hours alone and used them to relieve the tedium. When she'd barged in during his trysts, she'd shuffled them with such relish.

It was so long ago and now seemed so frivolous. In his flagrant womanizing, what had he been hoping to accomplish? He could scarcely recollect. He'd been a prolific libertine, but since he married Ellen his prior tendencies had fled, and he was so different from the person he'd been—and so chaste!—that he could have joined a monastery and fit in perfectly with the other monks.

The desk had a single drawer, and he rudely opened it and poked around inside. To his consternation and dismay, he stumbled on a partially composed letter, where Ellen had attempted to put her feelings for someone down on paper.

I love you, she'd penned. *We could make it work. . . .*

He picked up the page and read it over and over; then he crumpled it in his fist.

He'd refused to believe James's stories, yet here was hard proof! While he'd been waning in London, heartsick over their split and half-dead from his wound, she'd been courting in the country. Why . . . she'd been carrying on in the very house he'd purchased for her!

She . . . she . . . loved another! She . . . who had never loved him. In all the times they'd philandered, she'd never once declared a strong attachment, had never provided the tiniest hint as to what her feelings might have been. The fact that she hadn't, but that she could brazenly reveal them to another, stuck in his craw.

From outside in the garden a ripple of feminine laughter drifted by. As he peeked out, he saw Ellen coming across the yard, a portly, older gentleman walking with her. He remembered James's remark about several of her suitors being *acceptable* as potential spouses. Was this one of them? Was this fat, bald lout the type of fellow she'd pick over himself?

While he didn't ascribe to much vanity, he had some, and his fury spiked. Lest he rush out and beat the man to a bloody pulp, he struggled for calm.

Ellen was very fetching in a green dress and matching straw bonnet. Her cheeks were rosy, her eyes merry. Her companion thought so, too, which was clear from how he was ogling her. Ellen's head was cocked toward him, but what was the man confiding?

Was he professing his undying devotion? Why would she listen to such nonsense? Had she no respect for her vows? For her husband? Or was Alex naught more than a nuisance she could toss aside on a whim?

The pair disappeared around the corner of the house, and he grappled with a swell of emotion that had him perplexed and annoyed. Why was he so disturbed? What was it to him if she shamed herself with every Romeo who stopped by?

His aggravation was so out of proportion to how removed he perceived himself to be. Why?

In an abrupt burst of insight, he realized—with a terrible certainty—that he wasn't so detached, after all.

He loved her! He did! He always had and always would. He'd told her so on that horrid night when she'd been determined to leave him, but the words had rung false for both of them. Later, with how events had escalated, he'd convinced himself that the confession had only been romantic drivel, despicably spewed to gain a few extra minutes with her.

With the recognition of how desperately he cared, a huge weight was lifted from his shoulders. Why had he buried his feelings for her? Why had he denied how much she meant to him?

He wouldn't part with her. He couldn't. Regardless of how badly he'd treated her, or how low her opinion of him, he could win her affection. He had to.

Their chatter floated down the hall as Ellen and her friend neared. Momentarily, they sauntered in, though they weren't aware that Alex had arrived. He boorishly concealed his presence, lurking at the writing desk, and intending to eavesdrop and use whatever he learned to further his cause. They seated themselves on a sofa, and they were positioned by the hearth, their backs to him, so his opportunities for spying were elevated.

"What a beautiful day," Ellen said.

"Not as beautiful as you are, Lady Stanton," the man answered. "May I have the honor of calling you Ellen?"

Alex rolled his eyes at the man's pitiful flirtation, and his anticipation spiraled as he awaited Ellen's reply. Would she welcome the advance? Or would she punch him in the nose?

"Mr. Martin"—she untied her bonnet and laid it on the table—"we've been through this before. It wouldn't be appropriate."

"Why not?" Mr. Martin pushed. "It's not as if you'll be married for much longer. Your husband couldn't possibly mind."

"I'm sure you're correct," she responded with a sigh.

"He's mad to let you go."

"Yes, he is."

"He's a cad! A libertine!" The man definitely liked to exclaim! "He never wanted you! All of London knows it! When will you admit it to yourself?"

"I suppose it is foolish to keep dwelling on the past."

There was a lengthy silence; then the swine seized Ellen's hand and clutched it to his chest.

"Tell me I have a chance!" he begged. "Tell me that when you envision your future, you see me in it."

"Mr. Martin! I had no idea. Please, you're—"

"I love you, Ellen. I love you!"

Alex was so enraged that he was afraid he'd strangle the man, which he daren't consider, so he did the only other thing that occurred to him. He scooped up Ellen's cards and shuffled them. Loudly.

There was a shocked pause; then Martin snapped, "What was that?"

Alex shuffled again; then slowly, deliberately, he stood and stepped into view.

"Cards, anyone?" he inquired.

Martin leapt to his feet and demanded, "Who are you?" as Ellen groaned and muttered, "Oh my Lord."

"Are you acquainted with this . . . this . . . interloper?" Martin asked her.

"Why, yes, as a matter of fact. Allow me to introduce my husband, Alex Marshall, Lord Stanton."

"Your . . . your . . . husband?" Martin's voice climbed an octave.

Shooting visual daggers, Alex stomped over. "Is there some reason you're surprised that I'm visiting my wife?"

"Why . . . why, no," Martin stammered.

"You seem to be laboring under the impression that Lady Stanton is free to entertain you."

"Well . . ."

"Let me assure you that it is a *mistaken* impression."

"I understand," Martin mumbled.

"It's not mistaken," Ellen interjected. "You've been gleefully planning to be shed of me, so you have an incredible amount of gall to come in here and prance about as if you're some sort of injured party. You have no right to bully me or Mr. Martin."

"I have no right?" Alex hissed. "*I* have no right?"

"No, you don't," she said. "You relinquished any privileges toward me when you sought your blasted annulment, so I suggest that you scurry back to London and leave me be."

"I'll just be going," Mr. Martin offered, though neither of them paid him any heed, and he slithered out.

Frozen in place, they stared each other down until the front door shut behind him, then Alex crossed to her. Bristling with fury, he towered over her, but she wasn't intimidated in the slightest.

"Well, well," she taunted, "you've finally decided to grace me with your fabulous company. To what do I owe such a dubious honor?"

"Your brother stopped in town to inform me of the mischief you were perpetrating."

"The mischief! What am I doing?"

"You're being deluged with swains, who are sniffing after your money, and you're encouraging every one."

"My brother told you all that?"

"I was certain he was lying, but I had to investigate

for myself. Imagine my astonishment on discovering that his tale was true."

"Oh yes, James is a veritable fount of veracity."

"How many are there?"

"How many what?"

"Suitors."

She frowned and seemed to be counting. "I'm such a *femme fatale,* it must be at least a dozen. Isn't it amazing what a bit of property and cash can do for a woman? Thank you for making me so desirable."

She gave an odd chuckle and turned to walk away, but he grabbed her and pulled her to him. She gasped, and tried to tug away, but he wouldn't release her.

"You're finished," he stated. "It's over."

"What is *over*?"

"Your pathetic attempts to find someone else."

"Perhaps I'd like someone else."

"No. From now on, there'll be only me."

They were so close, and he was assailed by her heat, by her smell, her essence washing over him like a fragrant blossom. He crushed her to him, as he leaned down and captured her lips in a sweltering kiss. He hadn't meant to try such a dangerous, wild thing, but she was like a fever in his blood, and over the period they'd been separated, none of his attraction had waned.

He wanted her more than ever, and he was astounded that, where she was concerned, he could have been so obtuse. Through blind stupidity, he'd nearly lost her.

He loved her, and he had to show her how much. She was his wife, and she had to start behaving like one, just as he had to start acting as a husband ought.

His hands were in her hair, his tongue in her mouth,

and he reveled. During the months of his recuperation, he'd been so unhappy, but he hadn't been able to figure out why. This . . . this . . . rash, exciting tumult was what he'd been needing, what he'd been missing.

With great effort, she yanked away, and she gaped at him as if he were deranged, as if he were some stranger on the street who'd recklessly embraced her.

"What are you thinking?" she challenged.

"I'm *thinking* that you're my wife and it's been much too long since I kissed you. Apparently, you've forgotten how good I am at it. You'll need regular reminding."

"Hah! Don't flatter yourself into assuming that I'm awed by your amatory skills. Besides, I'm barely your wife—as you've worked very hard to guarantee—so I can't fathom how that enormous pride of yours could have led you to conclude I'd be amenable."

"I don't hear you complaining."

"Then you're not listening very carefully." She shoved him away, creating space, erecting boundaries that he had no intention of observing. "Explain why you're here—and make it fast. I have a bevy of additional beaux about to arrive, and I won't have you interfering with all my fun."

"I'm here because the annulment is off."

"Says who?"

"Says me."

He went to the alcove and retrieved the note she'd been drafting. He flattened it out, straightening the wrinkles from where he'd crumpled it; then he returned and dangled it before her. "There will be no more of these. From this moment on, I'm to be the only man in your life."

"You've been snooping in my desk?"

"Yes, and I found this." He tore the letter to shreds

and tossed the pieces over his shoulder. "Whoever he is, you'll have to break it off."

He left her again to snatch up the documents he'd brought, the ones that would have severed them forever.

"This is the last section of the annulment contract. I'd planned to have you sign it, so that it could become official, but I've changed my mind. It appears—my darling bride—that I'm not splitting with you, after all."

He ripped the papers in half, and they fluttered to the floor.

Her confusion was humorous to witness. "What . . . what are you doing? Our marriage is to be ended. It's what you want, what you've always wanted."

"No, it's not."

"It's not?"

"I was wrong to push for it; I was wrong to forge ahead. I convinced myself that you were better off without me, but the problem is, Ellen"—he reached out and brushed his fingers across her soft cheek—"I don't want to go. I'm so lonely without you, and I can't bear that we're apart. Can you forgive me and come home?"

She began to shake. "Come home?"

"I've been a total ass. I admit it. I've been inflexible and difficult and oblivious, and all I can say is that I'm sorry. Forgive me. Please."

"You *have* been an ass," she agreed.

"But I don't mean to be. I'll mend my ways. I swear it." He was terrified that she'd send him packing, so he hurried on. "After my brother—" He simply couldn't utter *almost killed you,* so he swallowed and started over. "After I was injured, I was too enfeebled to contact you. Then, when I was more recovered and considered it, I was too ashamed."

"I wrote several times," she divulged. "When I was at the hotel."

"You did?"

"Yes."

"I didn't know. I never received a single letter."

"The housekeeper responded for you. She claimed you were fine."

"I wasn't."

"I waited and waited, but you never asked for me." She glanced away. "I thought you didn't need me."

"Not need you? Are you mad?"

"You never said anything."

"I'm saying it now."

"But . . . but why?"

"Don't you know?"

"No."

"I love you."

"No, you don't."

"I do." Her trembling increased, and he rubbed his palms up and down her back, trying to comfort, trying to warm and soothe. "I've always loved you. I think I knew it from the first, but I was too stubborn to realize it."

She studied him, searching for prevarication, and she murmured, "You're serious, aren't you?"

"Of course I am. Are you supposing I'd travel all this way on a lark?"

"No, but I'm scared to believe you."

"Why would you be?"

"I can't imagine why you'd love me."

She blushed, and he could sense her self-doubt, her apprehension. She'd been on her own for ages. Perhaps she couldn't conceive of anyone loving her. She was so silly.

"Give me another chance, Ellen. I'll prove to you that my sentiments are genuine. Let me show you the kind of husband I can really be."

She mulled and fussed; then she acknowledged, "I never wanted an annulment."

He exhaled a heavy breath. "Good."

"I want to be your wife. I want to build a life with you."

"I'm so glad."

"I've been awful, too, but I didn't intend to be. Events happened so fast, and I couldn't slow the momentum so that I could reflect and make the right decisions."

"All is forgotten and forgiven."

"And that . . . that blasted letter you found in my desk?"

He tensed, fearing she was about to declare her eternal devotion for another. "What about it?"

"I was writing it to you."

"To . . . to me?"

"I composed a hundred versions of it, but I couldn't figure out how to . . . to . . ."

She flung herself into his arms, and he hugged her tight.

"Yes, yes," she begged, "allow me to stay with you. Don't force me to go on all by myself."

"I won't, Ellen. You'll never be alone again. I'll always be by your side."

"I love you," she finally confessed. "So much."

"I know."

"Let's start over, and this time, let's do it differently. Let's do it better."

"Absolutely," he replied. "We absolutely will."

"We have to set some rules before we commence."

"Such as . . . ?"

"You have to sell the property in the country where I was . . . was . . ."

"I already have."

"I don't want to ever see Lydia. Or your brother. I understand that they're your family, but—"

"You'll never have to see either of them. I promise."

"And I wish you would try to be civil to James. I realize he can be difficult, but I need the two of you to get on. For my sake."

"James and I will manage just fine. Don't worry about us."

"I insist on having many children."

"I hope we have a dozen."

"I'll expect you to be a true husband to me. I'll expect you to be faithful."

"Which shall never be a chore. I give you my vow of fidelity."

Could she actually presume he would desire another woman over herself? Her confidence was so low, her trust in him so tentative. He would have to spend several decades demonstrating how much he cared. She was everything he'd ever wanted, everything he'd ever needed, and he'd have to dote on her, would cherish and spoil her until she was positive his affection was sincere.

"Come with me." He took her hand and led her to the alcove, where he scooped up her deck of cards.

"What are you doing with those?" she queried.

"You won't be needing them anymore."

"I won't?"

"No. You'll be much too busy."

"With what?"

"With loving me."

He escorted her to the fireplace and tossed the cards

into the hearth. There was a fire burning, and it quickly devoured the stack. He watched until they were beyond salvaging; then he turned to her and smiled.

"Now then, I've never been in this house before. How about a tour? With you as my guide. I'm especially interested in the location of your bedchamber."

"You are, are you?"

"Yes, so don't dawdle. I'm in a bit of a hurry."

"Suddenly," she said, smiling, too, "so am I."

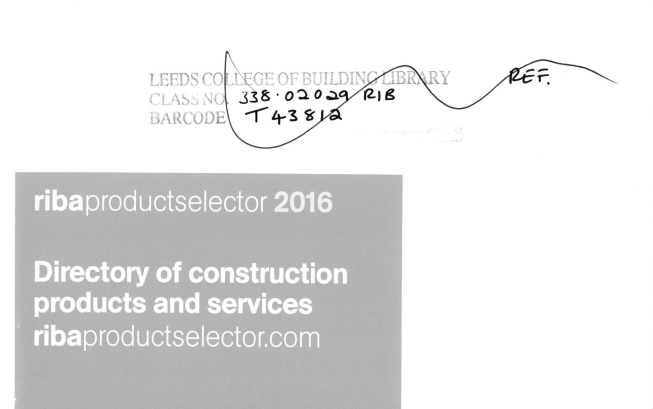

ribaproductselector **2016**

**Directory of construction
products and services**
ribaproductselector.com

RIBA ⊞ **Enterprises**

Acknowledgements

RIBA Enterprises acknowledges assistance from many sources during the compilation of the RIBA Product Selector, not least the willing cooperation of manufacturers. Every effort is made to ensure accuracy, but RIBA Enterprises does not accept liability for errors and omissions, nor for damage resulting from the use or misuse of products listed.

Colour origination and typesetting by Dennis Barber Ltd, Print & Publishing Consultancy.

Printing and binding by L.E.G.O SpA, Viale dell'Industria 2, I-36100, Vicenza, Italy.

British Library Cataloguing in Publication Data: a catalogue record for this book is available from the British Library.

ISBN 978 0 90712 561 7

ISSN 0265-8739

Cover image: Elaborate structure.
Photo: © Getty Images/Auke Holwerda.

RIBA Enterprises Ltd
66 Portland Place
London W1B 1AD
T +44 (0)20 7496 8300
editorial@riba-insight.com
ribaenterprises.com

NBS
The Old Post Office
St Nicholas Street
Newcastle upon Tyne NE1 1RH
T 0345 456 9594
info@theNBS.com
theNBS.com

Editorial

Advertiser Information Coordinator
Jonathan Last

Editors
Georgia Sanders
Stephen Platts

Production

Production Director
Kate Mackillop

Production Manager
Nicola Haywood

Design
Phil Handley

Sales and Marketing

Sales Director
Ben Councell

National Sales Manager
Belinda Beake

RIBA Insight Customer Service Coordinator
Sorrell Fullarton

MIX
Paper from responsible sources
FSC® C023419

At the end of 2016 please recycle your RIBA Product Selector!